THE BIG BOOK OF DEATH, SEX AND CHOCOLATE

Di Reed

TWO RAVENS
PRESS

Published by Two Ravens Press Limited
1, Fivepenny, Port of Ness, Isle of Lewis, HS2 0XG

ISBN: 978-1-906120-67-2

British Library Cataloguing in Publication Data: a CIP record
for this book can be obtained from the British Library.

Designed and typeset by Calum Kerr
Cover design by Donald Smith Graphic Design
Printed in the EU

Contents

Dedication

As always, for Mike, Madelaine and Al
For Tricia Feber
For Rosemary Shrager, Sue Gaisford and
Anthea Morton-Saner

And in memory of
Dorothy Ingham, Ruth Moore-Start and
Tony Minshull

1
PROPORTIONAL REPRESENTATION

Let's get this straight. She's a tiny organic scrap on a *very* small island on a small planet in a small solar system, where living things are an amusing and transient departure from the usual rock. Most everything surrounding her is some sort of rock, or a derivative. She lives out her tiny, fragile existence atop a molten fireball, stuck between hard and wet, supported by rock, sustained by water, and if you want to be melodramatic about it, continually under threat from both. While she dodges the day to day risks of things that might kill her, her planet sticks firmly to its orbit, incapable of dodging the millions of small and large projectiles that regularly cross its path and threaten to bring about large-scale tragedy or mass extinction. Earth is the child in the Milky Way playground, clutching its treasures in the face of a gang of intergalactic bullies, pelting her with cosmic conkers. It's a miracle either of them exists at all, but here they are, getting on with it.

Her time scales differ vastly from those of her home planet. Her place in time and space is infinitesimal. Even the dinosaurs, with their 200 million-year innings, constitute barely an afternoon's light entertainment on the earth's vast playing fields. By comparison, with its five or six thousand years of recorded history, its pyramids, its mountain climbers and deep sea divers, of which it is so proud, *homo sapiens* is a mere streaker.

So we'll take it from there.

I

Picture this: a desert scene in North America, a late nineteenth
century scenario. Think Western, the spaghetti sort. The sand
is yellow-hot, burned to fluorescence by the noonday sun. The
air is still, thick with heat. A lizard blinks on a rock, soporific.
The lizard is a bit predictable, and sometimes reminds her of a
fag ad, but she likes them, their rock-like stoicism, their other
worldliness, so there it is, a particularly large and handsome
iguana, on the rock, blinking.

For several moments, the scene is unchanged, while she
gets into gear, fixing the images in place, determining a path.
Should she come into the field of vision dead centre, or
approach from the far left? Which is more threatening, which
gives the greatest impression of serious intent? Does she
practise the looming confrontation, so it's spot-on by the time
she arrives, or has preparation become redundant? She's done
it so often now. Sometimes it works for her, sometimes it
doesn't. And her point of entry, like a wayward satellite
hurtling through the outer atmosphere towards a fixed
destination, is critical; it affects the progress of the rest. Like
everything surrounding her, it's a matter of life and death.

She comes over the horizon, a long way off, easy, measured, loping strides towards us. Today it's the middle course,
straight into the camera's eye. The cameraman shoots low on
the ground, so her denimed legs appear colossus-like in the
frame, the open canvas trench coat swinging rhythmically as
she walks. She may be a man today. She is so tall, so lean, so
full of strength and vengeance, there may be whiskers on the
leathered face that is coming into view. But more probably she
will be herself, lift the battered Stetson when the deed is done,
and let her hair, long, and white-hot blonde, the way it used to
be, tumble down around her, triumphant and satisfied, the
killer punch.

This is a good version. Today it's going to work, powered

10

by her anger, disciplined by her attention to detail. Its strength invades her mind and she disappears inside it. Now the object of her journey is coming into view, looming large in the foreground. A rough-hewn cage of branches, a scrap of tumbleweed trapped against it. A man squatting inside, a disgusting, drunken, stinking beast, chewing a tobacco wad, its orange-yellow juices running into his sticky beard. An almost-empty bottle of whiskey in his hand, he is leering at the approaching figure, insolent, unsteady, half-blinded. Don't ask how he got there. He just is, and this is her opportunity to turn the tables on him. He gets to his feet, stretches his mouth in a jeering, albeit uncertain smile, shows black and yellow teeth. She can smell the liquor-steeped breath.

As she kicks open the door, the sun is behind her – a very important detail – its heat heavy on her back. After an uncomprehending pause, he stumbles out, his arm up across his face, shielding his eyes from the burning light, and she backs off easily to give herself more space. He is watching her, looking for the gun, but there is no holster. Instead, her arm hangs loose at her side, and her hand cradles a rock. Slung over her shoulder is a heavy satchel. The thing is, *he* is in *her* shadow.

She savours the moment, takes a swig from the water bottle, feels the sweat stinging her eyes, running between her skin and shirt. He is too drunk, too bewildered to do anything except gawk. At the last moment, as her arm rises, he lifts the whiskey bottle in self-defence, and is struck down by the rock, aimed sure and straight at his centre. He grovels in the dust, coughing and spitting, and a second rock thuds into his splayed hand with a knuckle-breaking crack. He screams in sudden agony, tries to get up and make a break for it before the deadly hailstorm of stones breaks over him.

Take that. And that. And that.

The details are grisly, sadistic. Let's not dwell on them. She throws as many rocks at him as she has strength for, which varies from time to time, and she watches him crumple and bleed beneath them, the screams turning to groans and

11

indistinct pleadings. The stoning is more satisfactory than a simple shot, because she has made him suffer. She stands over him and chooses this moment to splice in the soundtrack, an electric guitar to the fore, a powerful swelling of strings and horns supporting it, underpinned by rolling timpani. Only at the point of death does she stand clear of the sun, and the molten fire and light pours on her victim, an incandescence so powerful, it obliterates him and purifies the space he once occupied. She opens the water bottle, slugs back liquid that is unrealistically cold and pure, and throws her head back, sinking into the exhilaration and exhaustion that overcomes her.

Then she turns and walks away, back the way she came, pulling the Stetson back from her forehead and yes, releasing her hair. She strides off, the hat hanging in one hand, a salvaged rock in the other. The sun's light, now warm and benign, rich and golden, reflects kindly on her receding figure.

The rock, four thousand five hundred *million* years old, is warm in her hand as she bestows a cool departing wink on the basking iguana. This is the absolute best she can do. It has been an exceptional encounter. She can't always fight him so convincingly.

Which is a pity, because when you're in the business of trying to kill a tumour, and all you've got to do it with is your mind, you just have to give it all you've got.

II

She is currently host to a colony of hostile cells, which will gradually increase in power and eventually overwhelm her. Her prognosis is two years. Her expected three-score-years-and-ten have been slashed by two thirds.

Wherever she goes now, she finds herself fascinated by the composition of living things, and their external shields, how they protect themselves from the outside world. Increasingly, she is obsessed by surfaces. This new curiosity has brought her to a closer scrutiny of her skin. This stretchy, waterproof exterior, with its clever, breathable fabric construction, protective hairs and regular sluicings of lubricating organic secretions, has betrayed her body. She can feel it opening and closing, like anemones oozing oils and salts, indiscriminately attracting and admitting whatever foreign organisms settle on her, allowing them to creep in under her surface and invade her good health. She should be crustacean, with a proper protective shell, not sheathed in this yielding, flexible covering so vulnerable to abrasion and laceration. Then perhaps the disease would not have got in.

Look how fragile it is, this skin that's meant to protect her from sunlight, from water, from cold and heat, from bugs and beasts and dangerous substances. Beneath it, sometimes so lightly skimmed they're visible, run her blood vessels, so close to risk from sharp, stinging edges, as they busily carry benign and malevolent cells that by turns cleanse and pollute her body.

Silence has taken on a sinister quality, heavy with things she can't know and doesn't trust. And no wonder. The disease has taken her by stealth, made her a sleeping victim of the worst kind of rape. She had no idea it was happening until it was too late. Now, left too long to its own devices, her cancer has consolidated its position and is growing, and she feels its malevolent energy as it builds up strength and begins to help itself to her fuel stocks. Having been raped, she is now being eaten alive.

As if that wasn't bad enough, she has fallen prey to the ravages of cliché, in exactly the situation where she expected to be dignified by a sense of individual power. But that's her all over. She wants to rise to the occasion, meet it with *sang froid*, or bravura – or at least bring something new to the genre. How *should* she feel about this? How *should* she deal with it? Naively, she expects the crisis to somehow reveal her true nature – so shouldn't that leave room for some individuality of response? Is it possible to strike out on her own, break into new emotional territory and come up with something new and different? Forget it. Death is as old as the first amoeba, and when it comes to being original about it, there's nothing new under the sun.

In fact, she was dismayed at the easiness with which the medical profession pigeonholed her as she faced this shocking, unique situation. The very fact that it had happened, and was happening, and would continue to happen to millions of others, actually seemed to make it worse, making the specialists complacent as they routinely tried to cushion the blow before setting her gently on the path of damage limitation.

It's all right, my dear, there's nothing you can say or do that we haven't heard or seen before. Shout and swear, commit murder, drive your car into a wall, stare blankly into space for the next twelve months – you can't shock us. All your responses are perfectly natural/understandable/ open to being patronised. It must be terrible for you, of course, but nevertheless, we have seen rather a lot of it all before ...

How dreadful it was to discover that no matter what her reactions, her doctors had already looked them up in a textbook and cross-referenced them to other cases, as if the emotions she experienced were part of the same package, and came prescribed along with the condition. Her status diminished by the hour as she heard about those thousands of others *who felt just like she did*. Instead of being placed at the centre of her own tragedy, she found herself being marginalised by others jostling for stage space, her attempts at dealing with the massive ramifications of her illness consistently devalued.

However you cope, however high you rise above this thing, someone else has been there already, and will go there again. That is a source of comfort. The unique, the extraordinary, the deeply personal challenge that must be conquered individually, is only a popular day trip that everybody gets round to eventually. Like Everest.

Before she had even sorted out how she was feeling, some well-meaning, percipient medic had got there before her, put it in a paper, labelled it neatly and taken away another piece of her identity. Was there nothing about this that she could call her own, that wasn't being trespassed all over by others in the same situation? Sure, she didn't want to be alone – but that didn't mean she wanted to be *the same*.

The anonymity of it was galling. She was no longer a person with a job, with interests, with special skills and a personality, with friends who came to dinner, with plans for the future and all the other things that made someone who they were. The person she was had been roller-coastered by cancer, flattened on the tarmac like the fall guy in a Tom and Jerry prank. She was now a two-dimensional patient, with a treatment plan and counselling sessions, and better not talk too much about the other things in life, because they may not be there for much longer. She's lost hope, the distinguishing characteristic of the rest of mankind. She's lost her future.

It seemed to her that while she and everyone else who had been tossed into the same boat was reeling like a drunken sailor and trying to hang on to their sense of self, the medical profession was still grappling with the concept of illness and individuality, as if there was some kind of radical, value-added novelty in approaching the patient as a person. It smacked of a marketing ploy, men in white coats suddenly being seized by the realisation that this wasn't just a tumour in a suit sitting in their office.

*Doctors! Do you treat your patients badly because you fear death yourself? If that's how **you** feel, imagine what it must be like for them! Are your terminally ill patients disillusioned and depressed? Are they unresponsive in your surgery – or even downright abusive? Have you considered that **your attitude might be making things worse?** Well not any more – because now you have the power to change. **YOU** can **make a real difference** by following our amazing four-point action plan. Learn to treat your patient like **a real human being** – and start to make dying of a terminal illness **a challenge for your patients**, not a threat. Call or write today. Send no money.*

It seems that some days, there's no end to the bitter internal diatribes she holds against doctors in the grip of the

15

blindingly obvious. And she knows, guiltily, that as far as her own GP is concerned, it simply isn't fair. However. Where was she? Oh yes – the blindingly obvious. It was the same with babies. Hadn't recent medical research just concluded that babies in the womb suffered pain during abortion? It was astonishing. How many millions of them had suffered while the profession chalked up savings on anaesthetics and disregarded its own stupidity while it waited for the sluggish research process to confirm the obvious?

Unless the procedure actually revealed something else about the medical profession, which exists to save lives, not terminate them. A mother who wants to abort a child is treated no differently to a mercenary out on a war gig, or a terrorist bombing a busy high street. Perhaps despatching the foetus without an anaesthetic is another way of punishing the mother – making her unborn child suffer for her sin. And as any mother contemplating an abortion knows, it isn't necessary for outsiders to offer a helpful contribution of guilt when you're already tearing yourself apart over the decision.

This is the twisted way her mind has started to work. Her trouble has always been that she thinks too much. That's what her mother used to say, anyway. As soon as you start to think about something big like dying, you begin to act out roles. And the more you experiment with attitudes, the further you seem to get from the laboratory of life.

The need to be different came later, when the shock had worn off and she began to come to terms with her new reality. At first, she had wanted to conform, because then all the books would have been relevant, would have been written for her. But all the books had been written about and by and for other people. She was perplexed by the lack of guidelines, ransacked libraries for information on proper codes of behaviour for dealing with such extreme circumstances. As a scientist, she was used to dealing in mathematical precision, and her work and life was measured in quantities and proportions. Even in her line of work, dealing with impossible equations of time and the unfathomable beginnings of the earth, there were structures and methodology, something to grasp hold of.

But when you are told you are dying, it's as if someone has started to unpick the stitches that hold you together. Everything becomes shapeless; priorities melt down and ferment into a mass. You can't think straight, because you don't know how to think. You lose your powers of reason because you are grappling with something that is quintessentially unreasonable. And you don't know how to feel, because you are told that everything you feel has been felt before, and you begin to suspect yourself of merely copying someone else's pattern.

She would never forget the moment of being told, the cold drenching that washed through her, the freezing sensation of the purest physical shock. And then the explosion of understanding, like Hiroshima happening in her head, the burn -up of everything she had previously known, and everything she had previously thought about the future. She would take that feeling to the grave. Shortly. The first coherent thought she remembered, liquid-nitrogened in the doctor's surgery, frozen with the sensation that her mind had seized, crammed up with too much information she couldn't process, was about jogging. *I used to run,* she thought. *I used to run to keep healthy.*

But although she understood, she didn't take it in, not really, not until her hair began to fall out. It was almost the worst thing. Turning up at the hospital for the first course of chemotherapy, petrified at the thought of the chemicals that would be pumped into her body, hadn't been enough to convince her she had terminal cancer. Throwing up for two days in the wake of the treatment hadn't been enough, either. But the morning she woke up and found handfuls of hair all over her pillow was the day the reality was sledge hammered home. It was the first visible sign that her body was falling apart. She was changing, not just on the inside, but on the outside, too. When she looked in the mirror, she could see the terrible knowledge in her face. She was dying.

That might have been why she went for a long, glossy

auburn tumble of curls when she chose her wig – another shock for her friends. She confronted them defiantly, as if she was announcing the formation of a new person from the ashes of the one being deconstructed by her new headfellow. She hates taking it off, having to face the faint, wispy spikes that are starting to sprout from her denuded scalp. This is when she misses her own hair, the hair she keeps for her fights with Terence. And it's days like this, when she is thinking too much, that the wig, the forlorn attempt to turn her back on her disease and pretend it's happening to someone else, bothers her. The glossy auburn curls are starting to work against her. She's still dying.

How big a deal is it? This has troubled her, given her usual preoccupations with the beginnings of time and the formation of the earth she stands on. She habitually imagines herself as a tiny part of a transient invasion that is having a temporary impact on its home planet, a tiny speck in a vast universe. She imagines a benign host tolerating a parasite that is rather thoughtless and selfish, but at the end of the earth's considerably long day, will do no real or lasting harm.

The disease is not quite the same. Its impact on her, the unwilling host, is much bigger, its ambitions grander – like some crazed Blofeld intent on no less than the destruction of its entire world. It is not on her, but in her, not in a place where it can be brushed off, but crawling through her, and she wakes every day with the awareness of its silent invasion.

What was she to do? Carry on regardless? How can she reconcile her own smallness with the massive impact of her own imminent demise?

III

What was curious – to her, at least – was the self-consciousness that overwhelmed her when she learned what was wrong, and what was going to happen. She was embarrassed to tell her friends, actually found herself apologising for being at the centre of such an appalling catastrophe. Dying at twenty-five! It's so pretentious! So melodramatic! Like some terrible soap opera looking for a ploy to write her out of ensuing episodes.

I'm so sorry, darling, but there just isn't a role for you anymore. We can give you a six-month contract and a death scene guaranteed to make the very rocks of the earth weep. I'm sure you'll agree that's a more than generous offer. You've been absolutely marvellous, a real treasure, but it's time to quit and let the show go on without you.

She vented her anger on the tumour, raging at it in the hope it would feel some remorse and take itself away. How can it countenance staying when the force of will against it is so strong? How dare it stick around, lolling insolently, gorging on her naive hospitality, when she has made it extremely clear that it is not welcome? For Christ's sakes, she even tried to have it cut out. How much plainer can a hint be that it has already outstayed its welcome?

But the tumour is thick-skinned, and has not taken the hint. It has instead taken over the spare room, the empty, tantalising space with the window that looked out over the rest of her life. She hears it at night, moving around the space, which is already too small, applying pressure to the walls. And it is grinning. The message is clear. Hostility, sulking, ranting and raving, brute force, withdrawal of privileges – these tactics are not working.

There's this thing in my head. I can't feel it, but I know it's there. It's a kind of madness, knowing it's there, but not being able to feel it, as if I'm being haunted by a figment of my imagination. Sometimes I hold my scalp, pressing my fingers in. I want to pull it out, get it out of my head, get this creeping, crawling thing out of my head before just the thought of it being there destroys me. As long as I've got my sanity, I can deal with this, but it's working against me all the time. I'm like King Canute on the shoreline, faced with the rising tide, but anchored in the sand. There's this thing in my head. I can't feel it, but I know it's there.

IV

Lately, she has tried to accept. Her new theory is that if she learns about her disease, gets to know all about it, its personal habits, particular foibles, she may come to a position of acceptance. Be honest, she's never going to like it, but perhaps she can accept. And move on.

The breakthrough in this strategy came when it occurred to her that the tumour was as innocent as she was. She already understands the indiscriminate nature of the disease, so there is no point in taking it personally. Why *not* her? Would she rather it had moved in with someone else? Well, yes she would, but by introducing spite into the equation, that makes her worse than the tumour, which is incapable of malice. It's just a lifeform that has found a suitable place to achieve its potential. The kindest thing you could say about it is that it's over-enthusiastic. In its eagerness to do its duty, it has gone over the top and, like an excitable child, doesn't know when to stop. It's like sharks. People always blame sharks for eating people, but they can't help it, it's just instinct, there's nothing personal in that, either. If they're hungry and you're in the water, they'll eat you. Life's a bitch.

She sits at her desk, the pool of light from the angle-poise lamp illuminating the specimen jar she is turning in her hand. It contains a tumour, the exact same sort that has moved into her brain and made itself at home. She got it from a friend, a pathologist, who found it in the laboratory storeroom and said no one else needed it right now. She found that funny, the idea that anyone could ever need a tumour. Medical researchers, though – what are they like, fascinated by the things that kill us or threaten us, obsessive about stuff that makes the rest of us frightened. He didn't want to give it to her, but she said she needed something to focus on. She needed to know what it was like, this thing that was slowly killing her. If she could see it, she told him, she might start to believe in it, and then she might be able to fight it more convincingly. He said he understood.

The tumour in the jar is very large. She wonders if hers will make it to such impressive proportions. Perhaps, as it's going to come out on top anyway, she should feed it up, draw comfort from trying to culture the biggest and best of them all. There might be an afterlife for tumours, where they meet up to compare weights and measures.

Hey, guys, Stella broke Paul's record!

Hell, all you ever think about is size. What about George? He missed the weight, but no one's ever equalled the density.

Oh come on, you know he got a lucky break with that radiation overdose.

OK, so you don't count the fact that Stella did a merger with Ricky from lymph, like some fatcat building society ...

But this temporary excursion into the black has little future. She knows, like everybody knows, that people are bankrupted of their humour stocks when the tumour enters the killing fields. She knows there will be a lot of pain. She knows there is itching, and a foul smell. And people find it harder and harder to look you in the eye, keep their patience with your moaning, keep from holding their noses.

The bit about the smell bothers her. It picks away at the insistent image of the gently declining, freshly-bathed martyr on a snowy bed – the received image of a terminal patient, spouting smug words of wisdom for the benefit of those to be left behind. She doesn't know why or from where this smell will issue, and she can't remember where she read it, so she's vexed on both counts. It's the kind of useless piece of information you absorb for no apparent reason, when the rest of the article has slipped from your mind. This little piece of valueless gore has tacked itself to her memory cells and stuck there, irritatingly, like a piece of chewing gum, a little, probably half-correct factette, that comes back to haunt her now it has become relevant.

It strikes her as a dreadful waste of some of her increasingly precious brain cells. Is it possible to discard the information and reclaim them for a more important use? How much more time would that buy her, trading in all the stuff she no longer has a use for? Think of all the useless junk she could shed that has cluttered up her brain since she began, quietly using up memory and energy in the hard drive! With the tumour elbowing its way into an ever-larger area of her brain, and available disk space shrinking by the minute, it's not as if she has the luxury of a limitless supply. She wanders into her head, a small, angry child clutching a penny in a sweet shop where everything costs a pound.

Hey, Tumour! You in the corner — the one eating away my brain cells! Can we do a deal?

(chomping noises) What kind of deal?

Say — you only eat the parts I can do without?

(blank incomprehension) How would I tell?

(She leaves, beaten, with no deal.)

In keeping with her policy of acceptance, she decides to call hers Terence. Terence the Tumour. Thomas the Tank Engine. The one in the jar is Deadhead, a punk who died in his prime, sated with chemotherapy drugs and boasting about how you should have seen the other guy.

So, she's realistic. This is the tactic for now. Lightening up. She might as well make the most of it, her fading opportunities to find entertainment in her condition. In this uneven war of attrition, she masses her armaments against an implacable and immovable force.

- Hey, Terence, you're not going to beat me down, you know. I've got weapons. I can fight. I've got jokes and drugs and nuclear power. I've got a great imagination.

- Don't make me laugh. You got no chance, doll. You need chemical intervention, it makes you throw up and your hair falls out. You can't eat. How you gonna keep up a sustained campaign? Me, I'm a natural. I don't need nothin. I got you, babe.

She is painfully conscious of the searching, trying to find the appropriate mechanism that leads to some kind of peacemaking. But appropriate for whom? And how can you make peace with something when you are its victim and the positions cannot be reversed? Whatever mechanism she comes up with, her friends can be relied upon to patronise her efforts and heap her with pity. The pity will surely kill her before Terence does.

After she had made her great revelation, she threw a champagne party. There was something about the hopelessness of her situation that made an extravagant, hedonistic gesture seem fitting. *Now I can wreck my liver,* she thought brightly. *And ransack my bank account. The only currency of any value now is time. I could sit here saving my strength, but what for? Why not beat against death's door in new clothes and a drunken frenzy, and announce loudly that I'm throwing my own party, thanks for the invitation, but I'm not coming just yet?* She splashed out on ten bottles of vintage Veuve Clicquot and invited her five best friends round, making it absolutely clear it was not going to be a hug and cry occasion. They went along with it, dressed up and laughed rather forcedly all night, but she could tell they were shocked. She wasn't fitting in with their expectations.

It's a defence mechanism, she could hear them say, taking even this refuge away from her by dragging it into the light and pinning it down with a suitably pitying identification tag. *It makes you weep to hear her, some of the things she says are frankly sick. She doesn't seem to be facing up to it and that's what she really needs to do.*

Oh yeah? Says who? Who's the dying one? Whose death is it, anyway? How can she turn that insidious pity back onto her well-meaning friends and hang onto her sick jokes with a clear conscience?

There's worse, too, because alongside Pity comes Euphemism. Her poor friends, destroyed by her condition, trying so hard not to compound the villainy by talking about her ... her *Illness.* She sees them struggling to avoid it, physically unable to say the word *cancer,* choking on it as it rises involuntarily from their vocal chords, savagely repressing it and replacing it with some dishonest, watered-down alternative. She feels so sorry for them, and that makes her angry. She remembers doing it herself. It's the way you try to make

23

dying people feel better. And all it does is make it worse, reinforce the awfulness of the situation you're in. The more her friends try to avoid it for her sake, the more they push the unpalatable facts down her throat, and push her even further away from them.

Why don't they just say it, and get on with the conversation – how can they possibly make it worse? It's as if they'd be uttering a curse, a destructive and malevolent mantra. She can see what they're thinking. If they don't say the word, perhaps they can lessen its impact, erode its reality. So they ask her how she's feeling, or say they've heard she isn't too well, or that she's a bit poorly. She understands that this is their unconscious way of giving her the lead, the choice of whether she elaborates on this and says, *Well actually, I'm not a bit poorly, I'm terminally ill and please don't patronise me.*

Everywhere she went she was strapped down into the patterns of Good Behaviour. The conversations with Patrick, her doctor, her sweet, kind doctor who suffered for her, inhibited the more aggressive emotions she was feeling. She could tell, right from the start, from the moment he started to tell her, that the news was bad. The poor man, he looked so wretched, so responsible – how could she vent her fury, her hysterical passion on him? He had done nothing wrong, missed nothing, acted promptly when she voiced her concerns. His voice was low, like a priest's, as if she was being given an early call for the last rites, and ever since that first appointment, it had not changed, as if he flicked a switch to modify his tone as soon as her name was called in the waiting room. She wanted to tell him to lighten up a bit, tell jokes like he used to, move more in sympathy with what she was currently trying to achieve, but she couldn't bring herself to do it. He already felt it was his fault she had a brain tumour – how could she possibly imply that his counselling methods were not up to scratch either?

That was the problem. Everybody expected you to be so well behaved about dying of a terminal illness. They've all watched too much *Dr Kildare*, they all imagine you expiring quietly on a pillow, pale-faced, smiling bravely at visitors, drifting serenely away towards the Lake of Eternal Peace, at one with God and the universe. If you say anything violent, or bitter, or spiteful, well, you're simply not coming to terms with it, not facing up to it, not taking it on the chin.

You know, everybody knows, that away from the carefully controlled world of television emotion, the grand theory of Human Ennoblement through Destructive Illness doesn't work. She's seen it all before, in a cousin struck down by motor neurone disease. No going quietly for him – he made everyone's life a misery with his bitching, his spite and his helpless, jealous rage as his ability to function gradually deserted him and everyone else around him was still walking around, still drinking pints without dribbling. When his friends ate pizza, and the cheese stuck in their beards, everyone laughed and made pig jokes. When it happened to him, someone picked up a napkin and wiped his mouth. At the very end, sure, when his physical strength had all been eaten away, and it was an effort to blink, he was obliged to lie martyr-like in his bed. But she could still see the anger burning in his eyes, the hatred of everyone who didn't have what he had, the refusal to accept and go with good grace. No one had been able to say anything that made him feel better about his short straw; nothing had helped him relinquish the savagery with which he fought for his life. Perhaps that was the dark side of hope.

Then there was her mother, always making excuses for the difficult old people she worked with. *They're tired, they're often in constant pain, they lose their capacity for tolerance,* she would say indulgently, after another crotchety old git had thrown a mouthful of sour, totally undeserved abuse at her. Her mother took it on the chin, but then again she could afford to – she was half their age, and there was nothing wrong with her. She learnt then that old age itself did not make people unpleasant, bitter and twisted; they were born like that. Old age simply threw their faults into sharper relief, when they saw less reason to bother about being polite and considerate, didn't care whether people liked them or not, and didn't care what they thought of them, either. *Selfish? Bad tempered? Mean spirited? Do you think I don't know that? Do you think I give a damn?*

Ah, but look at her mother now, so pragmatic with her elderly patients and distanced relationships – look at her now, trying to support her dying daughter in the same way, lift her spirits and get her to make the most of the time she has left. She's still affectionately bossy, humorously practical, but it's an act. It tears her apart, trying to communicate with her; there's so much she's hiding, so much she's afraid to let out. Neither of them has been brave enough to confront it, get The Big C out into the open where they can both look it in the face and give all their anguish and grieving free rein.

And God knows it's a tough one to swallow – no spoonful of sugar is big enough to sweeten the prospect of tumour-induced death. Terence, the primary, the one in her head, is the one that will gradually deprive her of her mental powers, take her sight, her hearing, her powers of speech, her motor capability. As he gets bigger, he will push her brain out of the way, dominate the floor space, squash up all the working bits into a corner where they will fuse together into a useless mash. That's how she pictures it, anyway, and this is what is very frightening. She uses her mind, exercises it, is creative with it, and the thought of it atrophying while the rest of her is still alive is terrifying. She fights the tumour with her mind, co-ordinates her attacks with it; it is her mental weapons that invariably give her hope, strength and the ability to toughen up against her foe. But, like a strain of bacteria developing resistance to antibiotics, Terence has his own built-in response to her inventive arsenal – he will simply get bigger, and that will be enough to disarm her. Both of them know the score. Cerebral creativity versus physical bulk – no contest.

Meanwhile, the secondaries are ganging up on her in currently neutral territories, threatening to turn her whole body into a war zone. This is pure overkill. One tumour can do the job perfectly well, given enough time. She tries to imagine what it will be like when she can no longer think clearly, when her limbs don't work anymore and she can't feed herself, when her brain is turning into mashed banana and she is totally exposed to the final onslaught from her assailant.

How much longer? How much longer before I start to slide towards this helpless, agonising, drooling conclusion?

V

She reads a lot about death just now, watches documentaries about it, researches the tiniest details, tries to find a picture of an afterlife that is convincing. She knows all about the different stages of grieving: Anger, Denial, Fear, Bargaining, Depression, Acceptance. Been there, done that, seen the movie, read the book, bought the T-shirt, had the tattoo. She found no mention of Apathy and Paralysis. The way she spent the first few weeks, watching the world go by as if she'd got off at the last stop and couldn't be bothered to get on again. The way it seemed impossible to function normally, without being aware of the futility of it all, and the pretence. Carrying on as normal is unsustainable when you've been shown the red card and asked to leave the pitch.

She watched the people around her, in the city, at work, things to do, places to go, people to see. She was already separate from them, even as she walked with them. Death was something that happened away from life, in a room marked *Quiet*. One minute you were part of the crowd, going about your busy life, the next you were siphoned off and you died, almost shamefully, somewhere where you couldn't be seen. The next day you were not in the crowd, and life accommodated the gap, fused seamlessly together again and picked up the pace. Somewhere else in this crowd, someone else is dying, too.

As long as death was around some invisible distant corner, you could still do things and believe in their importance. But

27

when you knew it was coming, and soon – brushing your teeth, eating sensibly, keeping fit, going to the movies, starting a fat novel, going to work – what was the point of all that? What was the point of anything? It was like playing a game where you couldn't follow the rules. You spent your life ricocheting off obstacles, trying to stay in as long as you could. You careered along, driving past other people's disasters, hearing about other people's terminal illnesses and near misses. Then it happened to you, and you either stopped playing, or took on a new set of rules.

She is still playing the game of life, but she has moved into Death Row. Appeals are pending, but increasingly desperate and lacking in conviction. Sentencing has been carried out, but the date of execution is not yet set.

But she is circling now, and has been from the start, ever-decreasing, increasingly frantic circling, trying to find a way out of the downward spiral. Her own death has become too big for her, too muddied, too hopelessly unconnected to any of the experiences and theories and stories she has been trying to connect it to. Whichever way she looks at it, she's still going to die.

Big deal. So is everyone else.

VI

But she can't go on like this, and like they sometimes do, even when you're dying, things get better. The turning point comes when she finds that it is possible to look beyond Terence and see something larger, less parochial. In the black holes between the black humour, she has thought herself up against a wall, and feels the psychological paralysis closing in, freezing up the precious time remaining, trapping her like a mediaeval prisoner in a dungeon well.

But some light has filtered down here, despite trying to

find the Meaning of Life in a transient world that deals in ephemera.

There is another way of looking at this. She has remembered that in the final analysis, everything comes back to rock. Accordingly, she has learnt to take herself away from the frenetic pace of the present and go backwards, away from everything she knows, all the way back to the volcanoes that shaped the first landscapes. More often now, this is the place she goes to rather than the stoning grounds of her nightmare encounters with Terence.

It's all hypothetical of course, an elaborate exercise in sustained bullshit, but it is this placing of herself in context that begins to help her view her position at a distance.

Too many people in her situation find God – all of a sudden. She isn't about to fall for the trite salvation package, but from her obsession with the tumour, the malevolent embryo developing apace within its chosen womb site, she's found a new way out, with the perspective she needs to move forwards. It is not in her nature to search for meaning in spiritual things, but give her something solid and enduring, and she can get a grip on it.

The chink of light comes from a small chunk of rock resting on a pile of papers to the left of her desk. The rock – Lewisian Gneiss – a favourite paperweight and concentration aid, is almost as old as the Earth itself, and seems to embody endurance and longevity. It's what you might call rubbing it in. It is always the first stone she casts when she is fighting Terence with her mind, always the one she searches out and retrieves when the battle is over.

But the rock harbours more than destructive possibilities. It is four thousand five hundred *million* years old. In that time, it has been thrown up out of fire and violence, has changed and cooled, been submerged and exposed, been crushed, cracked and broken away, and eventually been tossed by water, rubbed by sand and become sand in some part itself. But it is still around, and the millions of years of wear and tear are still revealing new facets of its nature and composition, like a maturing personality. It is a survivor. What she sees as an unchanging entity is in fact the end product of aeons of change. In the rock's slow and dignified metamorphosis, she is finding an opposite to the brief flash of her own life, and the violent, destructive activity of the tumour.

It is the length of time, the proportion of it that is so frustratingly impossible to grasp. At its core, the history of the earth is not about humans at all. It is about rocks. The entire existence of the human race is a mere blip in comparison, a flickering notion across the Earth's face.

The whole structure and fabric of the home planet, with its shifting tectonic plates, its volcanoes and ice ages and oceans, its grand scale geological activities, its countries and continents that move to their own agenda, regardless of political will, has created an elaborate system in which life itself may only be an interesting by-product. She and everyone else sets such store on *timeless* elements. *The timeless fascination of the pyramids, the timeless beauty of Helen of Troy, the timeless classics of The Beatles,* that are bound by such an absurdly short timeframe they throw the whole basis of our existence into a relief that is as sharp as it is comic. In ten million years, Greece, the foundation of our civilisation, our modern thinking, our social and political organisations, will have sunk back beneath the sea. It won't be there. A country littered with the remnants of what we call *ancient* monuments will be lost. The humans may not be there to see it, but the rocks will. Perhaps *they* are the superior beings.

Billions of humans, cats and dogs, elephants and dinosaurs and eels, spiders and fishes and ants and preying mantises. Species that have come and gone, part of a chain of natural extinctions as the Earth has matured. But extinction is a dirty word, something humans have adopted as their own shameful initiative, paying a collective debt of guilt to the Dodo and the tiger and the whale. Billions of humans, thousands of generations, countless acts of love and warfare, in a blip on a four thousand five hundred *million*-year time scale. Within this maelstrom, her existence is both atomic in size, and atomic in its rage at being cut short.

Look at it. The rock's hard, black, gritty surface is pitted with glittery spikes of mica, and broken by two patches of rose quartz, which look like wounds, as if someone has tried to expose a pink and fleshy vulnerability beneath the unyielding surface. It is like seeing what is happening under her own surface, a metaphor for her disease, a sculpture of atrophy.

When she is six feet under and rotting down to compost, it will continue its own metamorphosis on its own vast time scale. They will share the same fate, in a different form; both will remain part of the Earth. Death is a part of the process of change.

As a child, she used to lie awake in bed, waiting to catch the moment when consciousness became sleep, so she could say, *Last night I knew when I fell asleep, I was conscious of my unconsciousness.* Now she wonders if death will be like that, if she will be aware of the transition from being alive to not being. Will she know, try to stare death in the face? Will she fight, or will she be past caring? Or will the pain of leaving be fierce and bright, laden with thoughts of everything she never got round to doing? Will she worry that she left the cooker on, or didn't unplug the television?

Have I done enough? Have I responded adequately to the chances life gave me? Have I experienced enough, made the most of it? Did I make the right choices – or has my whole life been a series of wrong decisions? How important was it in the end that I chose x instead of y or z? How wide is the gulf between the choices I was offered, and the opportunities I seized? Have I passed?

She understands that death is final, but she can't cope with the concept of finality. There's still some part of her that expects to come back.

Even with her background, it is quite impossible for her to grasp the longevity of the experience, so used is she and every-one else to dealing with transience. Perhaps it is a protective mechanism, shielding her from the realisation that on the grand scale of things, she has not mattered. On a four thousand five hundred *million*-year time scale, a human life is a forty-five-thousandth of a second. *Who bothered to work that one out?* How can the world keep on turning, and how can she shoulder its indifference to her passing? How can she cope with knowing that she has not made any difference, except by believing that her absence, like her attendance, is merely temporary?

The rock, four thousand five hundred *million* years old, is warm in her hand, as if it still harbours a tiny fragment of energy from the earth's core. She rolls it in her palm, holds it to the light. She won't be there. Not now, not ever, never again. She will be dead, and everybody else she knows will still be alive. And once you're dead, you have no business in the land of the living. That is the difficult thing to understand. And that is why there is no comfort in the thought that thousands of others daily face the same thing, because like everyone else, she faces it alone.

Sitting by the window, anchored by the rock while she looks out over the rivers of people in the street, she closes her eyes and sees the horizon of a desert, somewhere in North America, and the sand burned to fluorescence by a white-hot avalanche of punishing light ...

2

IF I RULED THE WORLD

I

The Great Dictator Armando IV, having discarded most of
the better aspects of human nature at an early age, went on to
bully, then threaten, then murder his way through life, driven
by the might of an ideal. The 'IV' part was an affectation – he
was the fourth son of his family to be christened Armando,
but it did not reflect any leadership lineage. Dictators have to
seize power, then hang onto it like grim death, in the teeth of
fierce detestation. Curiously, for someone who had built his
whole life around killing and oppression, he had never thought
much about death. He tended to think in terms of *removal* and
control, steeped as he was in the politically correct vocabulary of
his milieu.

His assassination, therefore, had come as something of a
shock. Had it been a failed attempt, he would have wasted no
time in forcing his hapless security forces through the mincer
and indulging in some violent rhetoric, followed by an extended period of savage recriminations. But the assassination
had been a success, he was well and truly dead, and quite
simply, he didn't know what to do about it – who to shout at,
who to shoot at, who to slaughter. They were all still alive, and
he was here, impotent and frustrated, but at the same time
detached and in a way that surprised him, relieved that the
worst had happened. And it was not that nasty, really not at all
nasty, being dead. He found that perplexing. He had wielded

33

death as the ultimate punishment, used his people's fear of it to crush them. Were it not for the economic practicalities, he would have concentrated more on torture had he known.

The last thing he remembered was riding in an open-top car, being cheered by large crowds. It was his official birthday and his country was happy – or rather, his country had been *told* it was happy. He had been waving and smiling in his rather stiff, exaggeratedly dignified fashion, long used to these per-formances for the benefit of a people he regarded as little better than a herd of sheep. Then he suddenly couldn't see anything, and only heard the unmistakable cracking sound of firing rifles, screaming and mayhem around him. A few seconds later, he was drifting above the hullabaloo, trying to get a grip on things. His body, virtually headless after the bullets had exploded it into a ragged, splintered, bloody sac, was thrown back in the seat, bleeding indiscriminately. So it was immediately clear what had happened. A few feet from the car – imagine! only *a few feet from the car*! A woman's body was face down in the road, liberally peppered with machine gun wounds, and bleeding into the tarmac. He didn't have to see her face to know who it was, and he was suddenly overwhelmed at her determination, her cunning and her patience.

Presumably, after the assassination, his people would now *really* be happy – he was under no illusions about his popularity – and he was seized by a sudden curiosity to know what they would look like in genuine celebratory mood. Would he be able to spot the difference between spontaneous and enforced gaiety?

But none of that mattered now. He had lived his life as he had thought he should, and now it was time to pay. As he sat patiently outside God's Interview Room, waiting to be called, he was fairly certain that now it would be his turn at the sharp end.

He had already ruled out most defences he could raise for his actions. Pinning the blame on his parents with the *damaged parents = damaged child = damaged everything else* formula was both cheap and cowardly. In the hour or so he had had at his disposal since the shooting, he had decided to be candid about things, face up to them, admit his enjoyment of brutality, and hope to score points for honesty. He hoped he would be bull-jawed and grit-faced at the prospect of an eternity spent roasting on the end of a devil's spit, but accepted as realistic the proposition that he would be as terrified and agonised as the next man.

There was a military air about the place that soothed him. He responded to order, found it oddly relaxing that someone else was now in charge. *Who would succeed him?* he thought suddenly. He had not even begun to think about who would be strong enough, tough enough, smart enough and resilient enough to take his place. In all his years at the top, he had never seen any person with the potential to take on the task with any real conviction. He sighed, suspecting that there was the rub. He had borne the brunt of the decision-making for a very long time and the responsibility had started to get to him in the end. It was one of the setbacks of being a dictator. Not only did you abide by the rules you had set for yourself, but everyone else expected you to keep them with the same zealousness other legislation had been forced on them. To slip, to give the slightest hint of comfort in your position was to invite risk – at best, loss of face, at worst, assassination. Perhaps that's what had happened in the end.

At some point, maybe a few years before he died, the passion had deserted him, just as everything else had, and he had begun to regard his Grand Mission as a job, something that tired him and put him out of sorts. In idle moments, he began to wish that he could retire and go fishing – a more recreational kind of killing – potter about in the garden and breed Springer Spaniels. But he had a persona to live up to and a responsibility to his public. His rise to power had inspired several new dictators in other small countries who had seized power, but lacked the imagination to develop their own systems. He was under pressure to keep up the good work right to the day he dropped, lead by example. His imitators did not want to see the author of a new social order turn into a comfortable old man with pleasant hobbies and a yen to see the Pyramids before he died. He had to keep a grip on things.

Now he was dead, the fishing, gardening and dogs would never happen, and he had never seen a hieroglyph in its native surroundings. Just now, he was beginning to think about all the things he had never done, and what purpose his life had served.

It was always purpose with people, wasn't it? There was always a problem about the meaning of life. You could lead the most idle existence, or be the busiest person alive, and you would still ask yourself and your friends what it was all about, speculate on what you were doing, and how it fitted into God's great plan.

He had never been idle, but nor had he fitted into God's plan. Killing, torturing and oppressing were simply not part of God's vocabulary, unless you were on his side and doing him a favour. No, the interview to come would be a complete humiliation if he attempted to weasel round his beliefs and actions in the faint hope of a lighter sentence. His actions had been indefensible. In spite of himself, his mouth was dry as he watched the door and began to think about where he had come from, and how it had all started.

II

Raised – or more often than not, *not* raised by wealthy parents in a large white villa in the most privileged district on the outskirts of the capital, he was a singular and lonely child with nannies and governesses for company and a social problem with other children. He had often reflected on the random stroke of fate that had brought the Ramirez family to live next door. They had purchased a plot of land, and he had watched with fascination as the green field was overturned in preparation for the building of their new home. He became totally absorbed by the site, watched its gradual trans-formation from a pile of earth and a sea of mud into a pile of earth and a sea of mud with a gleaming, scrubbed new home in its centre, all dazzling white and glittering glass. The family moved in, a husband, a wife and three children, and the husband began his labour of love – the garden.

Mr Ramirez accepted no help, preferring to be his own landscape architect. Over the next two years, the young Armando had studied him as he sculpted the earth into borders and beds, rockeries and ridges, waterfalls and fountains. Gradually, the plants became robust under his fiercely devoted care, and filled the spaces with astonishing showers of colour, like living fireworks.

Armando saw the dedication, the labour, the persistence of creation, the way his neighbour worked to bring beauty out of desolation. But he saw the ruthlessness as well, the pitiless scourging of pests, the rigorous selection of healthy plants, the extermination of weeds, the poisoning of any infiltrating species on the sumptuous green velvet of the lawns. His own family, especially the women, and especially the youngest child, Maria, were disciplined in their activities, so that nothing should be spoiled. This man demanded perfection, and worked tirelessly to achieve it, remodelling where necessary, pruning, deselecting. A lifetime's work. As Armando's political ambitions began to take shape, the garden became his metaphor.

In the past, he had despised gardening as a soft option for elderly people past their prime. He had fallen for the sentimental portrayal of the sharing, caring gardener, a slave to his plant children. But when he spotted the grubby underbelly of the operation – and it was a life lesson, this, that there always is one – his interest was kindled. The selective kind-nesses for the plants and fauna he wished to accommodate were balanced by equally selective brutalities. This disciplined individual, striving for his particular image of perfection, was both saviour and sinner, deliverer from evil and righteous executioner. The garden was a Holy War. In it, he saw his own future, and how he would go about the business of achieving his goals.

Armando had learnt half his lesson about the power of brutality by watching the irascible, over-protective Mr Ramirez and his relationships with his youngest daughter and his beloved garden. Once, encouraged by their mother while he was away on business, the three children played a throwing game in the garden. Maria, then aged seven, and unused to freedom, grew giddy on it, threw the ball wildly. It sailed past the desperately outstretched arms of her mother and crashed into the border, snapping off a primary branch of a shrub her father had cosseted from seedling to shaky adolescent, and only just planted out.

The wayward trajectory horrified her – she ran sobbing towards the house, already fearing the punishment that was still two days distant. But come it did, on the day of Pepito's tenth birthday celebration, a special garden party the family had been planning for months. While neighbours, school friends and relations all joined in the festivities, Maria was placed on a checkered rug in front of the ruined plant, which was now sited, for its own protection, in the most distant corner of the garden, and forbidden to move from the spot for the duration of the party.

Armando watched her ordeal with fascination. He saw the way she submitted unquestioningly to the dignified fury of her father, her steadfast contemplation of the cause of her punishment, the desertion of her brother and sister, who had, at the scene of the crime, compounded the villainy of betrayal with merciless sibling condemnation. He also saw the iron-hard, unrepentant will with which Mr Ramirez refused the entreaties of the party guests to set the child free, and his brazen indifference to their low opinion of him. He saw the way some of the women turned their backs on him for the rest of the afternoon, or failed to disguise the flashes of contempt in their eyes.

As the child sat, listening to the sounds of merriment drifting down to her from the terrace, Armando watched her weep, and felt the first thrill of seeing a human being utterly subdued. Then a defiant relative walked down from the terrace, all the way across the grass, under the full glare of Mr Ramirez's disapproving stare, knelt beside Maria, and slipped her a small bar of chocolate, and Armando learnt that the smallest act of kindness brought with it hope. Maria's face changed, her expression set as she ate the chocolate calmly, slowly, in a secret act of dissent. Armando stared across at Mr Ramirez, his unconscious role model, and was not surprised to learn later that Maria had been punished a second time for accepting the gift. She was never the same child after that, and he wondered what would become of her.

III

He was this far gone in thought when the door he had entered by opened cautiously and a woman came in. He was surprised to see her – he had expected anything as grand as a judgement from God to be delivered on a one-to-one basis. Let's face it, he had been a fairly influential figure in his time, and his name would go down in history. Surely this merited individual attention?

She was an old woman, tired and haggard, thin and frail. He adjusted his big, meaty, well-fed frame inside his greatcoat. All his life he had had a horror of poverty, squalor, signs of deprivation. As ruler, he had learned to recognise the value of the poor in example setting, and they disgusted him all the more. The present comparison was too crass; he expected better of God than to try to make value judgements by pushing up starving, inconsequential peasants against someone of his rank and calibre. Then he looked at her again, recognised her, and thought he understood. This was Adela the guerrilla queen, the woman who had assassinated him. She had got her own back after years of patient waiting. Armando might despise the sheep that constituted the bulk of the people living under his regime, but at least they were easy to control, could be herded where you wanted them. Adela and her like were rogue rams, endlessly butting their horns against the shepherd's crook, refusing to fall into line. She was not, at least not initially, driven by finer feelings and high ideals. Her motive was revenge. Armando had personally ordered and supervised the torturing and shooting of her husband and children.

Oh, it had been a trivial episode, many years before he had gained notoriety and power. He had been a soldier, sorting out some sordid episode in a distant, pestilence-ridden outpost. There was no time to waste on politics, so, with a detachment and efficiency that had earned him several commendations at Headquarters, he had taken the initiative and tackled the problem at its source. Only time revealed that his punishment had not gone far enough.

It was years later when he learnt the second half of his lesson about brutality, when Adela taught him just how far you had to go with some people to drive your point home. In her case, his mistake had been a failure of judgement, the magnitude of which he only realised later, when Adela had become almost as well guarded as he. Her husband had been shot – that was routine for suspected guerrillas. Her children were tortured first, then shot. He couldn't remember how. In fact, he didn't actually *know* how. Even then, the details of the cruelties he and his men inflicted were of little consequence. To tell the truth, it was all rather tiresome. He liked to settle problems swiftly, and torture, which tended to be protracted and unpleasantly noisy, made him uncomfortable. He was a thinker, a planner, a man who conceived on paper; he had no stomach for witnessing pain.

He had had an afternoon engagement after this appointment, and he had no sadistic interest in the screams and pleadings and blasphemies and curses that came from Adela and her three children, who were, let's say, disfigured before they were bayoneted to death. And of course his men insisted on raping Adela afterwards, just to labour the point. He could see himself now on that bright, sunny lunchtime, smoking, leaning against the wall, one eye on his watch, while his men took their turns. He was worried about missing the afternoon engagement – it would look bad if he turned up late – but to interrupt now would be churlish, bad for morale. After all, rape was one of the perks.

When the last of them came out, he glanced through the doorway at the woman on the floor, emotionally if not physically disembowelled, weeping hysterically over her bayoneted children and her slumped husband. He said, "You should clean up this mess. Women like you should devote your time to the home – see what happens when you neglect your family and turn your thoughts to revolution."

He sauntered away from the little house, because it was important to look unhurried, thinking he had left a broken woman who would probably drive herself to death within a year. He did not see the hard centres of her eyes, like almonds set in bitter chocolate, that would not be crushed by cruelty or injustice or devastating grief. He saw that now. He had seen it before, with little Maria in the garden. He might have put out the fire, but he neglected to stamp on the ashes.

But if God was trying to make some sort of obscure point about servitude and cruelty, he had rather missed his mark. Far from being a helpless victim, this woman had been a thorn in his side for years, sabotaged many minor operations and assassinated many fine officers. Shooting her family was supposed to break her spirit in the early days of the regime, but of course, when he had come to power, the conflict had become personal.

While she continued with her small-scale guerrilla-type tactics, he moved on to ever-grander expressions of power and control. His genius for strategy removed him at an early stage from the hands on missions, leaving him free to plan the kind of operations that left people in no doubt of his intentions and ability to achieve them.

It was the strategy – the bit he had real talent for – that was rewarding. But the administration accompanying it was another matter entirely. Another matter *entirely*. It was one thing to develop an idea for oppressing a group of people, whether it was a long-term project or a quick-fire solution to something that was bothering you. But the fine detail, the hours spent in clandestine meetings or talking in ridiculous codes over the telephone, the problems of co-ordinating supplies when the people supplying them had no idea what the materials were for, these were all hard work. The constant agonising over who he could trust, and the monitoring of the chosen few to ensure his judgement had been correct. The way a single forgotten detail could throw the whole thing out of kilter for a month or more – these were the things he had no patience with.

He could see in his head whatever it was he was planning, so clearly, so bright and sharp in every detail, it was almost painful in its perfection. There it was, precise in every detail, running from start to finish through his mind like an expertly directed film. Why couldn't others share that vision, grasp immediately and exactly the completeness of his idea – and go away and sort it all out? These were the things that made him lose his temper, and display the unreasonable and violent aspects of his character that he preferred people not to see. It was the pressure. It was understandable, his panicked aides would say afterwards, when they had scuttled into his office after the outburst with a jug of his favourite lemon barley water, and made arrangements with the medical authorities or mortuary facilities for the collection of the unfortunate victim of the fallout.

No, it was tough being a dictator and orchestrator of military and political enforcement. People forgot – or it simply didn't occur to them – that there was a great deal of sheer grind to the job of bending a population to your will. Outsiders saw the sensational bits, the culmination of months of paperwork and statistical analysis. A child could blow up a family, or a policeman or a hospital ward – and several of them had proved the point. *His* talents lay in the large-scale, and people rarely appreciated his efforts. They didn't understand that it took a lot of dull, routine office slog to kill ten thousand people.

Well, look at it like this. The administrative implications of doing anything in volume are massive. First you have to develop and refine the idea. Then you have to sell it, and its feasibility. Then there's the strategy. Then you have to mobilise the necessary forces, only a certain proportion of which are military. All the while, secrecy is a top priority, so that's another headache. Eventually, you get around to killing your ten thousand people, give or take a few hundred either way. But that is by no means the end of it, oh dear me, no. In the aftermath, you discover how good your cover-up operation has been. It's simply not the done thing for a dictator to be seen to be responsible for a massacre. You shouldn't have to admit to such a thing even being necessary. The world interprets it, and proceeds to market it as a sign of failure, that a lot of people must be disagreeing with you if you have to keep killing them to keep them quiet.

Although he had generally regarded killing and oppression as a means to an end, like many dictators, he found it difficult to think in terms of actually achieving the stated objective, which would be total compliance, if you were honest about it, not peace. If everyone did agree with him, then ruling the country would rather lose its edge. Even though killing did not seem to take up an awful lot of time for his men, most of his job was bound up with some form of oppression. What would he actually have to do if there was no longer a need to keep his people in line?

But that was ludicrous. There would be a great deal to do. Developing diplomacy, initiating trade agreements, speaking to countries which would become friendly if he made his terms attractive enough. His aides would do all the paperwork and negotiation, but he would have to start the ball rolling and front it all. The trouble was, Armando had never been much of a diplomat, or much of a thinker. Oppression was his particular talent.

He sighed. The killing – all right, he would admit it, the bit he was good at, the bit that interested him – was such a very small part of being a dictator. It was all these other things that had begun to wear him down. They had started to make him actually listen to the new liberal types who kept suggesting from safe enclaves in other countries that killing was not, when it came down to it, a very efficient way of achieving an objective. On particularly bad days, he found himself slowly coming to the conclusion that you could manage a country much more simply, enjoyably – and cheaply – if you were a bit more laid back, a bit more tolerant, and a bit less paranoid. You liked to delude yourself that you were God, but you weren't. It was going to be interesting to meet the person who actually carried the title. Perhaps he could learn something from him.

His thoughts returned to the woman who had come into the room and disturbed his train of thought. Perhaps she didn't recognise him? But surely she must. She raised her head and they regarded each other, the Great Dictator and the putative Little Victim, and he suddenly realised why she was here at the same time as him. Had she enjoyed the spectacle of his death – he still wasn't altogether clear about what had actually happened (well, you're not exactly in a position to take notes, are you?) – before her own demise? Or was she cut down by the machine guns before she knew she had got him? Either way, the scores had been levelled. This last glorious act of revenge would mean a lot to her. He was a dead dictator. She was a martyr.

Her eyes were heavy and uncannily expressionless as she said, "Now you will get the punishment no one on earth could give you. And I will be here to see it."

As he listened, Armando thought he understood – again. The Divine Retribution would be accompanied by a more down to earth punishment at the hands of the one he had punished. He sighed. It was all very biblical, very predictable. Why had he behaved as he had, when he knew all along what was coming? A few stiff remarks and a swift despatch to the burning pit. Or was the afterlife run along more sophisticated lines these days? Perhaps some subtle form of psychological punishment, or maybe, after careful consideration of costs and other logistics, God had decided to update with the Everlasting Electric Chair?

He was plunged into sudden gloom. His had been, after all, a wasted life, long on effort and short on results. The punishment he had visited on the millions he had taken a dislike to was, in the end, disproportionate to the pay-off. Was this how God felt?

IV

In his office, God sighed heavily as he heard the words spoken by the woman. It was complicated enough, he thought, without situations like this. He couldn't put it off any longer. He had stalled for the last twenty minutes, but this was it. Another couple of tricky admissions in prospect, another confession, another series of explanations and justifications. He didn't like dealing with the dictators. They made him uneasy. They were too much like him – taken off too big a bite, and hopelessly ill-equipped for the task.

The restructuring programme wasn't helping, either. However you styled it, bureaucracy was still bureaucracy, cumbersome, time consuming and inefficient. Heaven, just like any other vast, unwieldy corporate giant, creaked along, hopelessly overburdened by clients, dreadfully understaffed and crippled by low morale and poor systems management. Nick, the boss, was asking for his honest opinion about the feasibility of introducing Total Quality Management – it was all the rage in the Western World, and a sure sign to God that everything was beginning to fall apart. After the initial amusement with the current fad for throwaway shorthands like TQM, LOMBARD, DILLIGAS and LABATYD, he had begun to hate acronyms. Nick, boyishly enthusiastic about *everything*, loved them.

His eyes strayed to a fat wallet placed carefully on the end of his desk, a newly published report about the state of the planet. It was his carrot to get him to the end of the day, his reward for the grind of the admissions procedure. He was a geologist first, a bureaucrat second. Creating the world in six days was stretching the point, of course, but the principle was along the right lines. He couldn't have done it single-handedly, and he couldn't have done it with a purely philosophical background. It was his practical streak as a scientist that had pulled it all together, and his hands-on work for the Creation was the last time he had really got stuck in. But he certainly didn't get Sundays off, not since the appearance of mankind. Heaven was seven days a week, twenty-four hours a day, and you didn't get Christmas or bank holidays. It must have been five hundred years since he last had a day off. And now Jupiter was up for grabs – a wonderful, messy, enormous, thrilling challenge. He might still be stuck in a tiny backwater of the universe which not many people were interested in, but he couldn't think of a more exciting planet anywhere than Jupiter – stormy, unformed, crying out for all the devoted geological attention he could pour on it. The frustration was terrible – he was trying to put together a bid for the work in the midst of all this infuriating spiritual sticking-plaster stuff for a human race he wished he'd never invented. He sighed again. One day, he'd like to give it all up and go fishing. But still, not today. He rose to his feet, crossed the roomy, comfortable office and opened the door to the anteroom.

A large, ruddy-faced man, who gave the impression of possessing boundless energy, approached them. Of the myriad persona available to God on these occasions, this was the most reliable in both putting people at their ease and keeping them in their place. The woman remained seated. Given her fervently religious background – part of the problem in the first place – Armando had expected her to be rejuvenated in God's presence, jump to her feet and sing and clap her hands, or indulge in some other such over the top expression of pleasure. But she simply sat, eyes glittering with anticipation. Armando cleared his throat, adjusted his greatcoat, and faced him, man to man. He was immediately taken aback; he had expected a thunderbolt to start off with, followed by anger, disgust and a red-hot poker. God's face, however, did not wear the expected expression. Where Armando looked for stern approbation, cold dislike and formal distance edged with revulsion, he found warmth, and intuitive understanding. The backs of his eyelids began to prickle.

It wasn't so much a handshake as a clasp, firm, sincere and full of compassion. The Great Dictator nodded stiffly, flummoxed and floored. God then turned to Adela, took her hands, and pulled her to her feet. Her eyes searched his, and he got the message. *Whatever you do to him, make it more vile than I have the power to imagine. Do this for me. Avenge me.*

God looked meaningfully into her eyes, gave her a particularly brilliant smile, and said, "Come, both of you," before ushering them into the office.

When they were seated, deeply cushioned in soft leather, and God was opposite, in a slightly higher chair, Armando wondered again if there was some complex, devilish mind game at work. God now looked uncomfortable, as if he had difficult news to break that he knew would reflect badly on him.

"I am so very sorry," he said eventually, "that both of you have led such – difficult lives."

Surely we – I – made it difficult for others? Armando thought, but held his tongue.

"The world as you know it" – God winced involuntarily and thought, *I sound like something out of Star Trek* – "operates on a balance between good and evil, right and wrong. From the greatest heroic deeds to the smallest breaches of honesty, from the smallest acts of kindness to the greatest betrayals of everything mankind considers correct."

Armando and Adela, still refusing to look at each other, fixed their gazes on God and nodded.

"It is a complicated project," God went on. "To some extent, it is still in its experimental stages. Mankind has brought an interesting new dimension to things that we had not allowed for when we began. But we have established a kind of code of practice, if you will, that enables us to see how the balance we seek is affected by different levels of contributory factors."

God stopped, put a hand thoughtfully to his mouth, and appeared to start again. "I will, if you'll allow me, discuss these issues in isolation, for the sake of simplicity. The many other managerial complexities of the Earth are handled by separate departments." His audience of two made no attempt to disagree.

"So, we are talking about the need for balance. War and disease, for example, different kinds of government, environmental circumstances, dynamic people who become catalysts for change, and so on." God drew a deep breath, watching Armando and Adela, the die-hard opposing factions, losing their footing on unstable ground. They were riveted now, held in thrall by a situation that was unfolding in a completely different direction to their expectations. "We are particularly interested in how people respond to hardship and suffering, both as individuals and groups. If people are to reveal their strengths, they must be tested by painful circumstances. In order for us to arrive at an acceptable balance, someone has to suffer, and often, someone has to perpetrate the suffering and bear the responsibility for it."

In the silence that followed these words, God felt their sudden, incredulous half-grasp of what was coming, rush between them, binding them together for a fraction of a second, before bursting upon him in a torrent of outrage. The Great Dictator, his voice rendered husky by a sense that he was no longer in control, said, "We were chosen?"

"I am afraid so. Just as we must appoint people to set good examples, so we must appoint those who set bad ones."

God raised his hand, blocking the two-pronged protestation. "There are queues of people lining up to be the good guy," he said. "Believe me, nobody wants to be the bad guy. I wish there didn't have to be any. We all do. But until we complete our research into definitive human characteristics, there is no other way. As I said, the complications your race has introduced were not expected, and we have to make the best use of you we can. It is vitally important that when the pendulum swings in the wrong direction, there is enough momentum to ensure it swings back."

"So contrary to popular belief," The Great Dictator said with uncontrollable sarcasm, "you are the driving force behind the evil in the world. You have been my mentor."

"It's a difficult one, I know," God said. "There's the question of expectations. You, for example, expect to be punished for your crimes, yet you cannot be held responsible for them. I induced the behaviour, and your life has therefore become forfeit to wrongdoing. Adela here" – Adela seemed so gripped by shock at this point that God did not include her in the conversation – "quite rightly wants you to be punished for all eternity for what you have done to her children and her country, but it is I who must bear her wrath. And you have performed an invaluable function in that you have taught the world about evil and demonstrated how far its boundaries may be stretched. That in turn galvanises the forces for good in the world, and makes people redouble their efforts to ensure that evil on such a scale is more difficult to replicate in the future. In short, we have much to thank you for.

"Now, it's a slow process, I know, and a certain amount of learning done in one generation is unlearned by succeeding generations, as memories dim and attitudes change. And of course, the world is a large and diverse place, and lessons learned in one culture are not necessarily transferred to others. So while, for example, the Western world learns that genocide against the Jews is undesirable, another culture will quite happily persecute another race by deconstructing the general arguments against genocide and reconstructing a different code of sanction. The recent events in Eastern Europe are an excellent example of this. Good is quite a general characteristic of the human race, but it is also often a weak one, and easily perverted – a flaw in the developmental process. That's why massive acts of destruction have always occurred which are driven by small minorities. Eventually, it is our hope that the good within individuals will become tougher in character, and become a primary instinct, not a learned response. Then we'll be getting somewhere."

Armando, The Great Dictator, the man who killed millions and then hankered after a river in Montana, a nine-foot fly rod and a Hornberg Caddis, is shrinking by the minute. His power, his ingeniousness for destruction, is being removed, piecemeal, by the Supreme Being. None of it was his idea after all. His greatness has been borrowed, a copycat act masterminded from above.

God smiled at him ruefully. "You have, it's true, been manipulated by our needs, but it also means that your life has served an extremely positive purpose. And we do operate a compensation scheme here. You will have a happier experience next time around."

Armando's first response was that he didn't want a happier experience, merely an original one. "Is there nothing about my life that can be called my own?" he asked angrily. "Does everything I've worked to achieve have to be put down to an automaton-like response to some kind of pre-determined auto-suggestion?"

"Not at all," God said smoothly. "You are given a certain set of circumstances with which to play. How you respond to your environment is not something that concerns us directly. We put down a set of criteria, it's true, but the interpretation of them is down to the individual. There are, fortunately I have to say, long gaps between people who respond to them as you did, and express themselves on quite such a grand scale."

He was mollified at this, and a small piece of him reasserted itself as he grasped at the shred of independent thinking God dangled for him. He could take some of the credit after all.

"Is there no punishment for him?" Adela said suddenly from her chair.

"As I explained," God said, a trifle brusquely, "his whole life has been a punishment, as has yours. People are required to suffer ordeals so that others may learn from them. And you have seen your fair share of killing and cruelty – from both perspectives."

Adela, nursing dashed hopes of watching a scene of vicious reparation, sat shaking her head, trying to think of something to say. Why was argument suddenly so difficult for her? When she opened her mouth at last, she heard herself say, to her own astonishment, "I would like to see my family."

God smiled. "Of course we can arrange that. We try to give people opportunities to tie up loose ends before the next round." He stood up, concluding the interview. "Now, I think that will do for today," he said. "You will, of course, have other chances to meet with me and other members of staff to discuss your next placement, but in the meantime, I would concentrate on losing some of the baggage you've been carrying around." He smiled reassuringly. "This is a healing place," he said. "You'll find everything you need to help you progress. I think in a few days you will both be feeling much better about all of it. Remember we have been talking about the need for balance."

At the door, and almost through it, Armando paused, turned and looked once more into the face of God. His eyes were troubled.

"There is something you need to ask," God said.

Armando cleared his throat. "Yes," he said, and stopped, still uncomfortable with his new role of subordinate. "I want to know – " he stopped again, wondering why the question needed to be asked.

God waited patiently.

"We are a trouble to you," Armando said. "You have said as much. Your manner is dismissive, somehow. I wondered – when you look objectively at mankind – what do you consider to be our most significant achievement?"

God smiled suddenly at the unexpected question. "Magnification," he said, without hesitation.

Armando stared at him.

"The ability to see," God clarified for him. Armando shook his head. God cast around, looked down at his desk and seized the chunk of Lewisian gneiss resting on top of the geological report. "Because when we see, we understand," God said. "If you look at this, you see a piece of stone. Am I right?"

Armando shrugged and nodded.

God held it closer. "But when you truly *see* it, you understand the building blocks of the planet you inhabit, the very foundations of where you came from." He regarded the Great Dictator thoughtfully. "It is not a question of scale, as so many humans think," he said gently. "Not creation. Not destruction. Not discovery. Simply the ability to see. Because when we see, we live our lives as we should. Do *you* see? Do you understand?"

After a moment, his voice very small, Armando said, "And what is the worst thing?"

"Differentiation," God said, and smiled a sad smile.

Armando nodded. That, at least, needed no clarification.

V

God closed the door behind him and rubbed the palms of his hands over his eyes. The problem was trying to accommodate the ordinary people as well as the ones who made themselves disagreeably singular. Dictators! he thought wearily. They were the worst. And their victims weren't much better. Both arrived with totally wrong-headed expectations. Both were a threat to the smooth running of the unit. He was now well practised in keeping a straight face as he delivered his welcoming speech.

And it wasn't that he couldn't view the dictators' predicament with some sympathy. As he knew only too well, if you were in power and trying to rule your corner, none of the options were easy. Victims of paranoia and irrational prejudices bolted onto disordered, confrontational personalities, dictators chose the hardest route of them all, convinced it was the easiest, that eventually everyone would capitulate if they had enough tantrums, and they would get their own way. The astonishing, simplistic egoism "I think, therefore I'm right" carried them through until they were shot by exasperated, driven people acting from a variety of not always altruistic motives.

By choosing evasion, God generally had little trouble. After all, the package he was offering was very attractive. He could cut short the initial interview by pleading pressure of work – his daily quota was fifty – and then he relied on the pleasant conditions to do the rest. Few people were going to argue with the chance to do exactly as they liked for as long as they wanted. There was always the odd exception, someone who came back too firmly rooted in reality, who couldn't settle for bliss. So you got rid of them, put them back again, but tried to place them where they couldn't do much harm – the South American jungle was a good one. God had pinched the idea from the British, when he saw the use they had made of Australia, and he had to admit he wished he'd thought of it first.

Even before he closed the interview by selling heaven as a sort of paradise achieved through Alzheimer's, he usually had shock on his side. Sometimes he was ashamed of the way he took advantage of people. They arrived knackered, dis-illusioned, or smug. But all of them were in a state of shock, stunned that they had died, stunned to find he really existed, even the religious ones, and stunned that he really wanted to see them, and received them in what purported to be a contemporary environment. God, unlike many of his followers, believed in moving with the times. The attention to ancient rites was touching, of course, but ultimately caused problems. By the time they got their act together and wanted to argue, God was no longer in a position to speak to them. Half of them left convinced they were dreaming and would wake up.

Neither did he see everyone. It would be impossible. Not

to mention dull. He tried to concentrate on the specials, the potential troublemakers. His brief was both broad and simplistic: to reduce problems.

In the midst of his reverie, the intercom buzzed loudly.

"Are you busy in there?"

God sighed. "No, Nick. I've just processed Armando IV."

Nick tutted sympathetically. "Oh, him. Any trouble?"

"No. I did the double with Adela Marquez. Worked a treat. What can I do for you?"

"It's just that I've had a referral from the gate – someone who's complaining about dying and says she wants to go right to the top."

"She means me, not you," God said in exasperation. "I'm God, for Christ's sakes. Who is she and what's the problem?"

"That'll be a screw-up in Reception," Nick said apologetically. "It's all very well developing new training initiatives, but if middle management can't supervise the new recruits, we've had it. I'll get on to it right after this – we probably need a new mentoring programme."

"Angels with brains would be a good starting point," God said tersely.

"Look, it's just a quickie. I know you've got a lot on. Mrs Theresa Burns wants to know why she died two days before her daughter's wedding when she'd gone to the trouble of having a cardiac bypass last year. She says it doesn't seem fair and she wants to go back."

God sighed impatiently, tapping his fingers in a measured rhythm. Eventually, he said, "Tell her she may well have had the operation, but I cannot guarantee immunity from physical damage caused by her flagrant consumption of cream cakes and her penchant for smoking. When the surgeons have had such an impressive impact on her chances of survival, a similar commitment from her would have been sensible, not an immediate return to old habits. She certainly can't go back – I'm not a miracle-worker. If she is not happy with that response, I'll see her at four o' clock on Thursday."

"That sounds fair enough," Nick said. "I'll give her the

option, but you know how it goes – four days on chocolate éclairs and Woodbines with no repercussions, and she'll probably come round to the idea. Did you get that memo? Give me a buzz about it later if you need to."

There was a pause, and God knew there was something else coming.

"I don't suppose the pandas are extinct yet?"

"You know they aren't," God said tiredly. "And neither are the whales or the Siberian tigers or the other dozen or so specials."

There was a sigh. "It's just that – well, you know we can't get on to the next stage with all these hangers-on."

"I know, I know," God said. "It's my lot again. They keep coming up with salvage plans. They don't get it, the way it's supposed to work, and I can't do a lot about it. It's insecurity, really, they're trying to save other creatures in the hope they'll work out how to save themselves. They've seen what happened to the dinosaurs."

"They haven't – you know – worked anything out yet, then?"

"Oh no, they're miles off," God said. "Some of their theories are seriously entertaining. But they *are* getting better. Especially about the rocks. But they won't get anywhere until they get into the middle, and that won't be for quite a while yet. We'll just have to watch them."

"Well," Nick said, trying to sound brighter, "we always said this would be an interesting one, didn't we? I must get on. Keep me posted, won't you?"

"Will do," God said, and turned to survey the mountain of paper on his desk, searching for Theresa Burn's details. There were more and more of them, people demanding explanations, threatening tribunals and legal action, punitive damages and the like. Heaven had avoided being sued so far, but God could see the day when a legal department would have to be set up. There never seemed to be a right time to die – in fact, nobody seemed to accept that they should die at all. Dying was not seen as part of the deal, represented a drop in standards, a failure of systems. He sighed. Where on earth had they got that idea?

After two thousand years, the challenge had lost its edge, and he was getting fed up. Most other Divine Beings had been able to retire and go back to more interesting things, as faiths waxed and waned. God was a survivor, as was Mohammed down the corridor, victims of their own popularity. Some of the tribal religions went back even longer, of course, but you could cope with the numbers, do it on a part-time basis. And it could be hurtful, when a deity was finally rejected. Ra, Isis and all the Egyptians had taken it very hard after such a long run, and relocating them had taken a good deal of counselling and post-trauma support. Ra in particular had begun to believe in his own publicity, really got into it and began to identify with the persona created for him. He was quite the loaded gun before he entered reconditioning and was able to accept the way things really were – that he was a high-up in Heaven, but there was really nothing more mystical to it than that. God rubbed his hands over his eyes. There was a board meeting later in the week to discuss the overwork and if there was any possibility of restructuring. And he wanted Jupiter. He needed a holiday, a thousand years to reconstruct priorities, a change of scenery. He'd certainly earned it.

And what were they, after all – surface relief, literally, that created a diversion from the real business of the planet and its long-term future. What had happened, that their massive numbers, their triumphs and atrocities, petty passions and annihilating conflicts had come to almost swamp other affairs, the structural matters, the contingency, the equatorial concerns, the internal combustion calculations? They had done it for a bit of fun, knocked up some carbon-based rudiments and then sat back to see what happened. Absolutely every other species was fine and sorted itself out. It was the humans, the ones with brains and imaginations, who turned out to be insecure, immature and constantly seeking approval.

Mankind was the first species to acquire the basic intelligence to question, and try to work out, or not work out, what was going on, what it was all about. And that was the fundamental problem with all of them. No one wanted to blast them out of existence, because they needed to run their natural course like every other species had done, but there were so many of them, and even allowing for their indecently hasty development, it was still taking too long. And the longer they stayed, using up precious resources and administrative time, the better they got at adapting to the challenges of life on earth, and the longer they would stay. Even the dinosaurs, who had lasted infinitely longer than the fast and furious blast of the Age of Man, were not a problem, and left everyone able to get on with their jobs. Once they got religion out of the mix – and that meant removing Man from the mix – God and the rest of the heavenly corporation would be far from redundant. Everyone missed the dinosaurs. Mankind was not like that. In their desperation for reassurance, humans would kill, torture and oppress, bend others to their beliefs in the grip of a powerful uncertainty that translated as its opposite.

Dictators who killed and induced others to kill on a grand scale were really off the scale. If the object of the afterlife really were punishment, it would be impossible to atone for the sheer volume of suffering engendered by one person and his dream. Torture was a thoroughly uncivilised response, and prohibitive in terms of cost and manpower. They'd all had a good laugh at the primitive images of men descending into pits of fire – *What on earth do they take us for? one of the appointed deities had asked* – being roasted on spits, eaten alive and countless other inventions. But the humour in the situation had petered out when they realised that of course, these ideas were man-made, and could only come from the imagination of a species doomed to live out their lives in a state of confusion and uncertainty about what they were doing, and why they were doing it. Whatever they imagined God would punish them with in the afterlife, they tried out themselves on the living first, just to make sure it was really going to hurt.

God sighed. Every day he was confronted with growing evidence of human cruelty, and every day he wondered how much longer it would go on.

As now, dictator and oppressed – the dual interview technique was something he had pioneered – could be shepherded out of the door in a state of confusion. People tended not to get into arguments with him. The religious baggage they had acquired on earth, even the atheists, could always be turned to good effect when the time came. It was a challenge compared to dealing with the usual round of petty suburban jealousies, football hooliganism or schoolboy wanking. Then he remembered that it would not go on forever and sooner or later the planet would perform one of its spectacular reinventions, and they could start again with a new set of dynamics. Give me a rock, he thought, any rock, and its complexities will keep me happy for hours. Give me back geology. He clicked the monitor to bring up his tender for the Jupiter project, then picked up the memo from Nick that had been left on his desk and read:

TO ALL DEITIES:

In response to numerous requests for reduced working periods and freedom to re-establish key structural surveys on rocks and minerals underlying the tectonic plates, interviews for five relief deities will take place next week. Please write recommendations for the posts in the space below. A list of interested parties is provided for your convenience. Asterisks denote those interested in job-sharing.

Please also submit a draft for an induction and training programme. These are to incorporate basic understanding of pre-requisites, so studying faiths to determine attitudes to areas such as forgiveness and punishment, moral codes etc is mandatory. I know this is a bit of a pain, but we have to make some attempt to deliver on expectations. I have all the relevant information on file and will download stuff as appropriate.

Depending on the success of the new recruits, incumbents should bear in mind that mentoring and overlapping are likely while the present levels of processing are sustained. Results are expected shortly on the probability research project being done into the projected survival rates of long-term faiths. Please submit any outstanding overtime slips along with your recommendations, and indicate your availability for conducting interviews.

Finally, I hate to encroach further on your good nature, but one of the Indonesian gods is looking for a short break – can anyone double up and stand in for him on processing duties just for a while?

RSVP ASAP.

Nick.

*P.S. Some of you have expressed interest in drafting one or two exceptional humans onto the deity training programme. I can't see this being practical, but if you feel strongly about the idea, I will review a list of no more than **three** additional candidates. In these cases, psychological profiling is essential, notwithstanding past performance.*

The submission deadline for Jupiter has been extended by one week. Presentations will be timetabled after the closing date.

Cheered at the thought that his holiday – he might yet get around to actually visiting the surface and getting a real feel for the place – might come up sooner than he thought, God flicked the intercom switch to find out who else had come into the waiting room, demanding to know the meaning of life.

3
I TOLD YOU I WAS ILL

I

Well, doctor, I'll tell you everything I've been feeling, and you may be able to tell me what you think it is. (Perhaps a light laugh here?) I've got my own ideas – I do try to think things through, so as not to waste too much of your time – but I would like your opinion about ...

Dorothy sits down carefully on the bus, as if too emphatic a movement towards her seat might dislocate the fragile body she has only just managed to hold together all these years.

It's this tiredness. I feel so exhausted all the time. I spent all day in bed yesterday, just to make sure I'd have enough strength to come in. This sore throat just isn't getting any better, and I find bright light is beginning to trouble me – you can see I've got my sunglasses with me. I do hope this diabetes isn't getting any worse – I've been very careful about sugar since I saw you. I really don't want to think there might be complications, but as I mentioned previously, I was wondering if it might be ... CFS?

The doctor is pleasant. So gentle and patient. Only last week she had taken a blood test to check for diabetes when she had complained of thirst, frequency and fatigue. She had caught the same bus, had had to buy a bottle of mineral water at the newsagent's on the corner because she was so terribly thirsty. And her frequency had increased in the last week – definitely. Whether or not it was before she saw the posters displaying her symptoms in large letters, she couldn't say, but she was certainly grateful to them for giving her a clue as to what might be the matter.

The phone call from the surgery had come yesterday teatime, asking her to come in for the results of the blood test. She was triumphant. *I knew there was something wrong!* Perhaps the doctor would thank her for her percipience, for describing her symptoms so well, they alerted her to the very real probability that she was ill. Since childhood, she had nursed a litany of complaints, never as well as her mother thought she ought to be, never quite ill enough to get more time off school. And later, her husband, now long dead, had wondered why she had never had the energy she was always blaming others for not using. Perhaps she had had this problem for months; she had been feeling particularly unwell since Christmas at least.

Mind you, she had been lucky to get a blood test at all. It had been very irritating, when, after describing her symptoms at some length, the doctor had shown more interest in the bruise on her arm from where she had banged into the door a few days ago. *Talk about getting your priorities mixed up,* Dorothy thought with a snort. *Here I am with suspected diabetes, possible CFS complications, and all you care about is a bruise.* The doctor must have noticed she was annoyed, because she changed tack suddenly and suggested a blood test might be a good way to start solving the mystery. The call she answered yesterday evening – a Sunday, think of that! – vindicated her insistence. Such efficiency could only have been brought about by her being firm, and letting the doctor know she was not about to be fobbed off.

Although diabetes can be a very serious disease, fortunately you have a mild form of it, which we can treat quite easily. Thank goodness we caught it in time, eh? (She couldn't expect to take all the credit, after all.) Now then, here is your syringe, and I'll explain exactly what you'll have to do ...

Dorothy smoothed a wrinkle out of her coat and sat in smug frailty amongst the other passengers, anticipating the frank intimacy of a consultation about her illness between two intelligent adults.

How much worse can this get? How much more do I have to take before I start running amok with a chainsaw?

While Dorothy makes plans for the forthcoming diagnosis, and mentally reorganises her tidy fridge to accommodate the phials of insulin, Sheila Mooney sits fuming in a traffic jam on the other side of town and contemplates the morning ahead with ill grace. The journey to the surgery had already got off to a bad start. Driving down the lane from her home towards the short stretch of dual carriageway that would take her to the outskirts of town, a stray sheep had suddenly appeared in front of the car, forcing her to jam on the brakes. The sheep regarded her insolently while she flung verbal abuse at it, chewing grass and refusing to move out of the way until she had nudged it with the front bumper. Cursing the farmer, who must have left the gate open, cursing the sheep, which was infuriatingly unmoved by its near miss, and actually looked suspiciously as if it had walked in front of her on purpose, Sheila thrust the car savagely into gear and drove too fast on the remaining distance to the end of the lane, stopping at the junction with an undignified squeal of brakes.

It would be bad enough if this was a usual Monday morning, with her caseload of urban sicknesses spread depressingly towards the distant horizon of Friday afternoon. But no.

This is a very particular Monday morning, a bitch-with-a-headache-of-a-Monday-morning, a Monday-morning-after-the-argument-the-night-before. She contemplates a task ahead that must be handled with tact and sympathy, even though her mood is vile and the first appointment of the day is with a woman whose first, carefully chosen, anxious, and somehow always irritatingly cocky words always propel her stress-levels through the ceiling.

I can't find a way in. I have got to do this, and I have got to do this right. And I can't find the way in, the right words to open the gap and start a dialogue. I could do it with anyone else. I have done it. So why –

She punches the steering wheel as the lights change for the sixth time, cursing as she inches forward to occupy the minuscule gap that has opened up between her and the car in front. No matter how much she takes it out on Bill, or tells herself she doesn't need this right now, the crisis has come and she must concentrate her efforts to bury her personal prejudices. After years of flooding her appointment book with an endless stream of medical trivia, the bloody woman has actually got something seriously wrong with her. And Dr Sheila Mooney, bruised from a bitter row, aching for reconciliation, and focused only on her own pain, can really do without that today.

Bill, who always understood the most subtle swings in her mood, and was usually maddeningly patient about them, had been pushed too far over this one. It was both incomprehensible and painful to Sheila that one of the worst rows they had ever had had been triggered by Dorothy Timpter. It was infuriating that Dorothy, who played so large a part in her professional life, was now cropping up to cause dissent in her home. Bill had accused her of irrational guilt, of paranoia – *I know you don't like her, but you didn't exactly culture the cells and push her onto the down escalator.* That was bad enough, but then he said, *Come on, it's not all bad – it means one less name on the register, about three appointments a week, and at least a dozen phone calls.* That was when she blew – not because Bill was being callous and flippant, but because the same thought had already occurred to her. She would be glad to see the back of her first, sorry she was not losing her because she was moving house second.

Sheila sighed in frustration. When she first knew she wanted to become a doctor, she equated entering the profession with attempting sainthood. She had no illusions that she was, or could ever be, a saint, but she knew the demands it would make on her, and she worked hard to live up to the set of impossibly high ideals placed on her by first teachers, then patients, and always, herself.

She was comforter to the dying and the bereaved. She congratulated the happy expectant mother carefully nursing her new treasure; she was sympathetic counsellor to the not so happy mother nursing ruined expectations. She was good at diagnosis, and knew her limitations; she had a strong instinct, but when she doubted, she was humble enough to recommend a second opinion, or consult a more knowledgeable colleague. Children trusted her and respected her honesty when they asked if it would hurt; relatives nursing the sick depended on her support and believed in her. She worked on committees, gave lectures to laymen and students, tried to establish and live by a strong ethical code. She was, in short, good at her job, but she was not perfect, and had discovered her Achilles heel. She was not good at Dorothy Timpter.

She had experience of malingerers, of course she did. People trying to sign on the sick so they could give up work, people so bored with life they had to invent complaints to give them a focus for their unused energy. They annoyed her, even though she recognised that the need to simulate ill health was a disease in itself – they wasted valuable time she could be spending with patients who really did have medical problems. But she tried to help them tackle the roots of their depression, tried to get them to direct their energies into something more useful than milking the system.

It's worth trying to put this behind you and get back on your feet, she would say, sometimes briskly, sometimes more gently. Depression is often caused by lack of activity and purpose. Having to work within the system all the time does limit your choices, and a job, or a constructive hobby would restore your self-respect and give you back your energy.

They rarely listened, preferring the paper chits that entitled them to cash without effort and couch potato heaven without guilt. *Look at the jobs market anyway, they'd retort. What chance have I got? Why should I work my arse off in a naff job and get paid bugger all when I can get the same money for staying at home?*

It was the ones who were enslaved by the system who carped most bitterly about it, she thought. Like everything else in life, they only noticed it when it started to work against them. If you didn't fight, you atrophied. It seemed there was nothing in between. The complex relationship between mental and physical health, environmental and social well being was always buried somewhere at the roots of the problem. Sheila saw it shot right through the social fabric, from the ones who had nothing, and never would have, to the ones who had everything.

Dorothy was the same. This need to sink into malaise must have begun at a very young age. Once it was established as a way of getting what she wanted, it was hard to change it.

How many times had Sheila seen it backfire on those who found themselves not only terminally unemployed, but terminally ill as well? She couldn't say for sure, but she knew the number was increasing. Suddenly, they were galvanised, gripped with outrage. *What, on the scrapheap before my time – and about to become landfill before my time as well?*

One chap had actually got better. With a year at the outside, he had stretched it to seven, and was still going. It would probably get him in the end, but at least he was making a fight of it.

Sheila liked fighters. She didn't like people who looked forward to being poorly and took pleasure in playing the incapable. She had a dreadful feeling that Dorothy would positively relish the prospect of a dramatic exit, her remaining days spent languishing away gently in a hospital bed, an insupportable martyr to *tiredness. If she knew what really lay in store for her,* she thought with sudden savagery, *she'd be less complacent about dying of cancer, less eager to want to be ill, and more understanding of the life she had frittered away on headaches and other tense, nervous pains.* She was like a sparrow, hopping nimbly between the starlings, pecking doggedly, eyes darting greedily, scavenging amongst life's grit for attention and sympathy.

Sheila snapped herself off short. This simply wouldn't do. Where was the natural sympathy that would so readily well up on mornings like this with any other patient? It was the role-playing analogy, the feeling that Dorothy had perfected playing her part as one of life's walking wounded. Sheila wanted to write them both into a Hollywood movie and make a great dramatic speech into her face, full of righteous anger. She wanted to make her see the light, punish her for her love affair with malaise, and get her to make life-changing promises that would enable her to face the end with dignity and calm self-knowledge. She snorted with derision. Dorothy was incapable of change. She would stare at her when she heard the news, finger the cameo brooch at her throat, repeat it, and …

This was where Sheila hit a brick wall. She didn't know what would happen next. She didn't know how to start, and she didn't know how to prepare. She would arrive at the surgery in a blind fury, instead of being in control of the ordeal ahead.

It always made her feel uncomfortable, being the bearer of such profound tidings. She had never got used to it. The ownership of discovery lay with her – it had yet to be shared with the person it would most affect. How each person met their death was a singular event, but however it came, it seemed wrong that it should be an outsider who heard of it first and had to pass on the information. It made her feel like a contemptible cross between the Grim Reaper and Mrs Tittle-Tattle, one hand brandishing the scythe, the other covering her mouth while she passed on the juicy details to the grateful masses who had ducked away from harm for the moment.

It was probably the most stressful task a doctor had to perform, and some of them were better at it than others. Sheila had run seminars exploring ways of breaking bad news to patients, and she well remembered the hostility expressed by some of the participants. When you're afraid of something yourself, something that's visited on someone else, there's guilt involved, and dread, and the desire to be as far away as possible from the source of the pain. While your patient sits there, numb with shock, unable to even take in what you're saying, or worse, in floods of hysterical tears, or worse, screaming at you that it's your fault and you should have spotted the symptoms sooner, you don't want the encounter to go on any longer than it absolutely has to. Like a soldier on a battlefield, your gut instinct is to cut and run, not stick around in the middle of the fray. When the accusations of callousness come, from the patients or their grieving relatives, already in denial, already looking for someone to blame, you can't tell them that you actually spent three quarters of an hour talking to the patient about their diagnosis, because they simply won't remember. They remember being told they're going to die. That's enough, that's quite enough, you could talk to them for the next four hours and they wouldn't hear another word you said. It's shock. They are incapable of responding to your compassion for days, while the implications of the news sinks in. And in the meantime, you're an unfeeling, brutal monster who has cut their lives short and can't give them the news they wanted to hear.

Death and the culture of blame had cropped up on more than one occasion in Sheila's lectures to students, as she tried to make them aware of the problems of a culture that constantly tried to deny death as an inevitable conclusion to life. These days, hardly anybody died unless it was somebody's fault, and doctors were right in the firing line. Even if your granny was eighty-seven and died of old age, somebody forgot to give her the injection, or gave her too many pills. And if it can't possibly be anyone else's fault, it has to be yours, and the finger is pointed accordingly. Sheila heard it time and time again from people dying of terminal illness.

Did I do something to deserve this? Have I brought this on myself? When I'm gone, will there be some smug bastard sitting self-righteously over his pint, shaking his head and saying to all present: "It's true, you know – you reap what you sow. We all know about the links between stress and overwork and brain tumours, don't we? We all know that if you smoke, you get cancer. I'm afraid she brought it on herself – it's an inescapable conclusion."

And we all know, of course, that whatever the trends in population, public health and social welfare, the death rate always remains exactly the same – one per person. The person who never lets a Mars Bar pass their lips, and the person whose idea of healthy eating is to reject a Magnum in favour of a Solero, are still heading for the same destination.

How appalling for the unlucky person, not just to die from disease, but to be held responsible for it too! *Well, she would eat beef/drink/drive everywhere/take risks/work herself to death in a stressful job/be a mountaineer/eat butter/sugar/chocolate/never open the windows. No wonder she died!* And you found yourself longing for the self-satisfied, preening jogger/health food freak/yoga fanatic/outdoor pursuits enthusiast/anti-television snob to drop dead at thirty-five, just for spite. But then, Sheila thought, those judges were simply expressing fear – they just couldn't accept that death was the only possible outcome.

In Dorothy's case, the *she brought it on herself* theory was simply too tempting. Sheila could feel it sneaking up around the back of all the other thoughts as the traffic eased up, and reaching the surgery before nine o' clock became a realistic proposition. To die blamelessly, you had to be killed by a mad axe-murderer who happened to be passing through, or run over by a drunk. People were blamed for dying because they spoiled all our attempts to live the lie of immortality.

Now there was Dorothy, who always flirted with illness, always hoped to be unwell, and was about to have her dream come true.

What made Sheila cringe was the way she had always wished illness on herself, arriving chirpily in the surgery with new symptoms, new theories and new suggestions for what might be wrong, and what should be done about it. She was the worst kind of patient – interested in being ill, fascinated by symptoms, alert to the tiniest signals given off by her rigorously policed body. Illness had become her survival mechanism.

The latest ongoing worry was that she was suffering from CFS. She had raised it several weeks ago now, timorously at first, then with growing confidence as she acquired knowledge about the condition and continued to press for signs from Dr Mooney that her suspicions might be well founded. She had mentioned ME at first, then started to use the new acronym, CFS, looking complacently at the doctor for acknowledgement of her up-to-date medical vocabulary. *Look, I even know the right word for it. I must have it!*

Sheila was cornered on that one, of course – she couldn't say one way or the other. CFS, she thought bitterly. However much it was a real and genuine misery for the people who least wanted it, it had also become God's gift to the self-obsessed. This wasn't the only self-diagnosed case she had seen from patients eager to attach the label of martyrdom to their flagging self-esteem. It saddened her that some of her patients were so lonely and dislocated that their only hope of being interesting to others lay in manufactured illness. But it made her angry, too. *For God's sake,* she had thought to herself, her head bent over her notes to conceal her irritation, when Dorothy raised the question for the fourth time, and she was running out of ways of skirting it tactfully. *Get a bloody life, not an illness.*

But it was too late for that now, even if Dorothy had gone through a sea change in her perspectives on life, the universe and the meaning of being ill. The irony was appalling. Dorothy was about to move from the rose-tinted realms of make-believe sickness to harsh technicolour reality, and Sheila guessed that she expected both states to operate by more or less the same set of rules. But she wasn't just going to be poorly, she was going to die.

Sheila always dreaded the moment of revelation, seeing what it did to people, the way you could see them scrabbling amongst the words for another meaning, struggling just to make sense of it, analysing every syllable for some scrap of hidden hope, that they had misunderstood, that they were stupid, that they didn't understand the terminology. She could hear the hollowness in the hope she tried to dish out in the face of such huge tidings. Not that most people heard anything she said in the first few minutes. She talked to fill the enormous silence, talked her way around the spectre of death that filled the surgery, suddenly shone in their eyes. Many of them died then.

What still made her go cold with horror was the fact that

she had almost not done the blood test. Dorothy had already been in the surgery for twenty minutes, pressing her case for more tests. The bruise had attracted her attention because it was still there from the last appointment – a large, dark, ugly discoloration that looked disproportionate to Dorothy's description of how it had occurred. Her suspicions had been kindled, but she had mistrusted the instinct, thinking wryly that it was more likely wishful thinking on her part that Dorothy might have a blood disorder. As it was, Dorothy had been so determined to get across her case for diabetes that Sheila's suggestion of a blood test had been interpreted as a final recognition of her own fears. Sheila, in turn, had had the compassion not to add to her concerns by telling her the real reason she had got out yet another syringe.

How is she going to take it? Will she cry? Please God, don't let her cry. I don't think my sympathy will stretch that far. Will she take it in? How many times will I have to go over it? She'll probably take it personally, blame it on me. It's happened before. What do they say – the nature of bad news infects the teller?

There was the problem of language. Did she use the proper terminology, or keep it simple? Dorothy loved the complicated words; it raised the value of her complaint. She repeated them before she left the surgery, until she had it off just right. Did she bother with the chronic lymphoblastic bit – or just stick with leukaemia? She wouldn't know the difference, and it would keep her busy finding out. What the hell, Sheila thought, whatever she calls it, it's still going to kill her.

Did she have any family? Christ, did I even ask? I must have asked at some point. What did she say? Obviously there had been a Mr Timpter at some point. Sheila racked her brains, and remembered something about her being widowed. Dorothy, now in her late fifties, had lost her husband before she had registered at Sheila's practice, so she must have been widowed close to ten years ago. She kicked herself. You always asked if there was someone who was close to the patient. Today of all days, she wouldn't want to go home and be alone. Had she asked? Or had she assumed there was no one, because for years she couldn't remember a single mention of another person – not when she was being admitted to hospital for tests, not ever?

While the traffic heightened her tension and distorted the poor image she had of her patient, Sheila struggled for some kind of balance. To break bad news, it helped if you liked the person, it helped if you genuinely felt compassion for them and their families, it helped if you wanted to make it easy for them.

But any rapport Dr Mooney might have built up with her patient had vanished early on in the relationship under the pressure of too many consultations, too many phone calls from bewildered colleagues – *Are you aware that Mrs Timpter was unhappy with your diagnosis and has turned up at my surgery requesting a second opinion?* – and a mountain of prescriptions she had written out against all her professional beliefs, because she couldn't bear the sight of her a moment longer. Dorothy Timpter might have been a bad patient, but Sheila Mooney really resented her because whenever she turned up for an appointment, she made her into a bad doctor.

III

There's a club I can join, wasn't it advertised at the bottom of that poster? There'll be little get-togethers where you can meet fellow-sufferers and talk about the problems you're having. I'm sure I could help – there's bound to be people who don't like the thought of needles – they've never troubled me, just as well really, with all the blood tests and jabs and whatnots I've had to put up with. And I saw poor old Fred go through the mill, didn't I just – so many needles and treatments, and so much nursing at the end, I don't think he appreciated all the efforts everybody went to. Me always going backwards and forwards, sitting about at the hospital while he just dozed off – there was many a time I wished it was me lolling about in bed all day instead of running for the bus morning, noon and night, I can tell you.

The bus was full now; glancing behind her, Dorothy saw

there wasn't a single vacant seat, and now an elderly lady was climbing up the steps, her stout legs supported by a stick, while she waved her pass truculently at the driver and turned to scan the passenger area.

Poor old dear. But so plucky! I've just managed to get myself comfortable, so the pressure on my bladder has let up, and I'll probably make it to the surgery with just enough time for a tinkle. I could stand, couldn't I – it's only a few more stops, and I don't think there'll be any sudden jolts.

Dorothy got to her feet with the merest suggestion of a wince and offered her seat to the old lady, who had taken up position just in front of her, and was capably gripping the seat rail. She declined gruffly. "I've stood all my life," she said. "Another ten minutes won't kill me."

Dorothy resumed her seat, casting a patronising and admiring smile at the woman next to her, who nodded briefly and turned towards the window.

All this time, knowing there's been something not quite right – well, I can allow myself a little point over the doctor. She's been very good on the whole, but when you think about it, she hasn't always – well, listened as well as she might. I should have known better, I suppose, I saw the same attitude when Fred was dying – and that was a long time ago now. I seemed to wear myself out telling them what would be best for him, but oh no, they had to see things differently. But I suppose they're so busy now, what with cuts and more patients and more people getting ill these days.

The bus creaked to a standstill at another stop. She stood to allow the woman sitting next to her to get off, then settled in at the window. Ahead, the traffic lights were red.

Dorothy gazed at the street with blank eyes. How many times had she taken the number 64, sat by the window and watched the view unfolding on her way to the surgery? Several times a week, sometimes more than once a day, if she had shopping to do as well. It kept her busy, all these appointments! It never changed. Whether it was quiet or the rush hour, the bus would arrive at more or less the same time. No new buildings had gone up, no new swings had been put into the park playground, no new shopping complex had been built. It was a comfortable, familiar landscape, with people she recognised amongst the shoppers, and folk who knew her when she went into shops to be served.

The drama of everyday human activity that busied itself along the pavements flitted moth-like, in and out of Dorothy's consciousness. This morning, a little boy was howling outside the newsagents, locked in dispute with his mother about a comic. A woman was buying tomatoes from one of the outside displays at the fruit and vegetable shop, cheerfully called *Bananas*. The bakery, *Hot Dough*, making its own bid for commercial individuality, was receiving deliveries of meat pies and sausage rolls for the hot counter; the supermarket shelves were being restocked with sugar and biscuits, and an elderly woman was leaving the wine merchant's with a large bottle of cider. The chemist was preparing for the patients leaving the surgery with prescriptions, and promoting a new treatment for cystitis.

Dorothy's interest sparked when she saw it. Cystitis! She hadn't had that for ages. Terrible business, it had taken years to work out it was triggered in her case by anything to do with blackcurrants, even bottled fruit squashes and tinned ones set it off. All those hot water bottles and never daring to go too far from the house because it was so uncomfortable to walk – and the council had refused her a home help because they said her illness wasn't debilitating enough. Dr Mooney hadn't been able to help, either. The antibiotics worked for a time, but the problem was soon back again and it had taken a lot of persistence to press for proper medical tests to get to the bottom of it. Mind you, it was a long time ago now, and it might be interesting to see what happened if she tried a little bit of blackcurrant juice now – she could buy a bottle of Ribena on her way back from the surgery, then give this new whatnot a go and see just how good it was …

Dr Sheila Mooney has finally arrived at the surgery. On her way through, she has been called over by the receptionist, and asked if she will have a word with one of Patrick's patients, a woman of twenty-five recently diagnosed with a malignant brain tumour. Jana still looks well, although she has begun to lose weight, and the striking auburn wig contrasts too vividly with the increasingly fragile face, pale as china, and the blue eyes rimmed with red and grey. Jana has had a bad night, is suffering from nightmares and thinks she might need stronger painkillers for the searing pains behind her eyes. She's still going to work, but concentration is getting harder to sustain, and her treatment programme is making her tired. She shares this information matter of factly, knowing Patrick won't be in until the evening, seeking practical solutions to the problems, wanting to get to her office at the university and finish the PhD thesis before her energy completely dries up.

Sheila asks if she wants to go to work, and promises to call when she has pulled out the notes and read the prescription details. Satisfied with the arrangements, Jana leaves. Sheila watches her get into her car, hopes the traffic has cleared, and heads for the doctor's lounge. She has seen it before, the gradual disintegration that signals the end of Jana's run of good health. Now the small symptoms will become more frequent, more intrusive, until she will have to face the fact that this is the beginning of being ill, in the final sense of the word. She has come off the plateau and turned onto the downward slope.

How much worse would it be for a woman of Jana's age, facing a drastically reduced life span? Sheila thought. Jana, clever, driven, her research incomplete, no partner, the eggs of her unborn children already zapped by chemotherapy, her whole future snatched away, a balloon pricked by a pin. Someone with plans and ambitions, and something to offer the world. She remembered thinking, when she was young, that perhaps it was worse for younger people to be dealt the hand with terminal illness in it. But experience had taught her different. People still expected it to be worse for the young, but in reality, nobody, no matter how old they were, accepted the news with *sang froid*. *Well, I've had a good innings. I can't complain.* Some of them said it, and no doubt wished it was sincere, but nobody meant it. And if she wanted further proof of that, she would have it, right here in her surgery, in a little over half an hour.

So. Sheila has dealt with the usual morning pleasantries with reception and her practice colleagues, has talked over visits and ongoing cases, and she is now in her room, running out of time. Dorothy will not be late. Oh, no. She will be too keen to hear all about the problem, will want to make a point of demonstrating her infallible punctuality. She will want to go home and play with her new prescription, count out the tablets, put them carefully into their proper place, and reorganise her life around a new complaint.

How do you organise your life around something that will require immediate hospitalisation, after which you will never be the same again? Chemotherapy, needles and itching, baldness, vomiting – and that was just for starters. Never mind the mental readjustment required, the arrangements to be made for the humdrum things of life, the demoralising blows as the secondaries started to invade her bones and organs. You had to be tough to take it on. You had to be able to accept and deal with real suffering. Dorothy had spent her life playing at it – but Sheila knew that the extended rehearsal wouldn't count for much.

Fifteen minutes before her arrival, Sheila is almost weeping with frustration. Then the phone rings. Her heart bounds with hope – a cancellation, an even sicker relative, an earthquake, a bus crash – *anything, please God, to stave off this appointment until I'm in a better frame of mind* – but it is not Dorothy, or someone ringing on her behalf. It is Bill.

"Darling? I'm sorry," he says, and waits. "I said unforgivable things. I shouldn't have said them just before your appointment."

Bill is simply terrific at apologising. His sincerity pours down the receiver into her grateful ear. "Thank you," she says, and she can hear the change in her own voice, the immediate reduction of tension, her body relaxing against the leather of the chair.

"You shouldn't have gone off like that," he says. "I've been worried as hell."

"It's all right. I just swore a lot," she says.

"Liar," he says, cheerfully, and Sheila wishes she was back at home, in bed with him, naked and uninhibited, enjoying life-affirming, ecstatic sex, far from the wastelands of sickness and imminent death. "Has she come yet?"

"No. I haven't come up with an opening speech yet. I've got twelve minutes and all I can think of is life's a bitch and then you die."

"Not good, not good. You'll think of something," he says. "You always do. Come home early tonight. There's lamb in the fridge – I'll cook it with rosemary, the way you like it. Let's drink champagne and make love." A pause, then, "The hell with tonight. Let's do it now."

Sheila, who wants to run for the door, undressing as she goes, abandons the fantasy and laughs, sparing a last vengeful thought for the arrogant sheep who got on her wrong side this morning. She has her carrot to get her through the day. "The traffic's appalling," she says. "I couldn't do that journey again, not even for you. But yes, roast lamb would taste particularly sweet this evening, after the run-in I had with a sheep this morning."

At the other end, she hears an insistent bleeping, and a sigh.

"I have to go," he says. "Ward rounds all morning. You can tell me the tale of the sheep later."

"Okay. Are you in theatre this afternoon?"

"Not so far."

"So far so good, then," she says, and prays that no late emergencies come in that day, for entirely selfish reasons. "I'll see you later." As soon as she replaces the receiver, the buzzer

sounds, and she flicks the switch to hear Marie's voice.
"Mrs Timpter is in reception."

4

THE LITTLE DEATH

I

In the same way that a long journey begins with a single step, so the journey towards sexual fulfilment begins with a touch. Hannah Dell, rising young actress, wakes on the morning of the day she will be acting out scenes involving sex, strangulation and death, and considers the issues of pretence, and distance. How far do you go?

Whether it's travel or sex, distance is relative. Some people will be happy with Paris, others won't settle for anything less than Macchu Pichu. Leaving the light on might be someone's ultimate sexual adventure – others pine for the full Marquis de Sade. Hannah, whose job it is to pretend, will today be at the mercy of another actor pretending to strangle her, having already pretended to have sex with her. Some people will watch the film, and that will be enough; others will go home and go on to mimic what they have seen, turning a celluloid fantasy into reality – a dream come true.

In Hannah's own bed, in real life, Rory, the man nestling in behind her, lays a hand on her flank, and kisses her shoulder. The caress is gentle, interrogative; he is asking permission to proceed. He waits for a minute or two, then moves his fingers in a gentle circling pattern. This small, rather sensitive and polite movement is enough to tell Hannah whether or not she is in the mood to respond. She can go one of three ways at this point. She can do nothing, which could either mean yes or no, or she can move towards him, which means yes, or she can give a quick, irritable flick to shake the hand away, which stops everything dead. The rejection must be hurtful, but all the same, it can't be helped. Sometimes, it's just the way she feels.

She wonders idly why the same hand, the same routine, can elicit such widely differing responses. The touch of Rory's hand can be as gentle and intoxicating as a shower of rose petals, or as irritating and undesirable as a swarm of ants. There are so many variables that can influence the pattern of events. Sometimes she thinks that everything comes down to mood. Other times, it's hormones. Or age. Or time of day. Or month. What happened the night before. What we talked about the day before. What has to be done today.

Ah. What has to be done today.

This morning, Rory gets the flick. He sighs in acknowledgement, and kisses her shoulder affectionately. He is extraordinarily tolerant of such rebuffs, something she forgets to be grateful for.

He says, "I just thought you might need the practice." The remark is impish, non-malicious. What has to be done today is on his mind, too.

In spite of herself, she lets out a small laugh and kicks him playfully on the leg. "Don't. You rotter. You know I'm dreading it." His arm crosses her, his lips brush the skin beneath her ear. It is this that turns her body towards him and switches her mood from incommunicative tension to erotic charge. It can happen this way.

As Rory begins to caress her, she makes a movement, closing her eyes, letting her head hang back, allowing herself to be persuaded. But it doesn't last; as his fingers trace the curve of her hips, she sighs, then breaks off, half-sitting up. Something has got between them, snapped the connection. Her irritation is palpable, puts the patiently arousing paramour off his stride. He stops, too, and she looks at him, fretful and preoccupied, the sexual imperative vanquished.

She slides back under the sheet, pats him as unerotically as possible on the arm, kisses him as androgynously as possible, and smiles as kindly as possible.

"I'm sorry. I just can't."

He gives the merest hint of annoyance, although he doesn't look too surprised. As he slips out of bed and heads for the shower, she sees the disappointed member drooping back to its original position and grimaces ruefully. What a waste. And what a comment on her – turning down the real thing so she can save herself for the pretend. But she can't call him back now – any sexual activity would be pure research into human behaviour, a gymnastics practice, a sound effects trial.

It's five-thirty am, and she decides to cycle to the studio and shower there. She pulls on jog pants and T-shirt, a thick sweatshirt – it's still pretty chilly this early on. She watches the clouds of steam issuing from the shower and is tempted to strip off and dive in the cubicle. She resists. After all, there's insult, and there's injury. And Rory has more of that coming in the course of the day.

While she crams down muesli before the short journey, she tries to restore some sense of normality.

"Rory? What do you think about that offer? Do you think I should take it?"

Rory accepts the peace offering, switches off the shower and appears, dripping, on the bathroom mat. "Maria Ramirez? Great part," he says, "but you won't get much pause for breath – shooting starts November, right?"

"That's not my problem. I still have three months to research and develop what I want to do. It's not as if I'll be finished with this one weekend and starting the other the next. I'm not sure I'm right for it," she says. "Maria Ramirez is older, and there's a darkness in her – I don't know if I could bring that side out of her convincingly."

"You're kidding," Rory says, rubbing the towel over his head. "You're not exactly Little Miss Sweetie Pie in this one, are you?"

"That's true. But Honey's younger, and she's in my field

of experience – I've got something of my own to draw on – well, not all of it, but something," she finished, as Rory threw her a mocking glance. "They must think I can do Maria, or they wouldn't have asked."

"It's a high profile project," Rory says. "Good production team, top-drawer director. And it's a hell of a story."

She grins. "I'm just thinking about all that chocolate."

"Not to mention the money – your biggest fee to date by quite a long chalk." Rory shrugged. "What more do you want? Cracking script, great team – all that, and as much chocolate as you can handle. Come on, you know you want to do it."

She shakes her head. "I'd love to do it. But it *is* risky. The character is so over the top anyway – if I fucked up, it's the kind of thing people will never forget. But if I did a good job, I could do anything."

"Exactly," Rory said. "It's the kind of project that opens doors. This one is going to have impact, and take you out to a whole new audience. From cult to mainstream – it's got a lot going for it. Trust me. I think you have to go for it."

"More screwing," she said. "And I'd have to put weight on again. She'd have to be fleshy and decadent, the forbidden fruit personified. I know exactly how I want to play her – it's just achieving it that's going to be hard."

Rory comes back from the bedroom, topless, wet haired, zipping his jeans. "Does the screwing bother you?"

"Sure it does. And it's worse because it bothers you as well." She goes to him, and they kiss. His hand rises to graze her nipple through the sweatshirt, and she wants him now, now it's too late and she can't have him. The kiss deepens, resolves itself. "It'll be okay after today," she says, her face pressed into his neck. "It's the worst one."

She pulls away and he makes for the bedroom.

"I'm setting off," she calls. "I'll see you on set."

"Hannah?"

"What?"

"Don't kiss him like that, will you? I'll have to smash his face in."

She laughs and disappears, shouting, "Jealous!" as she goes, then adds half apologetically, "You know perfectly well I'll have to."

"And you know perfectly well I'll be watching," he says ruefully.

Rory is the cameraman.

II

It is early, and there is still time to think it through on the way to the studio, in the dressing room, in the make up chair. She has spent most of the night awake, thinking about sex and choreography, emotion and authenticity, sexual chemistry and professionalism, prostitution and art. The differences between what she does in her own bed, as her own woman and Rory's mate, and what she will have to do with Matt Jordan, as an actress doing her job with another actor. Not that they've done anything yet – that is the barrier to be broken today. And the difference is that when they've spent all day at it, they still won't really have done anything. The trick is to make it look as if they have. That's what they need the director for. That's what the whole business is about.

However hard you try to be cool about it and treat it as another part of the job, all in an actor's day, acting out sexual behaviour is never easy. Forget that you don't fancy your partner and probably think he's a prick, forget you're being watched by a camera crew, a director, a soundman and a lighting technician, forget that you might well have to do twenty or more takes. Forget that what looks right to you and feels comfortable, probably doesn't work for the camera, and you'll get involved in complicated physical manoeuvres which feel totally unnatural, but look the exact opposite on the screen. Forget yourself, that you have to create different sexual behaviour to meet the artificial scenario, the character you're playing and the situation you're pretending to be in. Forget that you might have a headache, or a stiff neck, or the last thing you feel like at five in the morning is turned on. Forget that you're being asked to simulate lovemaking with an opposite sex you're not comfortable with. Even if this is what you normally do for the job, change behaviour, repeat yourself, submerge the mood of the day, it still makes a difference when it's sex.

Another thing – there is still the death of her character to shoot in as yet undecided circumstances. All she knows is that she is to be strangled, just one of the many ways she will probably meet her fictional end if her career is long enough. While most people only worry about their own death, and face it only once, she'll have to act many deaths through the eyes and experiences of people who were only born in someone's imagination.

She suspects that Richard Knott, the director, knows more than she and Matt. Today's scene, originally planned for an outdoors location, has been mysteriously moved inside at the last moment, rendering all the rehearsals not exactly redundant, but less useful than they should have been. Richard is known for not revealing all to his actors, until they need to know it. He has proved time and time again that manoeuvring them outside the carefully planned rehearsals is a way into authenticity. Some of these scenes, where the actors have been sprung a surprise, are printed after only one or two takes.

She counts herself lucky that in reality, she gets on with her co-star, doesn't find him repulsive, and shares a sense of humour about the art of pretence they practise. But rehearsals are one thing, and the business of filming another. They won't be laughing much this morning, not when the emotions being played are dark, subversive and verging on the controversial.

It would be preferable if the scene was comic. It's somehow easier to parody sex than try to reproduce it faithfully, easier to poke fun at the fleeting ecstasy of orgasm, that supposed peephole into a state of sustained bliss, than it is to take it as seriously as you do when it's for real.

What's bugged her since she started work on this scene was the slew of porno films she watched as part of her homework. Richard had not wanted her to prepare by watching actors who had the unfair advantage of actually performing the act she would have to simulate. Ever since, she had been conscious of the tension between 'serious' actors like her and Matt turning sex into intellectual fodder to make 'sophisticated' audiences feel better about watching it. If she and Matt really had sex, then it wouldn't be acting – so did that devalue the performance or increase its worth? It was beginning to irritate her, this idea that you could change sex from a verb into a concept.

Matt is familiar with sex scenes, has probably shot too many of them for his own good. He knows exactly how Hannah is feeling – it's a worse ordeal than losing your real virginity, the first time you sell yourself to the camera. "Remember, dahling, this is complicated sex," he said in his ironic actorly drawl, when they were together one afternoon trying to establish some basic choreography.

"What's that, then – more than two people?"

"Relax, Hannah, it'll be fine," he said, grinning. "Remember it isn't real." When she frowned, he shook his head and threw his hands wide. "Come on, that's supposed to be a liberating thought – you can let go, take a few chances – it's somebody else who doesn't exist. People in our profession do it all the time."

It's true enough, they do. And the fake frequently spills over into real life. Although they had never met before work started a few weeks ago, the marketing people believe that Hannah and Matt have a sexual chemistry which will ignite the screen. But although they get on tolerably well, there is no indication that, left to their own devices, they would ever get around to trying to set each other on fire.

All the same, everyone wants it to happen. The studio can create publicity around an affair, the press can sell papers and magazines, the media in general can pitch in for their share of the take. Whether or not the events are spontaneous, forced by the studio, or cooked up by the lovers themselves, doesn't much matter. Actors are doubly attractive propositions when they fall in love for real after merely pretending to do it for large sums of money. It's part of the fantasy the public buys into when it gets out its wallet for a ticket to the movies. They want their celluloid dream, then the actors cut up into little pieces on the sacrificial block for real.

It was difficult enough for actors, without the vampiric panting of the audience in their ear, demanding a fake affair with a bloody aftermath. In such situations, who falls in love with whom? Which personality is sparking the flame, giving out the signals of fatal attraction – the character, or the real person? And how long does it last before any counterfeit feelings are submerged by real ones, or before role-playing becomes the driving force of the relationship?

Acting was littered with relationships broken by a basic failure to perceive reality. Hannah had tried to minimise the risks of falling into the same hole. But she was constantly pretending to be other people, and the whole business of her life was rooted in deceit. Why should anyone believe in her?

How must Rory feel, facing the prospect of watching her fake erotic bliss with another bloke? Matt was undeniably handsome, and she wonders if perhaps she won't be able to help herself, if the scene suddenly gets hold of her, and she forgets that she's actually working. How mortifying it would be to really become aroused, instead of dishing out emotional counterfeits, of doing something outside the carefully planned manoeuvres because of pure abandonment! And yet authenticity is what every actor will tell you they most want to deliver. So would it be cheating if in the course of acting out sexual arousal, you really got turned on?

As if that wasn't stressful enough, real sex has not been the same since she began to prepare this scene, rehearsing the greatest intimacy with someone she only met a month ago, on the first day's shooting.

It was this that had come between her and sexual fulfilment this morning – a massive detour. The way she had moved in bed, the sounds she had made, the postures she had adopted – did they belong to her, or were they something she had developed for the scene with Matt? Or were they bound up with her sexual education, something she has learned and mimicked from other actresses playing sex scenes?

Every sex scene she has read or watched – and she's seen a lot of them in recent weeks – has begun to look like a list of erotic clichés based on a tired and unconvincing visual and aural vocabulary. There is prescribed behaviour for women approaching and experiencing orgasm, definitive movements for men trying to get them there – the old breast-fondling, nipple-hardening, back-arching, buttock-thrusting school of sex. Acceptable noises made by both parties – animal grunts for a man engaged in rape, stunned silence (with mouth hanging open) for a man engaged in sexual splendour. He may even manage a dignified smile as he is overwhelmed. Eyes closed to suggest ecstasy, eyes open to suggest boredom or an unexpected manoeuvre. A shake of the head – in denial of pleasure – a drawn-out sigh on cessation of movement.

It was beginning to come full circle, too, as real people took the initiative, stole back the sexual imagery and movement they have learned from watching actors and fed it back into their own experiments, filming themselves having sex. Life imitating art imitating life in a cycle of borrowed gestures, sighs and moans. What exactly can Hannah contribute to this pattern now that more and more of the audience is graduating from voyeur to performer?

At the moment, she finds it impossible to do anything to acknowledge genuine erotic effort without suspecting herself of aping the actress. And even when she comes, she watches herself, listens to herself, wonders how much of it is genuinely spontaneous, and how much of it is helpful signalling – *Look, darling, you've pleased me so much I'm having an orgasm.*

And that, of course, makes everything worse; she suspects that self-awareness is not, or should not be, part of genuine erotic bliss. It's true that the orgasm makes her feel very good – but how would she show the way she felt if she had never seen it done before, if she had no role models to copy? Would she grunt like a pig, or scream like a siren? Would she bother to make any noise at all? If she didn't, how the hell would the bloke know how well he was doing? Are the grunts, sighs and moans mere novelistic and cinematic conventions, or are they rooted in real human behaviour? How is she to simulate making love for a film without falling back on these trusty old patterns, which the audience recognise, respond to – and ultimately go on to imitate in their own bedrooms? Something she does this afternoon, while she is only pretending, could be picked up by people she doesn't even know, and taken home to be incorporated into the real thing for the rest of their active sex life. And so it goes. She will fuel other people's longings, other people's fantasies, become a catalyst for orgasm.

It was *The Joy of Sex* and all the other sex manuals that had not only brought sex out of the closet, but had also made enjoyment of it mandatory. Sex was for the happening people, the turned on and tuned in. If you didn't like it, you had problems, you were that terrifying word *frigid*, if you were American, you needed a shrink. Orgasms were mandatory too – and plenty of them, or your partner came in for a load of flack. Sex wasn't just something you had to enjoy, you had to be successful at it too. It became a talent contest, a point-scoring exercise, a source of endless insecurity, something threatening. Women walked round dripping sex appeal on the outside like Raquel Welch and felt like Diane Keaton on the inside, while men swaggered round like Burt Reynolds and felt like Woody Allen.

How long did you say? Only an hour? My goodness, he must be very quick on the draw! And only once? No wonder you're so tense and unfulfilled, darling. Here's a copy of The Joy of Sex to make you feel even more inadequate.

And there was exactly the same problem. *Sex manuals* were *porn mags* made respectable – educational pornography for inhibited people who could read about sex and examine pictures and diagrams – *where did you say I should put my head, darling?* – as long as they felt they were engaged in the experiment of learning, as well as enjoying.

Acting death would be no different. In childhood games of cowboys and Indians you had to roll over on your back and throw your arms out wide when you were dead, or it didn't count. Just like sex, it was hard to find an acted death you hadn't seen before.

The plot of the rather psychologically earnest, fashionably tortured and – she has to admit it – pretentious movie they are filming runs thus:

Honey, her character, is an artist who couldn't get mainstream acclaim, and became a critic instead. She comes from a working class background, and she blames it for everything that doesn't work out right. Her father periodically abused her before he drowned when Honey was fifteen. Painting, suggested by her psychotherapist, was supposed to channel her anger into something positive and help her develop away from her damaged upbringing and relationships. But she lacks creative power and is too bound up in the negative energies of her past to express her pain, her longing and her greed in a way that can translate into success.

Unable to validate herself as a creative force in her own right, Honey turns to critiquing the work of others, and finds her real skill, but it's not the skill she wants to be remembered for. She cultivates an outlandish image, a carefully controversial lifestyle, starts appearing in the tabloids, meets a lot of influential people and makes it to television, hosting a trendy review programme. All this does is underline her own failure in the art world as she faces up to a constant stream of modern, happening talent. All this while, she has flirted, prick-teased and never had sex with anyone. Her image as a cool media babe with a string of men in tow is pure fantasy – she's learned how to send out the signals, without ever having to deliver. She is so hollowed-out by the stream of disappointments life dishes out to her that she no longer has any emotional centre. That's when she meets Smash.

Smash is genuinely gifted, on the brink of *avante garde*

recognition, sexually precocious, everything Honey wants to be. She interviews him, befriends him, becomes his mentor and finally, agonisingly, his lover. She tries to find fulfilment as his protagonist, builds him up in the media, then turns against him when she can no longer control her jealousy. In a main programme feature, she denounces him for selling out and compromising his talent by becoming commercial – everything she could accuse herself of.

By this time, Honey and Smash are already in the grip of a destructive passion, and even while he understands the jealousy and hypocrisy of her actions, he has become dependent on her approbation. Smash is the first man she has allowed to break down her physical and emotional barriers, and the experience is revelatory, but she is unable to contribute to the relationship in any real sense. She uses him to bolster her failing confidence, starts to push him into more and more extreme sexual behaviours so that he begins to lose his sense of identity. As his adulation turns to confusion and resentment, he realises how much his association with the damaged Honey has changed him.

Bar a few niceties regarding the final impressions the audience is to be left with of the characters, that's the essence. Their story ends with Honey's death and Smash's release. But whether he has enough left to save himself, or whether he is doomed to slide into ruin or notoriety may well be left to the individual to decide, in a fashionably open ending.

III

What Rory is an expert at is working in difficult light. He has a gift for it, and in partnership with a director who is sensitive to the subtle nuances of mood and scene light and shadow can create, he can produce award-winning stuff. He knows how light can work for or against a character, can spot variations on a standard angle that can change the audience perception. He's worked with Richard before, and they are good for each other, firing mutual enthusiasm, intuitively understanding what they each need from every scene. Rory is proactive, lately he's been thinking that maybe he should take his camera expertise and his knowledge of light, and turn it to direction.

This latest production is a complex relationship story about two damaged characters who get together to escape the damage, and end up being destroyed by their separate destructive traits. So far, there's only one sex scene in it, roughly halfway through, but it's complicated sex, difficult for the actors, tricky for the cameraman, tough for the director, who doesn't want it to look like soft porn, and wants it to convey a variety of emotions for both characters and audience. Rory wants to shoot it at a distance, so there is a suggestion of privacy, but it has also to be clear – Honey is at last making out, properly, but he has to show that without resorting to the vulgarity of a meat shot.

In rehearsal, with the actors romping fully clothed on a variety of props, they tried to get the balance between the set and the action. Matt was relaxed and laughing, Hannah was serious, hiding her anxiety. Matt is disdainful of meaningful sex; sex is a doing word, not a thinking one – you either get your rocks off, or you don't. With his hunky good looks and charm, and commercial appeal, he's an easy target for the uptight luvvies who want everything, especially sex, to be cerebral. Richard agonises about the choreography, treats the actors sensitively, but knows exactly what he wants of them. This is going to be a bit of a baptism of fire.

Even so, Hannah is not going to be the problem from Rory's point of view, apart from the fact that he will feel like some masochistic voyeur. *Why does it matter at all, when he knows she'll only be pretending?* But Matt, too good looking, too eager to be seen as a great sexual athlete, may struggle with the complexities being demanded of him. Smash is being used, manipulated – has been, throughout the relationship – and this is where he has to face up to it, and begin the downward slope through depression, anger, desperation and revenge. At the very point where Honey and Smash should cement their feelings into a strong whole, the sex is destined to tear them apart.

Hannah is in her dressing room as Rory busies himself with the lighting technician, and the others prepare the set. Characteristically, Richard will clear it for a sex scene of all but himself and Rory, once everything is right. They've built a room with a large window, wooden and spartan, echoey. In the end, they settled on a leather chair, bottle-green and worn. Honey was sexually abused by her father in this room, so the scene, originally set in a neutral location which enabled her to break free of the tortured associations of the past, is now compromised by conflicting emotions. There's an old side-board with a half-drunk bottle of wine on it, and two glasses near the chair, one carefully overturned. In the background, there will be muted and infrequent traffic sounds. Richard is still deciding whether or not to labour the point about the father and cut in some flashbacks. The room is supposed to be three storeys up and looks vaguely continental, with shutters visible at the window. It overlooks balconies and apartments across the narrow street. This is distracting, because Hannah is already thinking about how she will have to change, both physically and psychologically, to become Maria Ramirez. In her mind, she now places the apartment in Barcelona's medieval quarter, where Maria went hunting with Luigi and Juanita for twists of candied orange peel dipped in bitter chocolate and new chocolate sensations in the chic cafes near the cathedral.

Rory, selecting lenses and lining up the shots, his thin, muscular frame leaning into the camera, is thinking about this morning. He thought it would be easier for him if he had really had sex with her. He doesn't for one moment think that Hannah would be attracted to Matt, but still, it's difficult. It was childish of him to want her this morning, but it couldn't be helped. He already knew she wouldn't be interested. She takes her work seriously, she wants to do this well. She has all the moves, all the feelings down. Sex this morning could have interrupted the flow, given her other ideas not compatible with Richard's. It will be all right tonight, when she has it all behind her. He's got this evening planned, mapped out in his mind. When she's spent all day pretending, she'll want the real thing at night.

IV

Behind the camera, rigorously professional, he slurs the film as discussed with Richard, so Hannah's climax is extended, drawing out her rapture as her head is thrown back and her eyes close, then open, and slide round to stare straight at camera – at him – and penetrate the voyeurism of the audience. Even though the take is in real time, he can see the final composite of the shot, the soft light changing to hard, Hannah's carefully rehearsed transformation from false ingenue to strumpet, defencelessness giving way to greed, a nightmare child of tainted purity. And Matt's perfunctory, disillusioned pleasure, done with the face, not the vocal chords, as directed. Matt does OK, he'll give him that, he's cool, understated, better than Rory expected.

It's never like this in real life. Hannah flits insistently across his field of vision in spontaneous scenarios at home, on holiday, away for the weekend, having regular, unchoreographed sex, her hair unwashed, or her fingernails broken, her legs unshaved. The images comfort him, remind him of the pretentiousness of what's going on here. People seem to want pretentious sex.

He films the kiss, asks for a retake, partly because he needs one to try something else, but also self consciously playing his professional role, showing them that he can handle this, while Richard explains the shot is very close up, he wants to see Hannah's lips yield to the pressure of Matt's. It's easy at times, the naked figures become visual elements in a framed composition, abstracts he juggles with, positioning them, sliding unobtrusively round them, looking for original ways of spying on the ersatz conjugal act.

He's on the job, watching Hannah's fourth attempt at orgasm, screwing the shot down from soft focus into sharp close up, concentrating grimly on the tilt of her head in relation to Matt's, and the angle of her raised knee, when there's a sudden gasp, an unmistakable release of involuntary authenticity. Richard, tense beside the camera, his little fingernail set between his teeth, is evaluating every movement and sound for artistic resonance and validity. He clenches his fist and ejaculates the single syllable, *Yes!* at this sudden joining of manufactured erotic fantasy with no holds barred bliss, when Hannah says, "I've got cramp. I've got to stop."

"And I thought I was getting somewhere this time," quips Matt, extricating himself from the camera-friendly position with only slight difficulty.

Rory grins, pulls away from the lens and relaxes, before walking over to her and taking hold of her ankle. "Here," he says, stretching her leg gently, and she grimaces, then laughs nervously, looking across at Richard. Rory resists the urge to tousle her hair, even though the need to reassert himself as hers is strong. Primitive territorial instincts, he thinks, self-deprecatingly, even while massaging her leg as pragmatically as he can. Like dogs pissing on a lamppost.

"How is it so far?"

"It's good," Richard reassures her. "Just keep doing what you're doing. I don't suppose you can make that noise again, can you?"

Hannah groans, freeing her leg from Rory's grip and flexing it. She screws up her nose. "Which one?"

"It'll be on the sound tape," Rory says, still grinning. "We can isolate it, cut it in over something else if we have to. But the take might still be good anyway."

That was the way of it. If people had sex just like they do in the movies, it would be impossible. What works for the camera doesn't work in actuality. Hannah, who looks terrifically well-honed and is performing as smoothly as a well-choreographed ballerina while she simulates orgasm in her job, is totally uncoordinated in real life. She has this jerk, a reflex action that can, and has, knocked him in the eye, or made him bite his tongue, or just caught him sharply on the head and all but ruined the moment. Experience has taught him to duck out of the way, but he likes it, it's a part of her she can't plasticise, he's not even sure she knows she's doing it. That's why he treasures it, the elbow in the balls, or the big toe in his eye. He knows he's got the real thing, and he's taken her so far out of herself she doesn't know what she's doing.

"Hannah," Richard says, as she limps gingerly back to her chair. "When we've cracked the sex, I was thinking we might go straight into a take on the death."

He stalls her pained expression. "I know, I know, this is tough enough," he says. "But it's working here, everything's right, and I like the idea of using the same light." He turns to Matt, who hasn't smiled all morning, and looks more troubled the more the scene takes hold of him. Rory sees that Richard wants to use that, the sense of disquiet that means Matt is submerging himself under the character, and it's not a place he likes to be. "Matt, you know how you're controlling her in this scene, taking her into the experience she fears, so we're shocked when she shows us that even though you've laid her wide open and made sexual pleasure possible, she still wants to use you to achieve her own ends? Well, I want her death to be like the sex for both of you, only you turn that emotion back on her – she relinquishes her power so you can overwhelm her – so you achieve a kind of murderous ecstasy together."

"So she's complicit in her own death?"

"Exactly," Richard says. "Think about it, she has always been the driving force behind her own failures, by wanting something she can never have. She can't get close to people because she doesn't know how to let go of her past, she can't be what Smash is, because she doesn't have the talent, and as soon as she experiences sexual fulfilment, she wants it to be more than what it is. She's writing her own ticket, which is both her tragedy, and what makes her unsympathetic."

"He strangles her," Matt says dubiously. "Wouldn't she be terrified? Wouldn't she fight him?"

Richard drops his voice to a low, treacherous whisper. "Not if she is enthralled at the same time."

"My God," Hannah says, articulating Matt's disbelieving gasp. "You mean – the choking thing? Coming at the point of death? Can we do that and get away with it?"

Richard nods. "Auto erotic asphyxiation, to give it its proper name. Beyond the little death," he says. "All the way. It's the only way she can go."

She stares at Matt. Actor or not, she feels the distance suddenly shrink between her real self, Honey, and the death about to be played out. So this is how far she has to go. While Hannah has always opted for the safe route to sexual fulfilment via traditional methods of transport, Honey is to plunge off the well-beaten path and head out into unknown territory, with her partner's hands locked around her throat.

Rory, squinting through the camera, sees the effect this conversation has on the next take of the sex. He has to hand it to Richard. Haunted by a glimpse of the end they must act out, Hannah and Matt play the scene differently. Now there is doom in it, a prescient quality that darkens the act, flattens the light. As Hannah reaches her sixth or seventh climax, both cameraman and director see fear in her widened eyes, as she reaches past the brief ascent and knows she has to go further, even if it kills her.

Richard is triumphant now, buzzing with powerful vibes. He begins to forget that he has actors here, thinks himself into the false reality as much as he can, capturing the dramatic essence as Hannah begins to disappear inside the role and work from her instinct and imagination. And Matt, his detachment edged ever so faintly with disgust and a dread of the inevitable, reaches his hands to her throat as she comes, and strokes it, his hand snaking up over her breast like a malevolent python. Rory trembles involuntarily, powerless to protect her.

"OK, hold this mood," Richard says some time later, and his tone of voice drags them back to business as he pushes them forward, to the end of the movie, the resolution of their association. "Rory, bring the shot right up close, light Hannah's throat so it's almost translucent. I want people to cringe away from what they're going to see, hold onto their collars for protection. Vampire movies stuff – that fear-threat-thrill thing. Matt, tell me what you're thinking about this, how is he going to do this?"

"So she doesn't have to ask," he says slowly.

Richard nods. "Does she want to be brought back, or is she knowingly giving herself up to the last ecstasy? Hannah?"

"It's like a seduction," Hannah says. "She knows, but doesn't want to know. He's her winged messenger, and her angel of despatch."

Richard nods. "OK, let's go with that for now. Improvise the lines, we can work them later." He stops. "What do you know about this? Ever done it?"

"Are you kidding?" Matt is outraged, the professional skin momentarily ruptured. "Come on, Richard," he pleads, "that's real fringe stuff, out on the edge. I wouldn't want to do it."

"That's OK," Richard says, unrepentant. "Neither does Smash. You know about sex, and you know about death, and you know about the little death. So you can bring those things in. All you're doing here is merging the three together." He pauses. "Some people are going to be fascinated by the idea of someone taking the ultimate risk for sexual pleasure – and some are going to be repelled by it. So the audience is going to have conflict about this – you have to make it work for both spectrums of feeling, somehow reconcile the two."

"What you have to remember is that it's like playing comedy. You need a fine sense of timing if you're going to pull it off." He pauses. "There's genuine danger, a powerful attraction to the risk. If you get the timing wrong, you die because you lose control over the strangulating mechanism. There are only a few seconds between retaining that control, and losing it to unconsciousness. If you're alone when that happens, no one can help you. Honey has already lost that control by asking you to take over."

"So it isn't the strangulation she fears," says Hannah. "It's her own rapture."

"It's turning that sense of abandonment against her," Matt says. "When you come, there are those few moments when you're laid right open, at the mercy of the other person. He's breaking her trust in the most extreme way you can – making her revel in her vulnerability, then exploiting her." He stops, then says suddenly, "I'll tell you something else. This is Smash's ticket to freedom as well, isn't it?"

Richard cocks his head, listening.

"How can anyone prove it's murder if they've been playing a dangerous game?" he says. "They've made the pact, but anyone coming to the scene will think it's just a game that went too far – it happens all the time."

Richard gives him a brilliant smile. "Quite so. The rebirth of Smash as a cynic," he says. "An innocent who learns from his mentor the value of manipulation. Good work, Matt."

In the short break between the discussion and the filming, Richard eats chocolate, discusses camera angles and agrees with Rory to try it in a single, static shot.

"I want them to find it hard," Richard says. "Uncomfortable. It shouldn't be a cheap thrill. Move the camera in."

"I don't need to," Rory says. "I can use telephoto."

"It's physical pressure," Richard says, shaking his head. "I want them to feel it, a sense of invasion. There's an alien force in what they're doing – if you're on top of them, they'll feel that intrusion, that otherness."

Settled back in the bottle-green chair, Rory thinks how conspiratorial Hannah and Matt look, almost naked, working out the position that gives them the best chance of making it through the take without too much repositioning. They look serious, talking in low voices about what's going to work best. If he was listening, he would hear Hannah say, *"We're ninety per cent naked, we'll have our hands all over each other, why don't we just do*

97

it for real? Why do we stop short of penetration, but make everything else legitimate? Aren't we just making it harder for ourselves, pretending when there's no need to?" And Matt, not entirely sure she is joking, says, *"You want me to strangle you?"* *"You know what I mean,"* she says. Matt, who is a professional as well, has asked himself the same question; it would be no hardship to fuck Hannah in the course of his work, but he's not sure he should look eager at the prospect. He stares at her. *"I know what you're saying,"* he says, *"but I don't know if I'm hearing right."* *"Maybe I don't know what I'm saying,"* she says, studying him. *"Maybe I'm just winding you up. I just want to know what difference it really makes when we've French kissed, groped each other and all the rest of it."*

Rory, selecting lenses, positioning lights and umbrellas, glances at them periodically. Hannah's arm is curled around Matt's neck, she's tilting her head in different ways, trying to find the way in to the main sequence. Matt is experimenting, trying to place a hand round her throat and a hand between her thighs, without it looking as if he's about to collapse on top of her. Rory sees the problem, takes a look through the newly positioned lens, and they watch him expectantly.

"You look unsteady," Rory says to Matt. "Try leaning more of your body against her ... No, hold on, I see the problem. It's not the upper body that's the problem, it's your legs ... move them forward, not back ... tuck them ... that's it ... can you move? Can you ... that's great, I can get all of you that way, and close in where I like. Hannah, you need to sit forward more, move into him ... that's it, you're not reclining now, that's better. You look as if you're contributing, not becoming his victim."

It works from the moment they start to shoot, Matt positioned to demonstrate penetration. Rory watches through the lens, the personal connections severing themselves as Hannah brings out the pathos in her unsympathetic, damaged character and succumbs to death.

Hannah is working with patterns, some learned in drama school, some self-taught, some instinctual. But it'll never be real. When someone drops dead in the street from a heart attack, what patterns does he fall back on? Hannah, pretending to come, pretending to die, has the luxury of detachment, experimentation, endless takes, of trying to imagine what can't be imagined, of looking good even when she's being throttled. The man in the street, pole-axed, dough-grey and sweaty, a dull, lifeless gleam in his eye, has peed his pants and will vomit over anyone attempting the kiss of life. He doesn't have the benefit of make-up stepping in with a powder puff, or Richard telling him how to behave, or a writer to help him deliver a cool, throwaway exit line. How is it that the hardest things to act are the most fundamental?

As Hannah works to portray ecstasy and death, she gives up on attempting reality and accepts the veneer of entertainment that will be slicked glossily over the screen.

Matt plays it close, claustrophobic, hypnotic, and Rory is amazed, his normally good-natured, superficial persona driven underground by this hurting, vengeful, calculating killer. His voice seeps into the air around them, soaking it in evil. Handsome, fun-loving, playboy Matt is metamorphosed into the angel of death, while Hannah begins to sink into ecstasy and release. Her eyes are wide until the last moment, Matt's body pressed against her, his fingers exerting pressure on that pale, naked, exposed throat, his voice soft, crooning, relentless as he takes her into eternity.

The sense of invasion increases as Rory watches through the Cyclops eye of the camera, playing the professional, analysing what he sees for shadow, light, dramatic impact. Watching Hannah invite her own death, he is struck by the thought that death demands the same kind of privacy as sex – the only place most people ever see either is on a screen, but the reasons for their fascination are different. Watching sex creates fantasies and the possibility of imitation. Watching death makes people superstitious – if they see it being acted out, they invoke the unlikelihood of coincidence and hope it protects them from the actual event. Perhaps that's why both are consistently dished up as entertainment – the forbidden fruit and the taboo, both as fundamental as you can get, yet consistently dressed up into allegories and loaded with deeper meanings. You can't just fuck, you can't just die, there has to be some kind of point.

"There's only seconds between being in control of the pressure, and losing it," Richard says from his director's chair, licking a small patch of melted chocolate from his fingers. "Don't spin it out too long. Matt, show us what you're doing to explode her into infinity. Come now, Hannah, and start to go."

Matt's arm flattens against her, his hand downwards, buried from view, his wrist flexing gently, his thighs moving in slow rhythms, his other hand at her throat. Then she goes into her sequence, and her arm suddenly kicks out at Matt, catching him in the eye, and she lets out a wild, inarticulate cry. Totally uncoordinated. Rory, fixed behind the camera, stares at this woman he barely knows, and an action that is completely familiar.

Richard catches his breath, hisses, "Don't stop, for God's sakes keep going," and Matt doesn't flinch, playing the action through, still talking in that strange, gentle, haunting voice, showing the camera that his grip on her throat has intensified the moment Hannah closes her eyes and lolls her head. His hands, both now choking off oxygen, somehow still manage to convey a tender support, and he keeps talking. God only knows what he's saying, he hasn't got a clue, he's just taken a huge flyer and is doing his best to run with it, as far as he can go, until he's sure she's crossed the threshold. Rory leaps from the camera, swings the arc lamp and changes the light in a flash of technical inspiration so its brightness bleeds the colour from Hannah's face, and takes another half minute of film, while Hannah and Matt hold their positions.

Richard stares greedily at the montage, then stands abruptly. "Cut," he says. "Print it. Hannah, when my time comes, I want to go like that. That'll do for today."

Matt throws his head up, emerging from the scene like an underwater swimmer gasping for air, his eyes full of something he has never actually done, only pretended to. His hands fly

100

from Hannah's throat when he hears Richard's voice, and he holds her face for a second, his eyes troubled. "Did I hurt you?" he whispers, and Hannah crosses her eyes and pretends to gag. He laughs, and then briefly holds her against him and kisses the top of her head, resting his cheek against her hair. Of all the images Rory has captured on film that long day, that flash of unprompted tenderness is the one that stays with him the longest. Hannah, who has been pressed up against the back of her chair for too long, moves creakily, groans and eases herself back into life and reality. Rory tosses them sweatshirts, and Matt gets off the chair and pulls Hannah after him. They hold hands, still isolated from the crew, standing close to each other while everything is switched off. Within a few minutes, both of them have lost enough to attempt normal communication, sharing their triumph with Rory and Richard. They know it's a good job.

V

It's two o' clock in the morning when they get back. Both of them are past tiredness. They've spent the last two hours watching the rushes with Richard and Matt, scoffing down take-out pizzas, arguing over minor points of clarity, whether or not Matt should come too, but in general, it's a pleasing result. Richard opts to leave it, not wanting it to look too finished, too glossy, too manufactured. Critiquing the action has helped create distance from it. They all took refuge in humour, black, nervous cracks about nails banged into the studio beams, lengths of rope, how to go about tying up all your loose ends, the definition of a free directorial hand.

Hannah takes a bottle of wine out of the fridge and brings it to the sofa. She sits close to him and his arms encircle her. It's an hour before they open the bottle. He's kissing her, he can't stop kissing her, she's his again, she's back the way he knows her, the way he wants her, and the drive to possess her, override the corruptions she played, and bring her back to herself is overwhelming. As much as Hannah couldn't perform this morning, so the opposite happens now, as if they both have to replace the grim make-believe of the rest of the day. But there's something in Rory's eyes that won't go away, and while he touches her, his hand keeps straying to her throat, as if he's fascinated by its delicacy, as if he's touched something deeper than pleasure, has to acknowledge Matt's dark work in the studio. And Hannah, her eyes fixed on his face as his hands undo the work of the day, doesn't try to stop him.

As if he would. *As if he would!*

In the aftermath, he wants to ask, but he's not sure he wants to hear the answer. Eventually, the silence burdened with the unasked question is too much for both of them.

Hannah says, "It wasn't real, but it did get to me." She sighs, then says, "Matt scared me. Some of the things he said – he says he can't remember them, but I'll never forget." She laughs edgily. "I never thought I'd say that about him. I think he scared himself, never mind me." She stops, on the verge of confession, looks at Rory and grimaces. When she speaks again, he knows she's not saying what she really wanted to. "And it's weird, you know, you giving us directions before we started, telling us what to do with our bodies – it helped, I guess, it grounded me, helped me keep enough distance and remember it was only acting. But I don't think Matt felt that."

"There's something else," Rory says and she suddenly looks uncomfortable, as if she's been found out. So they kiss again, deep and close, and bury the unsaid further down.

He's embarrassed now, he doesn't want to describe that tiny detail, the way her arm kicked out as if she was unaware it was happening. He doesn't want to hear that she lost herself in the scene to the point of abandonment, and he doesn't want to hear that she orchestrated it, that wild little flick and yell, that she knew she was doing it, that she's always known she does it when it's with him, and it's for real.

"Forget it," he says. "It doesn't matter."

In those moments, he knows what Hannah has come to suspect, that sex can't ever be real because it's become artificial, full of mixed up bits and pieces borrowed from other sources, life imitating art imitating life. And he wonders if the only time people ever genuinely lose their self-awareness and their compulsion to imitate is when real death beckons.

He lets go Richard's insidious instructions, the sense that all day Hannah has been guided through patterns of behaviour that were never hers. He begins to touch her again, his fingers playing delicately on the soft, translucent skin of her throat. She leans her body towards him, her mouth finding his, his hand slides down to her breast, and he becomes his own director in a sex scene that will never be all their own.

5

KINGS OF THE ROAD

I

Nobody likes the night manoeuvres, especially in the winter, when the freezing wind seems to bite through to your bones. You need to be tough to handle it, which is why I insist on rigorous training, and don't let the youngsters out until they're ready. There's always a few hot heads taking foolhardy chances when they think my back's turned, but assuming they live to tell the tale, they only step out of line once.

It's not their fault, but when they don't come from the Island, like me, Mackenzie and Macallan, they don't have the hereditary survival instincts. They're not physically built for it, so they have to learn, and they have to be trained just to get up to basic competence standards. Apart from anything else, they're the wrong colour for night work, and lack our natural agility, so they get themselves killed more easily. And it's no doddle working with foreign conscripts either, so I have just as hard a time. Mackenzie's a mild-mannered soul who thinks I'm too hard on them, but I've proved time and again that it's the ones who do the least preparation who suffer most – and the dead are all around to prove the point.

I've had to earn their respect and then field the accusations of nepotism when Mackenzie and Macallan took the top command jobs. It's not easy putting a very small minority in charge of the vast majority, but I argued the case and because they're basically reasonable and, despite popular myth, not without intelligence, they soon saw the sense of it.

The blacks are bred to the land, I said, *we understand the terrain, we've got a grip on the weather, how to exploit its tactical advantages, how to make it work for us. Now it's nobody's fault, but to be blunt, you simply don't have that background. You've been imported from the mainland, you've had it soft, and so have your forefathers – mild weather, nice barracks, good food and plenty of it. It's not like that here. You get tossed out into the field from day one, and you've got to know how to deal with it.*

It's permanent manoeuvres here, all weather, no shelter except what you can find for yourself, and if you're going to argue about who's in charge, you look to your leader. I'm fifteen, and I'm still alive. I don't get caught out, I don't get captured, and I don't get shipped out. It nearly happened once, but I learned my lesson. I started this force and dedicated my life to making the genocide of our race as difficult as possible and I've still got lessons to teach that you can learn from.

The whites could easily have mistaken the practicalities of my arguments for a bit of a chip on the shoulder. We've been ostracised from our own land and the whites – through no fault of their own – have become the predominant population. This is our land. It was our land long before the humans came, long before they went their separate ways and began to hunt and kill us, and then breed us in death camps. What drew us, blacks and whites together, was the genocide factor – the fact that no matter what colour we were, we were all destined for the same fate. That tends to clinch it.

Being herded up by a yapping dog, squashed into a truck, driven in undignified squalor to line up and have your brains blown out by an execution squad – that's what we've sworn to avoid. We'd rather die than end up on somebody's plate. Well, you know what I mean. The first lesson I have to teach the naïve ones is about kindness – Crofters being kind to the newborn, freeing trapped brethren from bogs and ditches and brambles, are only doing it so they can kill you in the end. *He saved me from drowning when I was a lamb,* that's the kind of inexcusable twaddle I find unbearable – *of course he saved you, you pathetic wretch, he doesn't love you for yourself, he wants to turn you into hard cash*. Once they understand that, it dispenses with any maudlin sentiment – and you can start to create a disciplined fighter who'll be with you till the death.

They don't argue anymore – except when it's bitterly cold, your hooves are frozen into the heather, and the troops are complaining about the conditions.

As I've said, one grave disadvantage about these Incomers is that they're the wrong colour. You can't be that effective at night when your fleece is white and the headlights pick you out. We've done our best to try and even things up a bit, experimented with heather and kelp and the like, even a spot of mud-rollies, but we've established pretty conclusively that camouflage isn't very effective. Mackenzie, Macallan and I do as many of these as we can, but we can't deploy ourselves across all the combat zones and maintain realistic levels of activity – spread yourselves too thinly, and you never get anything done well. Being black, we add the critical element of surprise and have a much higher hit rate.

Night time is also when the humans have been drinking alcohol, so they're either less alert and complacent, or more jumpy and less inclined to get themselves out of trouble when we attack.

And yes, I do know a thing or two about substance abuse. When I've spent all summer training the youngsters for action, I can see my efforts reduced to nothing by one careless lapse of concentration in the autumn. It's our Silly Season, and there's always got to be a few who don't listen to the warnings, who scoff at you and say, *What's wrong with eating a little bit of fungus, anyway?* You know when it's starting, because some of the long-haired human types start getting out of their cars and scratching about in the grass like us. They call them magic mushrooms. I call them Killer Moulds, and double the patrols when they're growing. I caught one young wag who'd tried storing a few in a peat bank, and had to strip him of his rank. It's just a game to these youngsters – until they end up glassy-eyed in the middle of the road, thinking they can take on that fast-approaching vehicle because they've transformed into

Super Sheep and are invincible. But that's an aside.

What I try to teach is which type of action to use, depending on the vehicle, the driver, the time of day or night, and the approach. It's taken years to classify all the possible engagement scenarios, and the appropriate military responses – and of course even when you've done that, you still rarely get a text-book situation laid in front of you. But that's soldiering for you. Are they coming fast or slow? Are they looking out for you? Can you get out of the way when you've set the accident in motion? Will you saunter into view, or make a sudden dash across the tarmac? Can you fool them into thinking you're taking a quiet nap, or a bite to eat, before you spring into action? Or will you – and this takes the most daring, the most skill – face them head on in the middle of the road, and force a skid or a confrontation?

Sometimes you get unexpected help – if they lose concentration just before you appear, that increases your chances of a hit. As I've said, if they're drunk, it's a definite advantage. Whatever the situation, the risk is all on their side, apart from the fact that we may lose our lives to the cause. They're the ones with insurance. They're the ones who prize their automobiles above all else. They're the ones who have to pay up if they hit us, so even if we die, they still lose. Some of the older ones have formed a kamikaze unit, but that's extreme, I try not to encourage it, even though all of us have sworn the ultimate loyalty to the cause. It can have a negative impact on the cadets, too much talk about death. When you're young and fired up with a cause, you want to celebrate your victories, not end up a mangled mess at the roadside before the first shout of triumph goes up. Don't get me wrong – death in combat is an honourable thing, not something the ones left behind mourn, but good soldiers are hard to find, and they should live to fight another day if they possibly can.

They've tried fencing us in, but you can't fence this land, it's too boggy, too lumpy. A few nights' digging and shoving will move a fence-post enough to create a breach in the barricades, and the Crofters – the perpetrators – never go out after dark, unless circumstances are extremely pressing. In the last couple of years, our tactics have been working. We've got a reputation. There are warning signs on the roads that we're about, Tourists are told how to avoid us, how to drive with caution in case they fall into an ambush. *Sheep with attitude*, that's what they call us. That recognition has made everything worthwhile – all the recruitment problems, the endless training, the high mortality rate, the racist remarks, the apathy, the unwillingness to accept reality. And it's culminating in this, an ambitious project to bring a Crofter to justice. They're the hardest targets by far, because they understand us the best, know our movements and habits.

Bringing a Tourist down is fine, and all the non-Crofters who live here – they all eat us, so I don't feel guilty that we're being indiscriminate. I suppose if you were being pedantic, it might class as a war crime, but I doubt it would stand up in court. Bringing down a Crofter is a particularly sweet proposition, especially when you're working in alliance with his dog.

This is a new direction for us, and it's taken top-secret meetings at the highest command levels to pull it all together. I'd like to take the credit for the idea, but it would be dishonest. I'd been banging my head against a brick wall for months, trying to work out why we weren't getting anywhere after all the work we'd put in. For all my knowledge and innovation, sheer graft and single-minded commitment, we still hadn't chalked up a significant hit. I'd invited military strategy experts, I held clinics, seminars and surgeries, and in the end it took the second in command in my own division to say the magic word: *Downscale*.

But I digress. First you need to know about Kip.

I've been after this dog for a while. I actually offered him a deal to come in with us, because he has a particular talent, which is not all that common. He can dash out from the side of the road and run alongside a car, so it looks as if he's going under the wheels. At the last second, he peels off, away from the car. I call it the Miss-Curve, a swift, seamless movement towards a moving vehicle, alongside it, and then a veer off in the opposite to the expected direction. It's sensational. It's just beautiful to watch, poetry in motion. Terrifies the life out of the drivers. If they don't want to report a dead sheep, they certainly don't want to have to tell an irate Crofter that they've mown down his chief henchman. Some of their avoidance manoeuvres have been spectacular, and the damage has been extremely satisfying. No deaths yet, unfortunately, but my goodness me, a few hefty insurance claims, and bills for new fencing and walls into the bargain.

But Kip was only executing these moves for his own amusement, with no political agenda. Sheepdogs are like that – they have some intelligence, but they lack morality, a sense of social responsibility. If only we had that skill on our side! I thought. So – and it was a considerable risk, I can tell you, the most dangerously compromising tactic I've executed – I talked to him. Mackenzie opposed it from the start – he thought the risk was too high, with the danger of me being caught behind enemy lines, but I talked him round and agreed to set up a rendezvous in neutral territory. I made sure it was at a distance, out in the field where I lured him far up an especially craggy hillside, so I could get into a position of relative safety, with him close enough to listen. *I'm not in the habit of recruiting mercenaries*, I told him, *but your impressive talents could really be of use here.* He cocked his ears, said, *I'm listening, Shaggy*, and let me go on. The Crofter was bellowing at him to get on with the job, so it wasn't easy for either of us to concentrate, and I had to keep a sharp eye out for any reinforcements that might have been sent in.

In the end, I couldn't offer him enough incentives to take him away from a cushy number up at the farmhouse, as much food as he could eat, and a Crofter who was kind to him. He was quite happy to carry out the runs, but he wouldn't enter into any treaty, or do it as part of a co-ordinated battle plan. He wasn't interested in any kind of solidarity with other four-legged species on a less lucky ticket, but from that day, I knew he was watching me, and our relationship underwent a subtle change. He made a better job of failing to catch me – instead of me really having to outwit him, he let me get away. I'd given him something to think about. Apart from anything else, I knew it was only a matter of time before he joined us, because of the way that Crofters work.

One winter night, he came to us. It was bad weather and I'd suspended manoeuvres for twenty-four hours after a particularly gruelling orienteering exercise on tough terrain. We'd organised a rendezvous on the road outside the local pub, where a high bank afforded shelter, and, as it was Saturday, there was always a chance we might score a hit without really trying. Four of the youngsters executed an almost faultless Indolent Facedown, sitting in the middle of the road and refusing to budge until the approaching vehicle had ground to a halt and then physically nudged them out of the way. I nodded admiringly – that's the kind of grit I like to see. No fuss, no histrionics, just good, level-headed teamwork. First class.

We were grazing without much hope on the brown grasses when a Landrover pulled into the pub car park below us and Kip's Crofter got out. My ears flicked – I could hear someone snuffling in the back, and thought I heard my name. When the Crofter, who went by the name of Tom Mackay, had gone through the door, I wandered over – and heard the low bark of a dog that didn't want to be heard by his master. It was Kip.

"What's doing, Kip?" I asked him. "Anything fresh?"

"I'm done for, Munro," he told me. "I have to get away tonight, or it's all over."

"What's the news?" I asked, although I had a pretty good idea.

"Later, Munro," he said gruffly. "Just get me out of here."

I called Mackenzie over, and between us we managed to work the handle of the Landrover's back door open. It was pretty knackered, and came down easily, and within a few minutes, Kip had leapt clear and was in our midst, staring at the car as if he couldn't quite believe what was happening.

"I have to find another place," he said eventually.

He told us that two nights ago, his Crofter had come home

with a new Border collie puppy. A new puppy in a house with a dog of Kip's age can mean only one thing. All dogs know it's going to happen, but the time for it is never right. Kip let out a howl of rage, sorrow and betrayal and spent the night in the kitchen by the stove, not in front of the living room fire with his master.

"I've got a choice," he said, with as much pragmatism as he could muster. "I can stay and train the wee laddie until he's fit to take my place, and then wait for the trip to the vet's. Or I can go now, and take my revenge."

It was hard for the dogs. The Crofters worked between dog and sheep, setting the two against each other, working one to an early grave, and raising the other for food. Sheep are expected to survive outside, and they need the Crofters for feed in the winter, but in general, we fend for ourselves. Dogs eagerly trade their independence for regular feed, a fireside and the company of men, which they seem to like. But they work for their privileges, and don't get the chance to die on their own terms, in their own time. Kip had few survival skills, and a winter in the hills without proper nourishment and the negative psychology that accompanies a sense of abandonment, would surely kill him. He was no use to anybody dead.

"We need a strategy that enables you to live," I said. "You're welcome to work with us, but you know living wild just won't work."

We reckoned that if Kip went back, he had some time – the wee laddie needed training, and Kip's Crofter, despite the barbarous practices he held in common with other Crofters, wasn't cruel. Kip had time to forge bonds with other humans – there were children at the farm, and a short distance down the road, a family of Incomer humans. I happened to know that these people did not subscribe to meat eating, and treated all living things with respect. If Kip started visiting them and giving out the Big Brown Eyes routine, they might just intercede when the wee laddie was fully trained, and the visit to the vet was looming.

Kip stayed where he was, befriended the youngster, and set about the task of training him. He was a professional and he did a good job, even though it threatened his personal safety. But he kept a watchful eye out, and started feeding information back to us about things that he thought might be useful.

He also began to innovate, and use his car chasing tactics against tourists, with very much better results. Crofters, after all, knew their dogs had the speed, manoeuvrability and common sense not to get themselves crushed under the wheels, while tourists, already nervy about driving the narrow, unprotected tarmac, were ripe for being pushed to their limits and committing errors. Kip came in for a good deal of abuse, but he took it in his stride. I was envious at first of the way he got direct recognition for his efforts. If one of my Incomers executed a carefully-practised movement into the road and forced a skid or sharp application of brakes, he was called stupid – whereas you could tell a lot of the drivers, even while they swore at Kip, were in equal parts infuriated and amused by his gung-ho and clever timing. The women – they're the ones with the RRP (that's Rosemary and Roast Potatoes to you) – were particularly infuriating. If one of my men walked into the path of a vehicle driven by a woman, she'd quite often brake, then smile benignly at him and say something like, "That was a lucky escape for you!" She completely missed the point – *she* was the lucky one for not ending up with her back axle sticking out of a loch. I despaired of ever reversing the psychology that always put the humans in the driving seat, if you'll forgive the expression, of them always insisting that *we* were lucky not to be *their* victims. Who controls these roads, after all?

Around this time, my relationship to the troops changed, in the wake of Macallan's revelatory suggestion of a new kind of manoeuvre. I knew my leadership was coming in for criticism because I had no real results to show for all the graft I'd put in. There wasn't a sheep who doubted I knew my stuff, but at the end of the day – what did I have to show for it? I'd always believed in setting our sights high, and for a year or two now I had been trying to work out the logistics of a large-scale operation deploying a couple of hundred troops. Mackenzie had pointed out that it was virtually impossible to co-ordinate such a large force, and if we were going to upscale our activities in this way, we needed clear objectives.

The truth was, I had become frustrated with the guerrilla tactics we had always worked with, the lack of fatalities on the other side, and the considerable risks we took to achieve very little. I met up several times with Fraser, leader of the neighbouring battalion, but the trips to his section of moorland took several days and even though Fraser was as experienced a campaigner as I was, we still couldn't come up with a workable strategy. The only alternative I could envisage was increasing the size of the divisions, and going out *en masse*. But then I couldn't think of what to do if we actually did.

Eventually matters came to a head, and it was Mackenzie and Macallan who took the initiative. Appropriately enough, it was Anzac Day, the day we honour our distant brethren, murdered in their millions in the great concentration camps in the Antipodes. Traditionally, we gather on the road near the bridge, face down vehicles for an hour, then meditate during a twenty-minute silence. It's a moving ceremony, reminds of our purpose, and enables us to pay our respects to the preceding legions.

"You have to be realistic," Mackenzie said at one of our regular tactical meetings. "This is a guerrilla force, it's the only way we can work. The lie of the land, the single-track roads, the infrequency of passing traffic – all those things work against us. We can't engineer a serious crash because the roads don't lend themselves to speed – and when they do, it's not the humans who get killed, it's us. You've been working on the right lines, keeping it small, developing the element of surprise.

If you change tactics now, you'll lose all the ground we've gained, and take us down a road that goes nowhere except wholesale slaughter – for us."

"I just wonder if there might be something we haven't thought of yet – "

"There isn't," Mackenzie said abruptly. "Your only chance is a coachload, and they don't come down this road. You'd have to be on the main road, and totally geared up for it – and the risk would be massive. If you got it wrong, we'd have huge casualties and nothing to show for it. And apart from anything else, you'd be on Fraser's patch. He wouldn't like it – he's got a new operation up and running and he wouldn't thank you for working over his territory. That section of main road is his prime training ground – there's a lot of youngsters on it, and he's got different methods to you. You wouldn't want them getting mixed up. And after losing his regiment, he's got enough on his plate, without having to worry about drawing up complex battle plans."

I conceded the point. Fraser's unit had taken out a Crofter last summer, written off the van and chalked up its first human mortality. But the price was high. The Crofter's widow, an Incomer, promptly sold the croft and sent all the sheep to an early appointment with the slaughterman, before repairing to the mainland. Fraser got out by the skin of his teeth, making a late dash into the hills during the round-up, and was now on the run, rebuilding his regiment underground.

Macallan chewed thoughtfully on a heather twig and shrugged his shoulders. "We're small scale," he said. "We have to accept that, and work within our limitations. We can never overthrow the system, or the humans. But if we can't throw a javelin into their hearts, what we *can* do is be a perpetual thorn in the side."

I immediately saw the sense of what he was saying, and wished I'd come to the same conclusion a lot sooner – we'd all wasted a lot of time. Perhaps if we used our tactics and skills on the scale they were originally developed, they would double their effectiveness.

"Look," Macallan said. "It's not your fault. We all know how much effort has gone into planning this operation. But like Mackenzie says, there's a lot of things against us. And it's not as if Fraser's tactics paid off. He might have got his kill, but was it worth all that sacrifice?"

In a word, no it wasn't. Casualties of war you expect, but few principles were worth wholesale slaughter. Fraser was still haunted by the despairing voices that floated back to him as the trailer was driven away. "Save yourself," they had told him. "Live to fight another day then we will not have died in vain."

"The other thing is, you're not getting any younger – none of us are. If we expect to make some kind of mark on this landscape, and give some hope to future generations, we need to score a hit soon. I really think we're getting close – and I've got an idea that might help you nail Kip's Crofter and give us something to run up our flagpole."

"Do we need Kip?" Mackenzie asked. I knew he was still uneasy about letting the sheepdog in on our military plans, just in case he was a spy.

"For information," Macallan said. "That's all. The rest we've done ourselves. It's just a case of putting a few elements together to create a streamlined attack."

I had to admit Kip had been an extremely useful source. In his role as double agent, he had been quick-witted, clever and able to supply all kinds of information about human habits. He had proved much more effective than any sheep we had used in the past to infiltrate Crofter colonies and supply information.

Ben was one of our early attempts to create a spy network. We had to go to considerable lengths to offer assurances to parents that there was a crack emergency team in place to get any spies out of danger before shipping. We explained exactly the situation to the recruit, so he was under no illusions about the risk. When he was still young, Ben was set up – put arse-end in a bog by the roadside as bait. He had been rescued by a Crofter, who eventually offered him to an incomer couple, who went on to raise him as a pet. *Pet* was the worst insult you could throw at a sheep, and you hardly ever saw one who had literally earned the name, especially on this island. But within three months, Ben was disgustingly well-fed, behaved like a dog and all but came in the house and lay in front of the fire. In the face of such excessive luxury, his resolve had caved in and he had turned traitor. In all my years as a commander, I'd never seen the like before. He was taken for walks, given chocolate buttons from the hand, and his doting owners bathed him with rose-scented bubble bath twice a year, and sprayed deodorant up his bum when he started to smell like what he was.

Leave him alone, was Mackenzie's dry advice, when I mooted the idea of storming his pen and bringing him back for court martial. *You don't want a recruit that doesn't like getting his hooves muddy.*

It was a long time before I had the confidence to try a similar thing again. It had been a mistake working in the field with unsupervised raw recruits, and the loss of our man was permanent — even if we had recovered him, a sheep so far removed from his natural behaviour was a terrible freak of nature that would never repay time spent in training.

I tried again, with older, more savvy volunteers, and this time we had better briefings. One or two of my best men had become pets as a means of working undercover, but one of them had deserted when he discovered that his owners were vegans and had no intention of ever causing him harm. The other was lulled into a false sense of security and despatched to the slaughterhouse when he unwittingly fell into a honey trap. The lure of being stroked backed up with a handful of doggie chocolate drops made him drop his guard, and the rope was round his neck and he was in the trailer before he knew what was happening. The woman cried about it, but sentiment doesn't cut much ice when you know you'll be coming back in an assortment of freezer bags and she'll be cooking you up with a bunch of RRP. That kind of sentiment comes cheap, I can tell you. And it was the end of the Pets strategy.

The other thing Kip did was watch television. He

debriefed us on all kinds of stuff about zoos and animal hospitals, but what really came in useful was the data he got on vehicles. There was a lot of fuss at the time about someone who had died in a car crash, and whoever they were, they had sparked off an enormous amount of debate about the dangers of going too fast. Kip's reports included a lot of figures relating to the velocity of moving vehicles, the impact of a crash on a vehicle's occupants, and the long-term physical traumas that resulted from being involved in a collision.

"It's to do with speed," Kip said, with authority. "It makes things heavier than they really are. If you're riding in a car and you hit something, the car stops, but you don't, and you keep moving because of the forces created by the speed. There are always three collisions in one crash," he went on, at risk of losing half his audience by blinding them with science. "There's the body hitting the inside of the vehicle, the internal organs hitting the shell of the body, and the internal organs banging against each other."

I was reminded of something Fraser had told me in the aftermath of the crash that had precipitated the loss of his regiment. As a fugitive myself, I knew the hardships he would face, and I thought the experience I'd gained over the years could help him survive. We met high in the hills on a warm night, when the midgies were rampant and bit our ears and faces, almost driving us mad. But it was a sacrifice worth paying – there was no danger a human, twice as vulnerable to attack as us, would come here. We had discussed the possibility of somehow using the midgies as artillery in an attack, but a strategy eluded us – we couldn't communicate with them, and their anarchy was so inbuilt, so instinctive, we couldn't imagine turning their considerable fighting power to any use requiring discipline. When they scented blood, they didn't care whose it was – man, sheep or cow, it made no difference.

That night, while I tried to dish out moral support, Fraser had talked of death – not of his own troops, whose deaths he did not witness, but of the Crofter they had brought off the road. *"It was the fear, Munro,"* he said. *"That's what took me by surprise. I wondered if humans perceive something different in death than we do. When I went to the window, I saw death in his eyes, but it was almost overwhelmed by the terror. There was no acceptance, no sense that his circle was completed, and it was his time."* Fraser shook his head, perplexed. *"So he fought – poor man, bleeding from his wounds, twisted and broken in his vehicle – he fought against the inevitable, and the fighting made it worse, tormented him all the more, made his exit undignified and ugly, a terrified mess."* He spat suddenly into the ground. *"It was the kind of death they force on us,"* he said, his eyes glittering with rage. *"That's what angered me. I saw what happens when you are deprived of your natural cycle, when death comes bidden by other forces than those intended. If I get nothing else from this life, I want to die at my allotted time. That Crofter showed me how central that is to everything we do."*

I returned to the debate. We already knew that in the winter, ice on the roads could force crashes. So people went slower. In the summer, there was no ice, and people drove faster. If they went faster, any crash they had would have more serious consequences. Macallan had picked up on this.

"We keep our best manoeuvres for the winter months," he said. "Perhaps we should try the summer."

"But we get the dark in the winter," I said. "The camouflage is better."

"Spring, then," Macallan persisted. "When it's still properly dark, but the roads are dry and clear of ice. When the humans are relaxed, and their guard is down. That's when we should strike."

"It makes sense," I said.

"Now," Macallan said. "Thanks to Munro, we can negotiate cattle grids in a variety of ways, we can survive the toughest conditions, we have experience in watching our quarry. What we don't do enough of is work black and whites together."

"Whatever combination we try, the whites always undermine the blacks," Mackenzie said.

"Because we always put them up front," Macallan said. He

looked at us. "Think about it. How do we deploy the whites? They're always up front, cutting their teeth on training exercises, with us in the background taking notes on their performance." He lowered his voice. "But if we work with them, and take the initiative instead of the back seat, we can score a hit."

The word hung in my mouth in disbelief, but I spat it out before Macallan.

"A decoy?"

He nodded slowly. "Exactly. Like I say, Munro, we've got all the training we need, thanks to you. This is a new way of putting it all together."

Four hours later, we had it. A location, a time, a strategy – and just two sheep. I had to hand it to Macallan. I had lost my way, trying to go for The Big One. His idea blew all that away and got us back on track. It was so simple it was almost perfection. It needed some refining, of course, some attention to the finer points of detail, but the basics were all there when he brought it to us. It required skill and considerable timing ability – but it could be done.

III

We were patient. None of us saw the value in rushing. It was still winter, after all, and the Crofters and all the other villagers were driving with due care and attention. The site we had chosen for the confrontation was the other side of a cattle grid, so I drafted Kilroy, an Incomer with a good deal of field experience, and together we practiced traversing it in all the ways we knew. The Roll and the Back Shuffle were straightforward enough as techniques, and so was the Hippity-Hoof, although you needed good balance and enough nip in you to get across quickly without stumbling, but The Bridge was a combination of surefootedness and a light hoof, with potential risk to the carrier. In the end, Kilroy offered to lay across the metal girders, because he had plenty of fat and muscle on him; I was thinner, more wiry, and also much lighter, so he had minimal weight to bear during the crossing. He lay, I walked, then he rolled the remainder of the distance. It was neat, swift and foolproof in the dark.

Towards the end of March, we agreed on a couple of dummy runs, just to get the timing right. No risks at this stage, just observing, calculating angles of approach and so on. The tragedy of losing one of my best men and closest allies was all the more shocking because none of us had allowed for the unexpected.

We had agreed the manoeuvre would take place late on a Friday night, because that was when most Crofters socialised in the pub before retiring. The preceding Monday, Kilroy and I set out with Mackenzie and Macallan to put the final pieces into place. It was bitterly cold, with a keen easterly wind blowing, so it was a considerable sacrifice being out in such conditions on training, so close to a major military outing.

We took our positions at the roadside, and waited. We had not been there long when Macallan gave the signal from his position in the ditch on the bend – he couldn't be seen from the road. A car had turned off the main road and was heading our way.

As the vehicle straightened out of the turn and approached us, I began to time it. It was a Ford van, typical Crofter transport. You could hear the tone of the engine rising as it accelerated towards us. I counted steadily, trying to fix the van against the markers we had set on the roadside – a lump of rock, a clump of prairie grass, some droppings. All very natural, nothing a crofter would notice. By the time I got to eight, he was crossing the small causeway. I sighed.

"Too much counting," Macallan hissed from the ditch. "Start from the causeway."

"Roger."

I was worried, but I couldn't put my finger on it. There was something not quite right. I glanced away from the Ford van, now doing a decent lick, and looked at the surface of the road. As the yellow glare from the van's headlights reached it, I understood. The temperature had dropped sharply. March was often cold, but if the wind was from the east, it could bring numbing frosts and late snowfalls that caught everyone unawares. There was black ice on the road.

I whipped round to warn Macallan, but it was too late. The van passed the last of the markers, hit the ice and skated off-course towards the ditch. I could hear the Crofter swearing, saw him wrench the wheel round with no effect. Suddenly, above the shrieking of the van's wheels, I heard Kilroy shouting, "Wire! Wire!" and I froze. Macallan had seen what was coming, had turned in time to clear the ditch where the van was heading – but he blundered into a tangle of rusted barbed wire just behind him and caught his back hooves up in it. I saw the measured, level-headed Macallan suddenly panic, pulling desperately against the treacherous wire and trying to force himself backwards – but he didn't stand a chance. He was half-out of the ditch when he suddenly turned and faced the van, which struck him full on the chest. The impact catapulted him clear of the barbed wire, leaving his back end hooves behind him as he landed in the heather.

The van crashed to a halt and the cursing driver threw himself out of the door and, after inspecting the damage, strode angrily down the road towards a crofthouse, where he could get help to drag his disabled vehicle clear of the ditch. He was not interested in us – to him, we were innocent bystanders.

"Scramble!" I shouted to Kilroy.

We stumbled over the heather to where the wounded Macallan lay. He was already near death, but his eyes were clear and peaceful.

"It's my time," he said. "It was meant to happen."

We made him as comfortable as we could, but we didn't disagree with him, or try to tend his wounds, or fight against his destiny. Humans go to all sorts of elaborate ends to cheat fate and avoid death, but we have a different attitude.

We stayed with him until he passed beyond us. He lay watching the stars, drifting between this earth and the next existence, contented and quiet. Sheep don't talk at the end of their lives – talking is for the living, for those of us who still have things to do, places to go, people to see. By not talking, they create the distance that's necessary to letting go, losing the things that aren't going to matter in the next round. We don't know what happens next, whether or not we have a future, but we know we can't do anything about it one way or another. That makes it easier to leave.

IV

We buried him with full military honours. We dragged the heather over his face, to try and protect his eyes from the hoodies – the hooded crows that scavenge on all our corpses in the end – said few words and left him to be absorbed into the living world.

When we returned, there was some discussion about whether or not it would be disrespectful to continue with Friday's planned manoeuvre, but Mackenzie in particular thought it would be a fitting tribute to Macallan, especially after all the work he'd put in. We all agreed that to give it up so close to fulfilment would diminish the importance of his death.

So it was that the following Friday, Kilroy and I were in position at the roadside, with Mackenzie on standby, clear of the ditch just in case. We weren't about to make the same costly mistake twice.

The Ford van turned off the main road and began to accelerate towards us. As it passed the bridge, Mackenzie said, "Now, Kilroy!"

Kilroy stood up, looking as casual as he could, and began to graze alongside the grassy edges of the road. The van slowed slightly.

"He's focused!" Mackenzie said. "Stand by, Munro."

We could see the driver watching Kilroy, who was havering as planned, picking disinterestedly at the grass, looking as if he might walk into the road. I moved into position quickly and steeled myself – if the driver left it too long, I'd be joining Macallan on the heather, with the hoodies pecking out my eyeballs.

At exactly the right moment, the driver moved his eyes away from Kilroy, the white sheep swithering at the roadside, to check on the road ahead, and reacted wildly. As Macallan had predicted, the white sheep had claimed his attention long enough to enable me to walk right in front of him, unnoticed. When his eyes refocused on the road, he saw a black sheep facing him down, yellow eyes glowing in the glare of the headlamps, horns proudly tilted backwards. The shock element was all we needed – all I had to do was hold steady.

I knew I looked magnificent, standing in the path of the hurtling van, all but chomping on a cigar and blazing an automatic at it. This was my big moment, and I knew I had him. I opened my mouth and bellowed, *This one's for Macallan!* The driver's instinct to avoid collision triumphed, he swung the wheel sharply and ploughed into the crash barriers on the bend, bounced off spectacularly and smashed into a large rock, the kind that are randomly distributed throughout the landscape. They harbour no malicious intent to sheep or man, but nevertheless are frequently implicated in accidents. When the din subsided, the silence was as thick and heavy as a fleece.

We stood and stared at the wrecked van, waiting for signs that the driver was alive, as the silence continued to stretch between us and the van, and extend along the road, where no other vehicles were in evidence to offer assistance. There was a brief, weighty stillness – the kind that comes when there is no wind, no signs of life from earth or sky.

And then the battered door of the van creaked and swung open and the Crofter emerged, unsteady on his feet, and surveyed the wreckage. We watched him as he turned away from the vehicle and saw the three of us. He was a young man, with dark eyes and short, thick, straight dark hair. He wore heavy working boots and a blue boiler suit – standard Crofter issue. We sized each other up from opposite sides of the road, and he stared at us for a long time, his face wearing an expression that was both bemused and amused. I knew he was wondering if we had actually intended this and worked it all out, and then talking himself out of such daft ideas, putting it down to a bit of concussion, and dismissing the notion as ludicrous.

Then suddenly he began to laugh. At first I thought he was laughing at us, but then I realised he was laughing at himself. He flung his arms wide to the sky – I think he had a little drink in him, not a lot, so that he was sodden, but enough to give him a sense of humour – and exclaimed, "Fifteen years, man and boy, I've worked with sheep and I've always got the better of them." He dropped his arms, then dropped his body from the waist into an exaggerated bow. He straightened and saluted, looked me straight in the eye, and said, with a shake of the head and an ironic laugh:

"Respect."

Then he winced, because his leg was cut, and his head was bruised – he was going to have a real shiner in the morning – and began to limp towards the cottage to get help.

V

So in the end, we didn't kill our Crofter. But from that day, in the wake of the deaths of Macallan and Fraser's Crofter and all those who had gone before them to so little effect, the killing became less of a priority. We still train and conduct manoeuvres, but the conflict focuses on disruption of traffic routes, derailment of vehicles and campaigns designed to limit the efficiency of the gatherings that take place prior to slaughterhouse convoy despatch.

And we have had an impact, with tangible results to show for all the hard slog. The young Crofter acknowledging my daring was witnessed by Kilroy and Mackenzie, and that endorsement of our tactical skills has done much to raise morale. Later in the year, after the summer and before the cold weather set in, a monument was raised on the bridge to alert drivers to the dangers facing them at that point. Set on a grey metal upright, there is a red and white triangular sign with an exclamation mark in its centre – and below it, a pretty passable silhouette of yours truly to commemorate the events of that extraordinary campaign. If you look at if from a certain angle, it looks a bit like an Incomer, but we'll let that pass. Modesty forbids me taking all the glory from that memorial, because it is, of course, also a tribute to the brave Macallan, who gave his life for the cause along with many others and lies buried close by.

The road ahead is long as we wage war against a regime that looks unlikely to change – but we remain united and determined to continue the struggle for justice against oppression.

Onwards!

6
THREE CRUSADES

I

Ban the Bomb! Girl Power! Flower Power. Black Power. Black Panthers. Power to the People. Fat is a Feminist Issue! Americans out of – well, anywhere they happen to be, really. Choose life! Meat is Murder! A woman's right to choose!

That's my mother talking. Well, all right, I might be exaggerating. Hyperbole is the prerogative of the terminally outraged. I need to paint it black. I've left out some of the exclamation marks, because after a while, they look as irritating as they sound! Don't they!! But you get the general idea. My mother is a walking ragbag of slogans that purports to have free will. She's like a patrolling sandwich board, with different signs to front and back that are always being painted out. A conformist parrot without a consistent cause. A fashionable rebel without a brain. She hasn't always been like this. It's all happened in the last couple of months, and it's something to do with me.

Save the whale! Even though she hasn't got a whale. *A dog is for life, not just for Christmas.* Ditto dog. *Save the rainforests.* She's got a limp yucca plant, and a dead window box. If she can't even manage her own back garden, how the hell is she going to take on an entire forest in Borneo? *Save the Children.* The hypocritical bitch. *Save Democracy.* Save any bloody thing you like, as long as it has nothing to do with real life, as she knows it. So how about save me? You've got to be kidding. That's too difficult, *definitely* too close to home and too much like cramping her style. Meat is Murder? Don't make me laugh.

She's not going to be my mother for much longer, I should explain, because tomorrow morning, I'm outta here. Given her attitude, this should give me some small cause for celebration, but after tomorrow morning, I will be incapable of reacting either favourably or unfavourably on the mother Fate has dealt me, or the joker she has slipped into the pack. I'm going to be stopped before I even get started. This isn't Ireland or South America and she's not Catholic, so I can't even fantasise about protection. This is all about her. Her choice. A woman's right to choose. I get sick of hearing about it. In my straitened circumstances, it's enough to make you turn to religion.

I used to think of us as *we*. My mother and I, bumping along together, easygoing buddies, a partnership. Now we're divided, she's turned against me, and I rock and roll around in this temporary lodging, at odds with my landlord, a tenant under notice of eviction.

The funny thing is that like I said, it wasn't always this way. I don't remember her having these feelings at the beginning. At first, when it was just a secret between the two of us, I got the idea she was contented with it, with me, with the whole idea of being a mother. She used to talk to me, when I was tiny, and not really able to understand, and her voice was warm, with sunshine in it and laughter. That's all gone now. She doesn't talk to me at all, except when she's had too much wine and she starts blubbing and going all maudlin on me.

One thing she does talk about with increasing frequency is mountains. It crops up a lot when she's arguing with Paul. She says she gave up climbing mountains to be with him, and that's as big a sacrifice as she could ever make. Somewhere in this sacrifice thing, I am being implicated. It makes me uncomfortable, and I don't get the connection.

Being incommunicado as I am, I don't get a say in the matter. I have no voice, not that she can hear, anyway. She is, as I suspect most of us are, deafened by her own ego, the strident voice that sees to Number One first, and can justify the most outrageous selfishness on grounds of *choice*. Forgive me if I sound a little bitter, and rather piqued. But I don't believe she's actually thought this through – she's not bright enough. She's simply strong-armed me out of the way to restore convenience. And I have not had my say. I'm sorry to keep harping about this, but it's important. Whether I am born or not born, she still has her life. But I do not rejoice in the luxury of that equality.

As an excuse, convenience is not the best she's likely to come up with, but it's certainly not the worst. It's just a bit – well, lame. Convenience? I'd be happy with that as an excuse if she was honest about it. *Sorry, but it's the wrong time for me to have a baby.* OK, it's a tough one to swallow, but at least it's straight. No, it's not the convenience I can't stand. It's the lying, the self -deceit, the persistent looking away from the shop window now she's chosen the goods.

I know all this because I've had to listen to her building up her stock of unconvincing reasons for the action she's about to take, painfully constructing a giant edifice of excuses. She talks about it too much, she keeps coming up with different reasons, she lies awake at night, she's started drinking, for God's sakes. That does me no favours, I can tell you. She gets up in the morning and both of us have got the hangover.

And she won't get on with it. The torture is relentless, I keep hoping the delay is indicative of a change in attitude, that I might yet get my shot in, that I might wake one day to find the teetering skyscraper of excuses has been razed, and she has seen through the self-deception. All the time I'm getting bigger, kicking her, sticking my fists in her bladder, giving her wind and heartburn, trying to make her focus on *me*. Sometimes I think I can shift the centre of her gaze. But I know I'm fooling myself. It's been painful to realise how deeply I am unwanted, for the most superficial of reasons. And it has been painful to hear my father, pleading with her not to go through with it.

All this has taught me a lot about words, and how language

is driven by the private agenda of the individual using it. My mother is incapable of confronting what her actions actually mean. This incapability is largely rooted in her chosen vocabulary. She's been encouraged in this myopia by the language of euphemism which the women surrounding her and the medical profession have developed to make the idea of *choice* more acceptable. They talk about a *termination of pregnancy*. That means you halt a condition, cease a bodily function. It shields you from what you are really doing. And this act, which would be categorised as murder a few months later, were I out in the real world and only slightly less dependent on her than I am now, is packaged and sold as *choice*, giving her a soothing belief in her own self-determination. Using the word *murder* in relation to someone not yet born is called *melodramatic* and *inappropriate*. By whatever term you choose to employ, it still stinks to me. It seems that once you take on the slogan *a woman's right to choose*, and you get pregnant, the choice is made for you – abortion is practically obligatory if you're going to prove your worth to the cause, because being pregnant makes you a victim. It's not *choice*. It's dictatorship. It's oppression.

And it's cowardly, too. It *is*. She's going through with it because she's been told it's the quickest, cleanest way to get rid of *the problem* and get her life back to normal. *The Problem*. That would be me. Another example of negative and non-specific language in action. But how can she ever go back to what she used to be? When you choose this option at this late stage in the game, you are asking someone else to take on the responsibility. She's made the decision, but someone else is going to have to take their dagger, do the deed, and clean up the mess. And what kind of mess she'll be in after is anybody's guess. But this *termination of pregnancy* is touted as the quick, clean, scientific solution.

She actually said goodbye to me tonight. I couldn't believe it. I mean, I knew she was going to, because one of her friends said it might help. She put her hands on her belly and said she was sorry, but she couldn't have me *now*. That's what her friend told her to say, so no marks, as usual, for originality. She couldn't hear me laughing at her. What on earth is that supposed to mean? *Now?* It's what I've been saying all along, she hasn't really got a handle on this. Does she think she can put me away in a box and pull me out later on, when she feels the time is right? It's *now* or never, my dear. Next time you get pregnant, it'll be someone else in here, at your mercy, hoping and praying that this time, it's going to be *convenient* for you. It isn't going to be *me*, because you're getting rid of *me* tomorrow morning. Unless you start listening to someone else, and give me a break.

I'm afraid of it, I'll be honest with you. All I feel now is anger, helpless, furious rage, but tomorrow I'll be very scared. I know what they have to do, and even while I rage against her, and fear for the pain I have to face – while *she's* fast asleep, I might add – I cry for the poor bastard in the gown and mask who'll have to dismember me and scrape out the bits. I am afraid they'll forget to put me to sleep first. I've been so dehumanised through use of the *choice* vocabulary that people who should know better are still unconvinced that I'm capable of feeling pain. It doesn't exactly fill you with confidence when you're going to be on the receiving end of the saline cocktail and ACME bone crushers.

Oh yes, I know what's going to happen. To their credit, they did tell her about it, and of course I had to listen, too, and they tried all the arguments that I've tried. Is it really going to be easy? How is she going to feel when she wakes up? And it will be too late then, they can't fish all the bits out of the bin and stick them back together again, and they can't guarantee that she won't come out in sympathy and go completely to pieces.

Perhaps that's why she cries so much, why she argues with Paul, why her reasoning sounds increasingly ragged and desperate. She's fighting with herself, and it gets harder to see why she is so determined to go through with this. Why is she putting us through this? Why am I such a bad option? Why can't she put me up for adoption, like one of her friends suggested? I could live with that, at least she'd be meeting me half way. If I understood that, I'd be able to make my own preparations for tomorrow morning. Someone told her, kindly, I think, that tomorrow never comes. I got the strangest idea she was saying it to me.

Well, you never know your luck.

II

Out of all this, the thing I find most difficult to believe is that I've been put in the same position twice. It's incredible. Helen – my wife – had a miscarriage. It broke up our relationship. And now Carrie wants to go through with an abortion. For the second time, I'm being denied fatherhood.

Helen bled so much. And she was in so much pain. I didn't know what to do. We'd had weeks of it, trying to save this scrap of life that was doing its best to hang on in there. She'd hardly moved, because when she stood up, she started to bleed. Not much, but still, enough to worry you. She wanted to go back to work, let nature take its course and deal with the consequences, but I said, how would you feel if anything happens? You'd never forgive yourself – and neither would I. What's more important – your career, or this baby? I think she knew that it was a lost battle, but she stayed at home for my sake.

The night it happened, we didn't really know what was going on. We rang the doctor twice before she called the ambulance. When Helen started to lose clots and stuff, it didn't dawn on us it was the baby – we were expecting it to come out in a recognisable form, not all these random bits we were flushing down the lavatory. We got to hospital at two in the morning, and they did a brutal examination – there were needles everywhere, and Helen was hysterical. The doctor was young and obviously didn't know what he was doing. Helen wouldn't co-operate until they gave her pethidine, she kept screaming at them to leave the baby where it was, she didn't know it had already gone. Afterwards, when the doctor tried to explain what had happened, I couldn't look at him. How could he do that to someone who was already suffering? Couldn't he see what he was doing to her – and me?

After a while, Helen got hold of herself and said it was obviously meant to be, she was glad all the worrying was over and it was a relief to know where she stood, and now she could get on with the rest of her life.

It was probably the pethidine talking, but I never forgave her for that.

I didn't have the benefit of a drug, so I cried for what we'd lost. I remember standing at the foot of the bed and one of the nurses telling me Helen needed me – not sharply, you know, but so I got the message that men were supposed to be strong, and it wasn't me taking the strain.

She did grieve, of course, once it was all over. The first time I saw her crying was when she put her Levi's on and realised they fitted again. I suggested making something for the baby, to remember it, but she thought that was overkill. She talked about it a little, but not as much as I felt we needed to. I think that was the reason we split up.

III

"On the overcrowded station platforms serving the great concentration camps during the Second World War, Jewish mothers who understood what was happening would slit the wrists of their sleeping daughters to spare them the horror of the gas chamber."

"When Central Intelligence informed Armando IV that a resistance movement was planning a revolt that his agents took seriously, he spent months and millions on infiltrating the key groups until he discovered the movement's plans to stage a mass rally under cover of a football game. His *agents, some of whom had gained the confidence of the movement's leaders, particularly encouraged the attendance of whole families, so he could emphasise the point that revolutionaries were not welcome in his country; if they did not like his system of government, they could go elsewhere. "We do not want terrorists," he said in a radio broadcast following the mass executions. "And we do not want their children, either. I believe this regrettable incident has annihilated both."*

"At the very end of the Third Reich, when Hitler and Eva Braun were dead and it became clear that the Nazi Empire was over, Goebbels, loyal to the Fuhrer, knowing he would face certain execution at the hands of the Allies, had the opportunity to send his wife and their six children to freedom. But rather than die knowing they would grow up without the guidance of a German fascist regime, he and his wife poisoned all the children, then poisoned themselves."

What was this? The strongest kind of love – or the most vicious expression of hate? Were the Goebbels passionate about their children – or their political ideals? Which was ultimately sacrificed to the other?

"The Kalahari Bushmen always suffocated newborn babies if they threatened the survival of the tribe – if they were born during a famine, for example. It wasn't relished, and the anguish was considerable, but it was undertaken as a practical measure. By the same token, a bushman who was too old to walk simply sat down and waited for death. The bushmen were – are, if they're still around - nomadic, and you had to be able to walk if you were going to keep up."

So now I'm trying to decide if Carrie is a Goebbels or a Kalahari Bushman. Or bushwoman, I suppose. Is she driven by some kind of ideal, or is there some kind of survival imperative? Whatever it is, she's deep down in her own exclusion zone, and anything I say or feel doesn't penetrate. She's heard me shout at her, and she's seen me cry, and she still hangs on to that decision like a drowning man – woman – clutches at a straw.

I feel helpless, as if I've lost my mandate, my right to speak. This is the day before she's going to do this dreadful thing, and there's nothing else I want to talk about. And she backs off into a corner, denies *my right to speak*, goes away from me, says she doesn't want to be judged. What does she expect? *A woman's right to choose* is all I get. It's insulting, demeaning, it removes all my *rights* as the father of the child she's carrying.

Helen lost her baby without even trying. That's all I can think about. It destroyed her – and she had no say in the matter. The baby died without her permission, and for no good reason. The sense of betrayal was terrible. I've tried to talk to Carrie about what it was like, how terrible it was to lose a baby without trying, and how much worse it will be to actually take that decision, but I don't think she understands.

I thought Jana dying of cancer might bring her to her senses. That sounds awful, but I thought it might put things into perspective, bring it home to Carrie about the finality of death. Oh, God, the finality of death ... just listen to it. It makes me so angry – the second most singular event in my life and I can only express my feelings through clichés.

Carrie hasn't been to see her very often since all this began, I don't think she knows what to say. She knows she'll have to explain it. Perhaps they've already talked about it for all I know. I can't think it would have gone down very well – it's not exactly tactful, is it, discussing abortion with someone dying of a brain tumour. Mind you, poor Jana probably won't know much about what's going on. She doesn't have very long now, she's in the hospice, and she's lost her sight. But of course if I say anything about it, I'm called spiteful and manipulative. You can't avoid it, can you, in this situation? Carrie's best friend is dying, through no fault of her own, and Carrie is visiting death on her own child. She hasn't made the connection. I mean, isn't there enough death in the world without making more? That's another cliché. I'll stop at two. There's never enough death in the world, of course there isn't, not until the last of us is gone.

All she can say is that this isn't the right time, and she doesn't think her head can handle it right now. Well, I'm sorry, but I don't believe it. I've seen Carrie go through some hard times, she was going through one when I met her, and I know she's more than capable of taking this on. I'll be here for her.

We've got a stable relationship – well, we had. She's got a very good job, and I've got skills as well. We can easily afford me to continue at home and take care of the baby. It's not as though I'm automatically expecting her to give up her job, if that's what's important. She can have anything she wants, anything, so long as she doesn't go through with this. But she says she doesn't want it. And if she does go through with it, I'm not sure I'm going to want her anymore.

Carrie's tough, but all of a sudden, she's trying to play the weakling. I don't get it. She talks as if she's going to fall to pieces if she has the baby, as if it's going to be the end of the world. What is all this? She's always spouting the feminist lines, the woman's right to choose, the women are just as strong as men bit – and then she says she can't cope with a baby. Is she really that fragile? Is she really that hopeless and incapable, that she'll be floored by a baby? It doesn't say much for women's aspirations of wanting to take over the board-room, and dominate the world of business, does it?

It's always annoyed me, this focus on one particular sex. All right, I can go some way to accepting Carrie's line that it's simply redressing the balance, but it's not helping anyone create a society based on shared values. Women start making a fuss about maternity leave from work, and then demanding that their jobs are protected, but they do it all as if the baby has arrived in their bodies by some sort of divine inspiration. It isn't just women who are affected by babies. They talk about equality, then before you know it, men are being treated like glorified sperm banks, used to provide the missing bits, then told to go back to being bachelor sexist bastards. Women are being blamed for the fact that it's them who get pregnant, but men are given no opportunity to support them because of the legislation. So who's really getting the worst deal?

But I don't think that's it, and that's what I told her this morning, the last day my baby will be alive. If she'd done it right at the beginning, maybe it would have been easier. But this is sheer cruelty. This is digging in, then rubbing salt into the wound. For both of us. Coming over all pathetic is just plain manipulative. This is the way she can get what she wants, and get people on her side. She's actually showing more strength than even I knew she had, as well as more determination, and more cunning.

She sat on the sofa last night, and ate chocolate. *You shouldn't be doing that*, I said, *you shouldn't do it. You've got to think of the baby. You've got to eat healthily for the baby's sake.* I don't know why I said it. She looked me straight in the eye and put another piece into her mouth, rolling her eyes and exaggerating her enjoyment of it. I was repulsed. I looked at her, stuffing chocolate on the sofa, and I thought of Hitler, dropping squares of chocolate into his coffee, while he planned the destruction of the Jews.

She's packing her hospital bag this afternoon, like some dreadful parody of an expectant mother. I'll be packing mine at the same time. I've run out of manoeuvres, you see, I can't think of anything else I can do to drive home how much this is hurting me, how much it has destroyed the image of the person I thought I lived with. When she leaves, so will I.

"When American pilots dropped napalm on Vietnamese villages, they flew back to base again, and were shielded from seeing the consequences of their actions. When killing can be conducted at a distance, greater atrocities become possible because the perpetrators do not see at first hand exactly what they have done."

IV

They said they'd do it to safeguard my mental health, that's the phrase they used. Now I wonder if they'd gone mad as well as me. I thought using my freedom to choose would make it easier, but the opposite has happened. I haven't come up with a single convincing reason that stands up to scrutiny. A lot of excuses, yes, a lot of personal politics bunkum, but nothing that makes me like myself. I've failed totally to make this a choice that gives me any sense of dignity, I've cut myself off from the baby and I can feel the sense of separateness that invades us.

But that's not all. We don't live in a vacuum, the baby and I, although sometimes I think we might as well. Pregnant and happy, and I'd be buried under an avalanche of helpful women, showered with boottees and shawls. But up for abortion and I'm out in the ice fields, scanning the horizons for the women who support my decision and are prepared to help me rationalise it. Someone came up with this freedom to choose ideal, lots of women put it into practice. So where are they all?

Where are they?

Within this sense of isolation, we live a life where there is a father to consider, a career to think about, and a political climate that says I should be rising above all this emotional blackmail that is pounding me to pulp from all sides. I should be clear-headed, self-centred, prepared to put myself first, think for myself, make my own decision regardless of everything else.

It's the novelty, I suppose, of self-sacrifice – how can I make my needs the focus of the problem, when the baby, who didn't ask to be put there, is rooted at my centre? It's a *fait accompli*. Here I am, it says, what are you going to do about it? I dare you to go to the ultimate extreme. A little Hitler, dragging me onto a new course, with my hormones massing their forces in sympathy. One week, a woman with a career and a balanced outlook; the next a pregnant mother with a foetus, an unbalanced, weeping, irrational bucket of baby-focused treacle.

I think this is the way people begin to go mad. When it's bad, it feels like piano wires, stretched across my brain, right through it, set between the temples and vibrating under a tension that makes my head sing. Next time someone strikes the wrong note, that's when they'll snap, and all the connections that hold my mind together will burst from their sockets and stick, needle-sharp, into any further attempts at rational thought. My brain full of spikes, disconnected and

137

hurting. The wires are so tight that I can feel them pulling between my temples and down the sides of my face. My jaws clench, my teeth lock against each other. I try pulling the Tiger face, a distant memory from yoga classes, a relaxation technique, and that pulls everything out of deadlock, but not for long. The wires tense again, they loop over my scalp, as if they're working through my blood vessels, sharp as steel guitar strings on unseasoned fingertips. The savage pressure around my jaw gives me a buzzing, tingling sensation that tells me my skull is too small for the overloaded brain inside. This is when I'm scared that madness is just a snapped piano wire away, it will happen any moment now, when the insides of my head blow apart like an Itchy and Scratchy cartoon, and splatter everyone with the mess.

This is how it's been ever since someone told me I didn't have to have the baby, I had a choice.

V

Will you look at all this! I've got all this stuff laid out on the bed – you should see it, it's ridiculous! Anyone would think I was going away for a fortnight, not just a few days. I can hardly fit it all in to the overnight bag. I bought it specially – look, it's got all these pockets and zips and things, I suppose I thought it would cheer me up. I've only got one nightie out – I had to buy that, as well. I don't usually wear a nightie, but you have to have one for hospital, I have to at least look respectable, even if I'm going to be treated like the scum of the earth. But I'm wondering if I might actually need two, in case I bleed or anything, I don't really know what it will be like afterwards, you know, how heavy it will be, or how long it will last. Anyway, I've got a packet of maternity pads. Perhaps I should have got two of those as well. I wish they weren't called maternity pads, but I suppose you can't really come straight out with it and call them abortion pads, can you? *Ease the discomfort and misery of heavy post-abortion bleeding with purpose-designed Abort-Pads.* Somebody would make a fortune. After all, there are 150,000 of us every year. That adds up to an awful lot of blood.

I've got a lot of toiletries, too. I got the tip out of a baby magazine. It says after you've given birth – which is effectively what'll be happening – you can feel very sore and sticky and sweaty, so having some nice smells and special treaty things can really make you feel better about yourself. I thought as soon as I can, I've promised myself a nice hot bath with some lovely expensive bubble bath and a big hot fluffy towel afterwards and body lotion and talcum powder, and a new nightie, and the moment I slide into the hot, foamy water it'll be like a new beginning, and all the horridness will wash away and I'll be able to put all this behind me and start again.

So that's what I did yesterday, I went shopping and bought all these lovely things, and as well as the new nightie, I got myself a summer frock as well, so I don't have to leave the hospital looking like a cross between a victim and a criminal. And now, of course, having gone a bit mad, and plumped for new underwear *as well*, I'm having real trouble working out how it's all going to fit in this little bag, never mind all the zips and pockets and things. Talk about retail therapy!

I did feel a bit sad in the chemist's, though, because of all the gorgeous baby things – but then if I *were* going to have the baby as well, I'd have needed at least one other bag for all her stuff! It did sort of bring it home to me about – well, anyway, what's the point in getting sentimental over it now, I've made my choice, and I think it's the right one. I've never been much of a one for babies. There was a while, when I was first with Paul, that I thought I might be, and he was so very keen for there to be a baby, and I thought it would sort of complete us, but well, it happened, and the longer it's gone on, the less comfortable I've felt with it, and it's got to the point where if I don't do it now, it'll be too late and I'll be paying for a brief period of indecision for the next twenty years.

It's not that I don't feel bad. It's not as if it's the baby's fault, and I know it's hurt Paul, but at the end of the day it's my decision – it's had to be, because Paul's not strong enough to make the hard choices – and I'm the one who'll have to give everything up. Paul's not up to it, he had a nervous breakdown when his wife had a miscarriage, so how could I leave a baby with him? He couldn't cope, he gets upset by what he sees on television, so how would he manage a crying baby all day? He hasn't worked since Helen lost her baby, so how could we give our baby the security she needs? I've got a good job, and I'd have to stay in it, and it would pay for a nanny, but Paul simply won't hear of a nanny, it's got to be him, making these elaborate atonements for a miscarried baby and a broken marriage that have taken away his self-esteem.

He's got this illusion that I was the one on the verge of losing my sanity when we met – he's always telling people I was nearly suicidal. It's rubbish – I'd broken up with my partner, that was all. I was upset – we'd been together six years, so no wonder – but I *was* coping. Paul doesn't mention that he was the one who actually took the overdose and spent ages in therapy. Which surprises me, really, because he's always been such an attention-seeker.

Now I'm wondering what makes people get together in the first place. You like to think it's love and mutual respect, and being attracted to each other's strengths. But the flip side of that has more to do with supporting our weaknesses, finding someone who fills in the missing bits, compensates for the parts of our lives and personalities that we don't manage so well. And then we use each other, until we don't need what they've got any more, and either grit our teeth, or move on. It's made me look at Paul differently, and now I keep asking myself why we ever got together at all.

It's not that difficult to work out, really. I was rebounding spectacularly and he was off the psychiatric list, and desperate to prove how capable he was. It was easy to get used to being nannied – that was my side of it. And he liked showing people he'd laid a career woman. We liked each other well enough, and we had fun together for the first couple of years. But when the original motivations wear off, you begin to work at papering over the parts you don't want your partner to see. It's much harder when all the paper starts peeling off and you're gradually exposed as someone who doesn't need nannying any more – me – and someone who actually can't cope without you – Paul. Now he feels trapped because he's worked out he has no power over me, and I feel trapped because I don't want our relationship defined in terms of power, especially when I've got so much over him.

It's the pressure he puts on me. This baby is being sacrificed to the fact that I will seriously go round the bend if I have to endure a full-term pregnancy with this terrible burden of Paul's anxiety. I can't stand the dependency. Up until now, I've thought he's worth it – it's flattering, isn't it, when you know someone needs you so much, they'll fall apart at the seams if you walk out on them – but hey, the Big Day is only hours away, and I don't know what I think anymore.

I have to stop this. It's my mind, it's racing away, I can hear myself gabbling like a lunatic, I'm probably closer to cracking up than I think. If I just stop, sit on the bed – but if I do that, I'll lose it, I know I will. You can't think any straighter while you're bawling the place down, then Paul will come in and it will all start again. I just need to go slower, strip away all the madness and see what I've got left.

At rock bottom, this baby is going to die because I have to protect Paul from facing up to his limitations. I've had to do all this myself. I couldn't ask for help. I know what he thinks of me for this, and I know what other people think as well. Paul would go to pieces without me, and I don't want to lose him. Or at least I didn't when I started all this. So losing the baby to protect us all was the best I could come up with. The alternative is to leave Paul, have the baby, go back to work and hire a nanny. I could do that, but it would be risky. Paul is so fragile. Or I can just give it up, go home and carry on as we were before. But I'm not stupid, am I? I've severed so many strands making this choice, the whole lot will probably unravel anyway.

Paul "copes" by reading books about the holocaust and reading out graphic descriptions of violent death. I've been through this so many times I have trouble identifying the real motives and the ones I've had to construct. I want the baby. No I don't. Well, maybe I do. Somewhere tangled up in all these real and *ersatz* arguments is a truth I don't think I can find anymore. And that frightens me. This is the kind of decision that you can't make a mistake about, and it seems that even trying to make a decision about it at all is a mistake in itself. Perhaps we really aren't meant to interfere in the hand fate deals us. Perhaps we should leave it up to God.

It saddens me to think how much the baby would hate me if it knew what I was going to do. If Paul had left me, it would have been different. I've pushed him so far on this, but he won't stand up to me and do what he thinks is right. I just can't – I can't do the leaving for him, I am so terrified of what it would make him do, I feel as if I'm caught between a potential suicide and a murder.

I hate what it's doing to me, I'm having to come out with all this political cant to try and justify my position. Paul's worked out that saying I can't cope with a baby is nonsense, but I can't tell him that the real reason for all this is because *he* won't be able to cope with a baby – and I won't be able to cope with him. He's blaming me, but he can't see that he's part of the problem, he's got to take responsibility for the decision I've had to make. I started off on this course of action to protect him, because I thought I should put him first, but now I'm thinking, Christ, he's a grown-up, he shouldn't need my protection. It's the baby who deserves that.

I kid myself I'm the one holding this thing together, but maybe that's not the case. Paul might be frail, but he's tenacious as hell. Look at the way he digs in for what he wants. He never lets it drop, I don't think we've had a conversation about anything else ever since I told him. Lately, we've hardly had a conversation at all. I can't deal with it. I really can't. I'm tired of always putting him first because he's so bloody incapable. But then I think – he isn't incapable, is he? He's got me running round after him, earning for him, keeping him, comforting him – what the hell has he got that constantly requires my devoted full-time support?

I've given up a lot since I met him. I used to climb, I loved it, I was good enough to tackle faces on my own, but I got into it too late. It gave me confidence, great self-reliance. I thought I could do anything. A crowd of us used to go off on weekends to crags and cliffs, practise and learn the techniques. That's where I met Dan. We went everywhere in this beat-up mini-bus, piled up with crampons and ice-picks and ropes. When Dan died after a fall, we were all stunned, we all lost a friend, but it didn't stop us. It gets into your blood, this idea that you can climb mountains. I look back at how I was then, and I can't believe I ever had that confidence and drive. I can't even decide what to cook for dinner now, or what to wear to work. I seem to have lowered my expectations of everything, lost this spark that made everything seem possible.

When I met Paul, he was so nervous about everything, I had to give it up. He used Dan to get his own way, the way he's using Jana now. Climbing was only the start of it – now I seem to have handed large chunks of myself over to him in great big packages, and he's got it all bundled together, roped up in a corner where he can sit on it. I thought he was worth it at the time, but now I think that if you think in terms of giving up anything, you're immediately defining it as a loss. You shouldn't have to lose things to gain things, not always, not if they're important to you. Not if they're linked to the fundamentals of what you are.

He's even started to use Jana against me, that's how twisted he is. I really did nearly walk out on him for that. I wish I had. The guilt is so bad now, maybe I should have been braver and just gone, taken the baby with me and started again. I wasn't going to tell Jana, but she guessed anyway. They say the dying become extraordinarily perceptive at the end. I'll miss her so much. I thought she'd judge me, think all the things Paul is thinking, but she said it was my life, and I had to do what would make me happy. I don't know what that would be any more. And I promised to visit today, later this evening, because I know I'm losing her, and by the time I'm over this thing, she might not be there for me any more.

This baby. Maybe if I just had this baby, and not Paul, and not anything else, it would be all right. In my dreams, I guess.

VI

The truth is, you get past caring, rock or no rock, organic transient or metamorphic fundamental. At some point, you realise you don't have the strength to fight it any more, and in a way, that makes it easier, as long as you remember to forget all the loss.

I've been watching the sleet meander down the windows. It looks like something you see under a micro-scope, little organisms creeping across the glass, trying to burrow their way in. That's an example of irrational paranoia, but all the same I can afford to smile at it. It could be Legionaire's Disease trying to get in now, and it wouldn't make any difference.

I have my chunk of rock with me, but I don't stone Terence with it anymore. No point. Terence's buddies have all ridden into town and staked out the saloon. I can see myself, the lone customer in the company of the bartender, aka nun, polishing glasses at the back, me sitting cool at the bar with the bottle of whiskey and the small tumbler, waiting for the showdown. I kid myself there's going to be a fight, guns blazing, me leaping High Noon style over the rooftops. But I'm too drugged to point a gun. I'll settle for finishing the bottle, and a bullet in the back of the head when I'm not looking.

But this kinda dying ain't that quick and clean. And you have to stare it in the face. Here comes Terence, swaggering through the doors, my filthy and despicable angel of despatch. He won't do nuthin until I rise and acknowledge him. In blacker moments, I forget to be dignified, and beg. Just do it. Do it now and do it quick. But he stands there grinning, malicious to the end, and sometimes I cry, because I don't want his ugly, cocky, taunting, told-you-so face to be the last thing I see.

You'll have noticed my lucidity. I never got to the mashed banana stage. The doctor stopped Terence getting any bigger with radiotherapy, and – whoop-di-doo – the tumour in my liver took over. So I kept my mind, and now I'm discovering that awareness of what's going on, the very thing I was so terrified of losing, is the least desirable feature of my condition. Mashed banana brain syndrome is something I'd like very much now, in vast quantities, pretty please with sugar on. I am now reminded constantly that the mind can only fight what is happening to the body to a certain extent.

I've had to tone the humour down a bit. I went one joke too far with my mother, and her pain shamed me into better behaviour. She'd just given me a rock. A luminous rock, the colour of the sun, shining like a sunset, natural not dyed, a wonder cut from the earth's crust and purchased at enormous, inappropriate expense to light my fading days. I'd lusted after this rock for a long time, since before I was ill, but I couldn't justify the cost. I stood like a kid with my nose pressed up against the glass of this shop, and took comfort from the fact that while it was still in the window, other people could enjoy it, too. When my mother flung financial prudence to the wind on account of my rapidly failing health, and arrived here clutching the precious stone, I thanked her by saying, "I should get terminal cancer more often." She almost threw it at me.

On the outside, the hospice works for and against you. It's peaceful, and everyone is kind, and no one seems to mind performing all the tasks they have to do for you, which get more and more ghastly as things progress. There's stuff coming out of my body I didn't know I was capable of producing. It's the connection with religion that makes the sisters serene in the face of all this messy suffering, I suppose, the faith that pulls them through, and that does rub off a bit. You start to think, if they're all OK with this, what is there to fear?

But it also reminds you of the false environment you're in. I mean, when did I last consort with nuns? When did I ever have to spend all my time in bed, because I've no strength to get up? But I made an effort today, for Carrie. Poor Carrie, looking so stressed out, she almost convinces me staying alive is a bad idea.

She wasn't in great shape when she arrived. In fact she burst into tears as soon as she sat down. I told her I knew I looked bad, but surely not *that* bad, but there was nothing to be done. She had to cry, and that was that. One of the nuns thought she was crying about me, and asked if I wanted her to leave, but I knew it wasn't that. Sister Catherine thought she might be upsetting me, but the truth is, it gave me something else to think about. She wanted my advice, I suppose.

I swore I wouldn't do this. I swore I wouldn't lie on my deathbed handing out advice to people. Just because I'm at death's door doesn't make me any better qualified to pontificate about the meaning of life, but people expect it, and Carrie's no exception. They want to leave you pocketing a gem of wisdom that will carry them through, and I can't deliver one, even though I end up thinking I ought to try, just to get people off my back. They seem to think that if you turn all wise on them, it somehow validates the fact you're dying and makes everybody feel better about it. Maybe it's the situation that fools people into thinking you've metamorphosed into some sort of guru. Sorry, but no. I'm not a guru, and having an illness that's starting to seep out of you, visible proof that the poison you've been harbouring for months is starting to gain the upper hand, hasn't turned me into a mystic. I'm just pegging out.

I didn't know what to say to her. About the baby, I mean. I could have gone out on a completely hypocritical note, but I couldn't do that, either. My instinct is that death comes soon enough, anyway, so why rush it?

But then again, you learn here that death sometimes takes its time, too, meandering off the point and losing concentration. Dorothy, the woman with acute lymphoblastic leukaemia, has been bad for two days now; they were talking about moving her because she's distressing the other patients. She's got the room across the corridor from me. She used to talk about her medication all the time, reel off all the doses, the way one drug does this, and the other does that, and this one balances out the side effects of the other two. She was fascinated by everything about her illness, how something that started off just in her blood had had all these other effects in other organs. You could tell she thought it was all going to go away, as if it was impossible she could ever have anything really wrong with her. Perhaps she'd always had good health before, like me.

I don't think she really had a handle on the gravity of her situation until the secondary in her jaw forced its way out of her cheek and started festering and oozing. Now there's a permanent dribble at the side of the wound because the tumour crashed through the salivary gland, and apart from making the skin raw, it keeps getting infected. She spends most of her time sitting in front of the mirror in her room, just staring. They can't snap her out of it. She just stares and stares at this nasty extrusion, how could something that horrible be coming out of me? Then she loses it, shouts and screams and says she doesn't want to have this wrong with her. The fear is terrible. You realise how much she's covering up when it bursts through like that. Today, it's hurting, and the pain relief isn't working. I can hear her whimpering when the nuns come to dress it, which they have to do every hour or so, to clean up the wet, and take away the smell. It's a dreadful smell. There's death in it, putrefaction, a horrible foreboding. It hangs in her room and drifts across into mine, fingering both of us. It's the one thing I'm afraid of.

It wasn't too bad, luckily, while Carrie was here. She has

her own preoccupations with death, but they aren't rooted in bad smells. In the end, I copped out. Like I said, at some stage, you just get past caring. I don't think I was much help.

VII

When I woke up, I thought, *she's really going to do it.* She got up early this morning – I was still asleep, so I knew straight away it was to keep the appointment. I was so scared. I really thought it was going to happen.

They argued while we got dressed. I kicked so much she had to stop for a while, and that made her cry, and that started Paul off. I felt pitiless – *sod them, sod the lot of them.* I'd already caused so many rows, what difference did another one make? I did it because I thought it might be the one that gets through to her. I did it because it's the only thing I *can* do.

Paul didn't cry, at least not at first. He was the Ice Man, Freezer Guy, his rage walled up in total contempt. I could hear it in his voice, any feelings he'd had for Carrie had completely died away. She'd always built her life around making him happy and this time she wasn't playing. I think it was the helplessness and the hurtfulness that got to him. There was a shift in the balance of power, as if she was finally standing up to him.

He said, "What can I say to you? Perhaps I've been going about this the wrong way. Is there something I can say that would change things? Is it that?"

I felt a sudden rush of anger. She said, and there was real venom in it, "*For once in my life I'm going to do something that isn't about you.*"

And he hit her. He had to cross the room to do it, and I felt the shock as his hand flicked out. She didn't see it coming because it wouldn't have occurred to her that he would ever resort to physical violence. I meant that much to him. I should

148

have been on his side for that – after all, he was on mine. Or was he? Had he ever been on anyone's side except his own?

She retaliated by throwing a tumbler full of water. Paul must have ducked because it smashed against the wall. Then there was screaming and shouting, the two of them hurling abuse, and me in the middle, feeling utterly wretched.

Maybe it's better like this, after all, I thought. Maybe this *is* the only way.

VIII

You can't help noticing the difference. The hospice and the abortion ward are working at opposite ends of the same spectrum. The blameless death and the murderess. I used to talk to Paul about mortality and how death brings us all down to the same level. But it's not true. There are too many variations on the theme.

I saw that last night, and again this morning. Jana is dying in quiet, shaded light, supported by sisters of God, her dying days framed by the huge picture windows that look out over ancient beech trees and dappled sunlight. The nurses tend her with soft cotton swabs and healing ointments.

When I check into the hospital to begin the killing process, it's all bright lights, scrubbed floors, brilliant white walls and glaring fluorescence. I am being invited to scrutinise my decision, search my soul, the interrogator's light shone full into my eyes. The ward is designed to bring it home. This is the harsh environment in which you will commit passive murder. My baby will die at the hands of rubber-gloved surgeons wielding shiny metal instruments. Somehow, everything reeks of last chances, as if lifelines are there waiting to be grasped. It's as if nobody will really accept your decision as final until you sign the damning forms.

I haven't signed them yet.

The staff are formal, unsupportive while they do all the routine stuff. There are women in the ward down the corridor who can't have babies, they say, without actually saying anything. People who would chop off their arms to be in your position. How can you insult them? Their whole lives have become extended grieving processes for the children they will never have.

The truth is, most of us simply aren't up to playing God.

The baby kicks furiously as I put my suitcase on the bed. The ward sister comes in. She's like a bloodhound, scenting indecision. My eyes are like footballs. I've been crying most of the night, and arguing with Paul ever since we woke up. Who the hell said abortion was the easy way out?

She doesn't say anything for quite a long time, as if she's letting me sense my own pain before she touches it. "Are you sure this is going to be the right thing?"

It was something Jana said. I don't think she was even particularly saying it to me, more like thinking aloud. She said sometimes there were too many decisions to make, sometimes you just had to let go and let things happen. We were talking about how complicated life gets, how sometimes you end up making decisions about things that nobody used to even think about. When women got married fifty years ago, they got pregnant and had babies. They didn't think about it, because that's what you did. If you got married, babies were part of the package. Now you can choose to not marry, choose to not have babies, and you think about it all the time, especially when you might have got it wrong.

"If it's so difficult for you to make this decision, then it must be the wrong one," Jana said. Her voice has changed, she can't form sounds as clearly as she used to, so you've got to concentrate if you're going to pick everything up. I told her she was being simplistic, but she went off about how making tough decisions is part of what defines us as successful people. *Was I doing this just to be tough?*

"It's the opposite," I said. "I'm doing it because I'm too bloody soft to stand up to Paul and tell him to bugger off."

"Oh well, then," Jana said, "So you're going to hide behind your unborn baby, who won't be around to make you feel bad afterwards." Even when the sounds are unclear, there's no mistaking the sentiment. Concentrating on the words so you can be absolutely sure you're being insulted makes you look like someone with zero IQ as you lean attentively forward, right into the stream of verbal abuse.

I jerked back as if I'd been scorched. "That's vicious."

Jana grabbed my hand, not very nicely. "Sorry and all that, but isn't all this because you've just worked out your bloke is a loser?"

I began to lose some of my romantic notions about dying people. Dying people aren't suppose to make you feel like shit when you've turned up to make them feel better. It's not fair. It's impossible to patronise someone who's shoving you face down into your own pile of mean spirited, lame-brained excuses. I thought Jana was going to take it easy on me, I thought I was going to be the one in control, that we'd spend most of the time talking about her.

"What's the point of talking about me?" she said with real scorn. "I have no decisions left to make. I've written the will, said what kind of funeral I want and bequeathed my unfinished thesis to the college. That's me done. You're the one who's still going to be walking around in fifty years, and I'd like to think you won't be hobbling around with a dead baby strapped to your back because you made the wrong *choice* [her italics] at the wrong time and saved the wrong person."

"Would it always be the wrong thing?"

Jana shook her head as vehemently as she could. "I don't know. You tell me," she said, then looked suddenly outraged. "Oh, no," she said, "no you *don't*. Don't you *dare* try to pin me down into a moral stance about the rights and wrongs on a grand scale. We're talking about you, and now, and what all this is going to do to you in the future." She looked at my football eyes and soggy Kleenex and took my hand again, and said, very gently, "Christ, Carrie, look what it's doing to you *now*."

And that was it. We talked about other things afterwards, and reminisced and when I got up to leave, she asked me to come back, whatever happened, because at least I'd stopped crying for twenty minutes and could still hold a reasonable conversation. When I left, she was holding a little piece of rock in her hand. She said it gave her perspective.

I found myself at the hospital in not much short of a trance. I must have gone onto auto pilot, because I couldn't remember anything about driving there. I remember a terrible row with Paul, the worst yet, and leaving him with an awful, desolate look on his face that frightened me. But as soon as the door closed, I lost him, and that's the last thing I saw.

It's funny how you're bullied by appointments and official things, isn't it? I think I turned up simply because I was booked in. *Oh – I must be having an abortion this morning, my appointment card says so.* You stop thinking about it, because you have an instruction. Then the baby stopped kicking. I suddenly thought, *Perhaps it knows. What if it can tell what I'm going to do?*

Then I remembered what Jana had said, about letting things go. So I tried to let go the decision and the baby and Paul and my mountain climbing and my job and the appointment card and Jana, and just as I was thinking that Jana had made me see mountains again, made me think I could still climb them, that's when the nurse came in.

And this is where I go out.

7

DEATH BY CHOCOLATE

I

It took a lot to reduce Detective Inspector Duncan Macrae to silence. Attending the scene of a death, he sometimes expressed his disgust or disbelief through the medium of expletives or blasphemy. But when he walked into the drawing room of the expensive eight-roomed apartment in a leafy Georgian street not far from the Portobello Road, anything he might usually have said died in his throat, a long time before it reached his lips. His sidekick, Tess Campbell, who had been eating a Mars Bar a few moments before, could only stand beside him with her jaw dropped in sympathy.

When the call came, from a woman blending exotic textures of Catalan and upper-crust English into a voice as rich and creamy as chocolate caramels, it addressed itself personally and precisely to Detective Inspector Duncan Macrae and advised him that a tableau of death awaited him at the given address. It was one of those voices that exerted a peculiar, magnetic charm, conjuring up an instant image of elegance, beauty, mystery and challenge. He found himself wanting to sleep with this voice that was imparting news of a death.

Given the bizarre nature of the conversation, he did not seriously entertain the possibility that this was a hoax. Perhaps he was already under the influence. Writing down the address, the phone crunched against his ear by his raised shoulder, he shook off the spell and tried to analyse the voice. The woman, who gave her name easily, was not distressed. In fact she seemed quite happy to chat. The death was – how should she put this? – an assisted suicide.

"We call that murder," Macrae said briskly, scribbling on his pad. If he thought this crude interjection would knock the woman off her stride, he was wrong.

He heard the sharp intake of breath and knew she was shocked, but not because he had hit on a hidden truth. "Oh no, you must not think that," she said. "Luigi wished to die in a most particular manner, and he needed our help to achieve that."

"*Our* help?"

"My friend and I have helped Luigi for several years. We have all explored his passion together, to the ultimate point."

"And what kind of passion is that?" Macrae said, feeling with increasing awkwardness that his habitual cynicism was out of place, and he was displaying the poorest possible manners in the face of such cultured politeness. He felt himself drowning in waves of information he could not understand, sucked under by a tide of unprofessional curiosity, beached by the flow and lilt of a glorious voice he could almost taste.

"You will see when you get there. I do not want to spoil the surprise. Luigi wanted it so – it is the last part of our bargain." She paused. "There are other things he requested, but I do not think they are realistic. All the documentation is supplied. I am sure you will want an interview, but you must not think we are criminals acting out of hatred. What you will discover in the apartment is an act of love. I wish I could be there to see it with you, and share your amazement."

The voice haunted him, all the way from the station to the flat. He couldn't get a fix on it. There was no hint of anger in it, or sadism, nothing to suggest there had been betrayal or revenge. Sadness – yes, there was sadness, but a pragmatism too, a sense of inevitability. If it had to be this way, then it was going to be done – what, properly? The woman's voice had the precision of one who speaks English as a second language,

154

yet her vocabulary was sophisticated, her modes of expression clear. He had no doubt that she was on the level, but there was a playful mischief in her instructions to go to the flat, a sense of fun, a sense that there would be some kind of entertaining revelation in store for him – not at all the kind of tip-off you usually got when there was a body involved.

He had braced himself for a slashing, a dismemberment, a Psycho shower scene, an apple-tree hanging, just in case her sense of fun was malicious in the extreme – but he had not detected that, either. As he turned the key in the door, with Tess behind him scrunching up the chocolate bar wrapper in her hand, Andy Bobby the back-up constable, Bruce the pathologist and Neil the photographer, he smelt the bitter-sweet richness of chocolate, and the woman's voice floated in his ear.

Duncan Macrae was prepared for anything. But not *this*. He sniffed, and the heavy, rich scent seemed to drench everything and lure him down the entrance hall like a siren song. It had a peculiarly disorienting effect, throwing the investigating police officers suddenly out of routine, giving them a sense that they were walking into something that seemed comfortingly familiar, yet incredibly dangerous. It was unsettling to walk into a room that you knew contained a body, and smell chocolate rather than death. Macrae's first flippant thought was to console himself by trying to remember what rooms with bodies in them usually smelt like, but it didn't work. The smell of the chocolate was almost worst, welding the anticipation of a commonplace pleasure to a nightmare revelation of death. Not for the first time that morning, Duncan Macrae had the sensation that he was about to enter another world, where different rules applied, where pleasure could assume the intensity of pain. It was a world that had the power to break out of its own confines and change the world of others. It already had. Shaking off the sensationalist notions that he felt certain were being induced by the unlikely perfume in the apartment, he walked briskly down the hall towards the drawing room, where the piercing light of a bright winter morning lanced through the open windows to illuminate the scene.

It was November, a bright, clear day, still a hard frosting on the pavements. The chill from outside had flooded the apartment, belying the warm, decadent scent that steeped the air. The windows had been thrown open, allowing the cold to pour in, a hard, ice-cube cold that caught in the throat and seemed to splinter in the eyes.

Andy spoke first. "Is that – uh – is that a body – _the_ body – under that lot?"

It was a fair question. They were assuming that the bath contained _the_ body, when the black-and-white-minstrel type spectacle before them might only be a grotesque complement to the real thing. Was it _the_ body – or even _a_ body – or was it an elaborate sculpture?

Macrae thought briefly, and with irritation, that Andy Bobby – a nickname the young constable had acquired after his small son tried to explain to a visitor what his Dad did for a living – had led a sheltered life. On the other hand, with twenty years experience in the force himself, he wasn't all that sure, either.

He stepped forward to study the open eyes, avoiding the glossy, rhythmic contours that formed a rippled pool of chocolate at the base of the frozen cascade pouring from the mouth of the body in the bath. "This is it," he said. "I would say putative cause of death is drowning, but –"

"Can't be," interrupted Bruce, opening his suitcase and starting to pull on surgical gloves. "He had to die first before he could be force fed." He flexed his latex-sheathed fingers with ill-concealed relish. Macrae shook his head, in a vain attempt to clear it. Bruce was way ahead of him. While he was still in gawping and gobsmacked mode, Bruce had already assessed the evidence and was drawing first conclusions. "Bit of a poser, this one, eh? Probably poisoned, or smothered to start with, probably already in the bath. And I would say," he added, looking for evidence of splashing and seeing none, "that there was co-operation, too, although of course the accomplices could have cleared away any signs of a struggle – it's obviously taken quite a lot of time and thought."

He broke off, bending close to the figure, and whispered, "Just look at this." On the shoulder, a spider was frozen in mid-crawl, its legs stuck fast in dark chocolate. Bruce chuckled softly. "Another pleasure seeker, by the looks of it," he said.

He made a few rudimentary examinations and said, "Seems a pity to spoil it, doesn't it?" He leaned forward. The face, set in white chocolate, had dark chocolate lips, a beauty spot positioned delicately on the lower cheek, and hair slicked down with a combination of white and dark. Delicate dark chocolate plugs stopped the nostrils and ears. "Remarkable," he said softly. "Look at the eyelashes. The detail is fantastic. This is extraordinary work. Whoever did this should be making a fortune in some other more acceptable field of art."

"Poisoned?" Macrae said. "What – cyanide or something?"

"No, no, you wouldn't want cyanide," Bruce said. "Far too messy. He'd thrash around, splash it all over the place, probably go all stiff. Awful business, cyanide. Quick, though."

"There's an air bubble," Macrae said, pointing to the middle of the bath. Bruce gave it a cursory glance, a single bubble of air held in thrall by a glistening chocolate dome.

"Oh, corpses, you know," he said dismissively. "Always farting."

Macrae sighed, and mentally crossed Aeros off his snack list.

"How the hell did they do it?" he said, stepping back and trying to take in the grisly pageant laid before them.

"Very slowly," was Bruce's cheery verdict from the edge of the bath. "They'll have used some kind of funnel, and waited for each batch of chocolate to set before they added another. You couldn't just pour it all in at once. And the same for the fountain effect. Look here – very faint spatula work, here – and here – to disguise the construction. They'll have worked from the bottom up. Very clever, you know, it really does look as if he's vomiting."

"They've done his hair," Tess said with horrified fascination. She realised she had twined her own red curls round her fingers as she gazed, as if she was checking it for adulterating substances. Her eyes strayed to the table in front of the bath and saw a fat wallet-style folder tied with crimson ribbon.

While Neil took pictures of the scene, Tess and Macrae scanned through the contents of the folder. The first item was a folded sheet of parchment, sealed with a blob of dark and white chocolate artfully swirled together and stamped with an intricate crest.

"I'm beginning to get the picture," Macrae said.

"Sir?" said Andy from over by the mantelpiece. "The candlesticks are made of chocolate." He peered at the walls. "And so is the flock paper."

"So are the bath's feet," said Bruce. "It's one of those cast iron jobbies, you know – the gryphon's claws for support," he added helpfully. "They've dressed the claws."

Macrae rolled his eyes. If the man's death was this much over the top, he must have been a nightmare to live with. He broke the seal on the parchment, which cracked into flakes in the freezing air and scattered to the floor, and read the letter, written in elegant copperplate script:

I, Abelard Luigi Belladonna Carlotti testify that I have planned and designed my own death. I administered the insulin myself ("Aaahh," said Bruce, admiringly, when Macrae called out the telltale word while he was still reading) *and was dead before my friends began work on arranging my corpse. It is my wish that my dear friends do not suffer prosecution for carrying out my instructions. It is also my wish that my remains are displayed in an art gallery in the form in which they are discovered. The whole is set on a plinth, which may be removed through the French windows. Any further information you may need is included in the accompanying papers. Signed –*

"I suppose that's what she meant by impractical," muttered Macrae, reading over Tess's shoulder. "I can see it in the Tate now, can't you? Not to mention *The Sun*."

"It's feasible," said Bruce, who seemed able to distance

himself from the reality of the circumstances and appraise them as the art form they were intended to be. "I mean, if a certain amount of preserving work was done, and the environment was cold enough."

"We've got a record here anyway," said Tess, delving further into the wallet. "Photographs, diagrams, sketches – everything. Setting temperatures, construction notes – even the amount of chocolate. They've done everything to the letter." She flicked to the back. "There's some sort of manuscript here as well. I'd guess a personal record."

Andy appeared from his tour of the rest of the rooms. "The bath in the bathroom is about 20% full of chocolate," he said. "And there's an almost-full bucket of it by the basin." He picked up a few of the photographs Tess had discarded on the table. "Bloody Nora," he said. "I mean – *bloody Nora* – look at them. Makes Mick Jagger's Mars Bar look a bit tame, doesn't it?"

"Surplus?" ventured Tess, returning to the chocolate in the bathroom. "They melted more than they needed?" She stopped. "Mind you, according to these figures, they calculated everything else so accurately, it seems a funny thing to get wrong by half a bath."

"We'll need to talk to them," Macrae said superfluously. The prospect of meeting the woman with the chocolate caramel voice and a talent for stuffing corpses with Cadbury's Bournville was distinctly unnerving. He turned his attention to the photographer with the air of a man who has seen enough and could do with some fresh air. The atmosphere of surfeit hung heavy on him, the sense of being gorged on someone else's favourite pig-out fantasy. "All done, Neil?"

"I wouldn't mind a couple of elevations," Neil said from behind his array of powerful lenses.

"What for?" snarled Macrae. "Think you might make the next Flake commercial?"

Andy snorted and made a bad job of covering it up.

"Lighten up, Duncan," said Bruce, who was still gazing at the body with profound admiration. "Neil just wants as accurate a record as possible, so when we're all accused of exaggerating, we can prove everything we say. He's just doing his job, like we all have to."

Macrae, who in the last hour had lost his sense of humour along with his passion for Yorkie bars, pulled his scarf up over his nose and strode for the door. Three reporters were being held at bay by two policemen.

"Hey Macrae, what's the story?" one of them asked as he headed for the car.

He pulled open the door with an impatient flick that stubbed his fingers agonisingly against the icy metal of the catch. For once, usual media curiosity completely stumped him. He stared at them, shook his head, and climbed inside.

"I think I've just given up Mars Bars," Macrae said on the journey back to the station, noticing that Tess, who always thought everything aloud, was being unusually introspective. "How about you?"

She shook her head, staring out of the window. "No." After a moment, she said, "Sir? Do you ever get the feeling you're leading a boring life?"

The fat wallet lay on her knees, heavy with evidence of lives she would never have dreamed of living.

II

Chocolate, chocolate, chocolate, Macrae read with an inward groan, as he gave himself up to the grim task of reading the manuscript at the back of the wallet.

My fairy godmother and hobgoblin, my blessing and curse, all my knowledge of sensual pleasure encapsulated in its liquid and solid incarnations. To live for, die for, die with, die in.

You must not blame the women. They acted with my permission, under my express instructions. We have done everything together these past years. When you examine the papers and photographs, you will understand how intimate we were, how well we understood each other. They did not contrive to kill me, they contributed to my death. I could not have achieved it without them.

Macrae sighed, annoyed at the flowery writing, even as he felt himself being pulled unwillingly towards and into this strange life with its macabre conclusion. The word *drown* surfaced in his mind, and he pushed it down again, as the image of the chocolate mannequin drifted between him and the page.

My earliest memory is of my mother eating chocolate. I was very young, perhaps only a few months, and I remember seeing her slip a dark, smooth chocolate lozenge into her mouth as if she was performing some sort of sacred ritual. I watched quietly, stilling my clamour for my own pleasure as I watched her take her own. I sensed a rival for her affection, a mystery, a connection. When the lozenge had dissolved in her mouth and dispersed its benign influence through her, she picked me up, smiling, opened her blouse and proffered the dark, swollen, chocolate-coloured nipple. I drank greedily, savouring the sweetness of her milk laced through with a tantalising bitterness, an exotic richness that stirred my unformed mind with unknown longing. Soon, even if I had been sleeping before she woke me, I could tell whether or not she had eaten chocolate before she fed me.

When I grew up, I learned that she had eaten chocolate throughout her pregnancy because she said it gave her strength, but there was much more to it than that. Chocolate made her feel special. It was the way she pampered herself, protected herself – it made her feel good about herself.

She let me in on her secret at a young age, as I have said. I was weaned on chocolate. As I grew, she gave it to me as a treat, as a blessing, when she was happy, when I pleased her, when the sun shone or the snow lay in sparkling splendour around the house. And when I displeased her, or she was sunk in melancholy, she denied it to both of us. In this way, my mother and I became inextricably linked by mood. Both of us had to be happy – or at least, not depressed – for there to be chocolate. Chocolate was not to be squandered on people who were miserable or naughty or bad in spirit. So just as chocolate became a deeply charged pleasure for us, so its withdrawal was the ultimate punishment. You should not be grouchy! You are not fit to receive chocolate unless you are content and your body is poised to experience its pleasures.

One of her favourite stories about my early days was how I ate. I was as disgusting as any baby with porridge or mashed vegetables or pulverised fruit. The waste products of my early attempts to get food from my mouth to my gut would slide down my chin, drip, glassy with spit, onto my bib and coat my fingers with a slippery, grainy residue. But whenever pudding was one of the coveted chocolate lozenges, I held it fast in my soft mouth, refusing to let even a single trace escape. Other mothers squealed about how filthy their babies were if they were given chocolate, so only rarely were they allowed to taste it. I, on the other hand, would stay clean, and showed the proper respect, relishing the rich nectar that steeped my tongue and slid down my throat like liquid gold. Perhaps I understood other parents' reluctance, and made doubly certain I would be allowed to continue to be favoured. The link between chocolate and extreme cleanliness was established.

In my young adulthood, I began conducting experiments into the coating properties of chocolate. I understood that these dabblings were not rooted in scientific principles, but in obsessional curiosity. I was fascinated by its viscous qualities, the voluptuous cling and fold of melted chocolate pouring from a jug into a bowl. I would interrupt the glossy flow by holding a metal spoon or my splayed fingers between both vessels, and then devour it before it set.

I became an excellent cook. I made gallons of chocolate mousse, chocolate truffle, chocolate ice cream, just for the pleasure of folding together the white silk of the whipped cream with the dusky satin of the dark chocolate. It was my first experience of real sensual awareness, and I would croon encouragingly as the cream yielded its opal purity to the decadence of black gold.

I filled a small pillow with cracked, roasted cacao beans and rested my head near it when I slept. Stimulated by its aromas, I dreamt about chocolate. Eventually, everything I ate included it. I dunked rum truffles into red wine, dipped the rims of champagne flutes into melted chocolate, and then chilled them in the refrigerator. I grated it over grilled fillet steak and chicken, mixed it with black pepper and tossed strawberries in it, poured hot oatmeal porridge over a nest of chocolate shavings. I put it on toast, beat it into scrambled eggs, made pasta and bread with it, made pavlovas and trifles and soufflé omelettes. And I drank it, rich and hot with goat's milk, or chilled with an ice cream float and all manner of chocolate decorations. My dinner guests adored receiving my invitations because I tried to make food an experience, and chocolate a revelation for them.

I became an expert at crafting objects, little teasing things that would make my house guests cry out with surprise at such novelty. I could even paint with it. I believe I could have made a career out of such trifles, but it was the darker, less acceptable side of my obsession that took hold and began to drive me in new directions.

I began to go further. I began to coat myself in chocolate. (Dear God, breathed Macrae, reading on with horrified fascination, and beginning, in spite of himself, to understand why Tess thought her life might be boring.) *I experimented with different parts of my body, varying the temperature, sometimes adding butter or cream so that it set, but stayed soft on my skin. Sometimes I dipped my whole hand, then sat in the chill cellar and watched it set, shiny and brittle, revealing the fingernails, pores and veins in exquisite detail. I learned that if I first painted my hand with lightly beaten egg white and then fine caster sugar, the chocolate coating would break off in satisfying flakes when I flexed first one finger, then another, then the knuckles and ligaments. I began to discover my body through my discovery of chocolate. My hair yielded particularly interesting results. Short, black and thick, I could massage white chocolate into it, then hang my head upside down until it set into thick, sweet spikes.*

It did not occur to me that I was celibate until I was in my early thirties, when I realised that all my capacity for passion had been expressed purely through my love affair with chocolate. I could temper chocolate and prepare it so it could be manipulated into exquisite artforms with the same sensitivity a skilful lover could arouse a woman and prepare her for the raptures of sexual fulfilment. But instead of choosing new adventures with women instead of chocolate, I sought to bring the two together.

I began to photograph my artistic dabblings, but the need to share my passion and its secrets became urgent. I was terribly nervous about this. I had to find someone who would share it, nurture it, take it further, not someone who would treat it as a joke. Above all, I wished to be taken seriously, I wished to document a shift from the purely scientific to the erotic.

III

I found them in the Ritz, in a small lounge where I occasionally took hot chocolate spiced with stick cinnamon, roofed with a dense cloud of vanilla-scented cream, and scattered with tiny dark and white chocolate pearls. That day, there was a measure of Irish whiskey to accompany it.

I had been searching for months, among my friends and acquaintances, and finally beyond them, for the person who shared my interests and had the creativity to take them further. When the two women came into the room and threw themselves into the deep maroon cushions of a small sofa, I knew at once. They had been shopping, and though their voices were low, their eyes, at once dark as cacao beans and bright as fireworks, glowed with an intensity of life that made them stand out as if they had stripped naked and danced on the tables. They ordered black mocha coffee with a jug of thick cream and a bowl of bitter chocolate shavings, and two portions of what I knew to be one of the most exquisite chocolate cakes in London.

This is how my instinct that they were right was converted to certainty. One of the women picked up her plate and the silver pastry fork with its three sculpted tines, and drew it carefully across the surface of the cake, which was thickly coated in a semi-set icing of chocolate mousse, then levered a small piece away from the plate. She held the loaded fork between them and they studied it, discussing its texture, its silky, glossy darkness, before she brought it first to her nose, then to her mouth, and placed it, like a divine sacrament, on her tongue. She wasn't eating a piece of cake – it was a ceremony, part scientific enquiry, part devotional act, part pleasure fulfilment. I loved her then, and felt the power of longing for her.

How to approach them? I did not know how to communicate my proposal to them without sounding perverse. Suddenly I realised I was racing ahead of myself. What was I thinking of? First I had to introduce myself, then get to know them. I noted the day – a Wednesday. I noted the time – 4.32pm. I noted the time of year – autumn. I was in a terrible state of indecision. Did I approach them now, strike while the iron was hot, or did I wait and make certain of my choice? No, no – I was already certain. There was nothing to tell me if they came regularly or were occasional visitors like myself. Perhaps they had never been here before, and would never come again. When I signalled to the waiter that I wished to take a small glass of iced mineral water, I asked what he knew of them.

Ah yes, the ladies. Occasionally they came here. They lived in Hampstead – together – when they weren't travelling. They shopped. They took refreshment here, sometimes dinner later. Here, they took chocolate. Always chocolate.

He went away with my request, leaving me to ponder my options. The word 'occasionally' alarmed me. It meant their attendance was irregular, they did not work to a pattern. They could not be trusted to turn up again within a reasonable length of time. At the same time, this very unpredictability bound me to them even more strongly, made them even more likely to suit the plans I had. I realised there were no options.

I glanced across at their table. The chocolate cake was almost half gone. When the waiter returned, I asked him to convey a bottle of Krug and six very special chocolates to their table. The chocolates were from Barcelona, delicate twists of candied orange peel dipped in bitter chocolate. I instructed the waiter to send only two glasses: if, as I hoped, the women invited me to join them, a third would be brought. If they didn't, I was contemplating an expensive gamble. The chocolates were a spontaneous choice – I was having to think on my feet – but as I waited for my gift to arrive, I knew they would be exactly right. After the rich chocolate cake, they would not want truffles; the candied orange would create a frisson, an aromatic, cleansing bridge between the cake and the dry, delicately fragrant champagne.

I continued my covert appraisal. That they were wealthy, I could tell from the bags slung over a nearby chair. Those told me too that they had cultivated taste, were not only used to luxury, but appreciated it with a critical acumen.

The waiter appeared, glancing across at me for permission to proceed. The twists of chocolate-coated orange peel, fastidiously arranged on a small salver, looked superb, the champagne chilled, the glasses dazzling, bright-sharp, as if they would lacerate you with their points of light. He had taken the liberty of adding two dramatic tiger lily blooms to the tray. It was splendid.

I nodded, masking my delight, and he approached the table, where the chocolate cake was close to extinction, its physical self exhausted, its spirit shining through the women's eyes. He leaned forward conspiratorially and I tensed, wondering if I should be looking, or if I should affect disinterest and avert my eyes. I looked, because already I was under their spell.

Both women listened attentively, and their curiosity seemed disarmingly good humoured. I was enormously relieved that they were not affronted, and did not appear to regard me as either a threat or a pervert. The waiter straightened and began the long walk back to my table. Perhaps the gentleman would be kind enough to accept the ladies' invitation to join them and help them drink the champagne?

I smiled and rose, hoping I looked calmer than I felt. I had no idea what I was going to say, but in the end, they made it easy for me. One woman had eyes the colour of bitter chocolate, the other, eyes full of the warmth and sweetness of honey. Chocolate and honey. It occurred to me that I could not have done this with someone who had blue eyes.

"You have chosen one of our favourite treats," the woman I already loved said. "It seems you know us already."

I bowed, and was horrified to hear myself say, "Chocolate is my passion. I hope I have found someone to share it with."

If she was taken aback, she didn't show it, but threw back her head and laughed. "Is this a proposal?" she asked. "Of marriage? We are being invited to share your passion before we have even shared a conversation?"

I flushed. "A proposal, yes," I said. "But not of marriage. It is a proposal of exploration."

She regarded me across the table as I assumed my seat, then turned to her companion, and I saw the light of adventure in her astounding eyes.

I had planned to say something cool and languid when I imagined how this encounter would take place. When it came to it, I could have lost my greatest opportunity through my foolishness. I said nothing else, and they asked nothing further. I worried briefly that in saying nothing else, I was deceiving them, but then again, it was never my intention to put them under obligation. I was delaying the moment of revelation, and of course, as is so often the case, there would be no need of revelation, a big dramatic moment of confession. After all my agonising, there was simply

166

understanding, and a natural progression of events. We loved chocolate. It
was as good a starting point as any.

IV

As Macrae sighed and pushed the bundle of papers away from him, Tess appeared at his elbow, smirking.

"Hot chocolate?" she asked, putting the plastic beaker on the desk beside him.

He accepted with a grin; it seemed to go with the material he was reading. It must be to do with expectations, he thought, the way the body responded to the mind. When you read about chocolate, you wanted to taste it; when your body rejected it, your mind had already decided it had had enough.

"What is it that makes people develop an obsession with a single thing?" he asked, staring out of the window at the anonymous urban landscape.

"But it isn't just a single thing, is it?" Tess said, sitting opposite him. "It might have started out as one thing, but it's turned into lots of other things as well, even if they've all sprung from the same source."

"Like the Hydra," Macrae said.

"Well, that's assuming that obsessions are always bad things." Tess flicked through the papers. "Look. Because of chocolate, he's travelled, he's learned to cook, he's developed a sophisticated palate and a high degree of artistic skill, he's developed his imagination, he's even developed his understanding of scientific principles. If you took chocolate away from him, would he have had half so varied and interesting a range of hobbies and pastimes?"

"But that's my point," Macrae said. "You're assuming he'd be nothing without chocolate. I'm saying he might have been so much more."

"The obsessive personality needs a trigger, a focus," Tess

167

said, "or it has nothing to feed on. It vegetates. He may have been considerably less."

"This guy ends up in a bath full of chocolate, looking as if he's vomiting the stuff up, he's got two women stuffing his body with it, he's overdosed on insulin – and this is something he *wants*? You can't tell me that's *not* bad, can you?"

"Perhaps you should finish reading it first," Tess said. "From what he said, and his woman friend, they had a lot of fun before it ended."

Macrae pursed his lips, trying to understand how the mind took a grip on something, then for whatever reason, refused to let go. "I just wonder how much fun you can really be having when it's so dependent on, or triggered by, one thing. How much fun are you *not* having when you swim in such a narrow channel?"

"It started when he was very young," Tess pointed out. "It's not as if he may have had a choice in the matter. His relationship with his mother was pivotal, I'd say. She was the one who created the links between the presence of chocolate and a sense that all was right with the world."

Macrae turned the pages absently. "He doesn't tell us what happened to her, does he?" he said, scanning the pages for a reference to the mother and failing to spot one. "But then why design a final image that's so negative, so indicative of self-disgust, as if he's overdosed on his own obsession?"

Tess pushed the open manuscript back across the desk. "It'll be in there," she said.

Macrae shook his head. "It won't be," he said. "That's like saying I can taste chocolate by reading a book about it. I can find out the physical mechanics of it, but he can't explain it to me. He can't make me *understand*."

"Probably you will never understand it," said a voice from the door, "but maybe you will come to accept that it was the only way he could express his feelings."

Macrae recognised the voice before he recognised the woman from the photographs.

She cut a surprising figure, not as tall as he had imagined

her, not as willowy. Not as beautiful, either, although he understood why Luigi had been mesmerised by her eyes. She carried herself with great poise, however, and was dressed like a movie star, highly tailored and artfully decorated. Macrae noticed her because she had recently poured molten chocolate down a dead man's gullet, and this increased her curiosity value, but even if you did not know that about her, if you saw her in the street, you would still assume she was capable of something equally fascinating. He rose awkwardly from the seat, gesturing for Tess to bring in another chair.

"It's Maria?" Macrae asked, while she gazed at him with calm detachment.

She nodded. "Ramirez, if we are to be formal about things."

"Where is your friend?" Macrae asked. "The one who helped – er – arrange Luigi's body?"

"Juanita Mendoza cannot be with us," she said, deliberately enigmatic.

"Oh? Left the country, has she?"

"In a manner of speaking, yes. But no, not really. She is dead, too."

Macrae tapped the tip of his biro irritably on the notepad in front of him, the tragedy of the double death utterly lost on him. "I suppose this was an assisted suicide as well?" he said. "Am I going to find her set in Turkish Delight in a double bed, choking on a chocolate dick?"

Even this did not disturb the woman's calm, although Macrae felt sure that the wince he saw was more at his choice of vocabulary than at the suggestion of murder.

"Oh no," Maria said. "Nothing so vulgar. It was planned. She did it all herself." As if to underline the point, she added, "It was her choice."

"Where is she?" he said tersely. "In the apartment?"

"She is in the bath," Maria said softly. "She died before Luigi."

Macrae pushed back his chair abruptly and strode towards the window, flinging it upwards to let the cold air and the

169

sounds of normality drift towards him. He ran a hand distractedly through his hair, letting the feelings of anger, confusion and frustration run their course. At least part of the sarcastic imaginings he had flung at her could well prove to be right. Well, what did he expect? A good looking woman with a voice that came from 0898 land and dubious creative talents. His thoughts were broken by the realisation that he was disappointed. Her manner, her refusal to show the appropriate emotions, had lulled him into a sense that she would have a reasonable explanation, that this chocolate thing was just a game that had spilled over into real life with horrifying consequences. He had wanted her to be less involved, more in touch with the consequences of her actions, less of a hat stand. Less of a woman displaying traits he associated with the criminally insane.

He turned back to the desk and picked up the phone. "Bruce?" he said after a moment. "Have you started yet?"

"Good Lord, no. Took us forever to get him here," came Bruce's voice at the other end. "We're just deciding on the best approach. Might be easier to warm it all up and pour it off, but you might lose evidence if the temperature of the corpse is altered."

"Whatever," Macrae said abruptly, not wanting to get into an involved debate about the logistics of Luigi's cause of death diagnosis. Bruce's professional excellence relied heavily on his talent for pedantry, but it was not something Macrae wished to apply himself to at the moment. "One of the women is here. She says there's another body below the surface."

"Really? Have to be quite a small one," Bruce said dubiously. "Although perhaps not, if she – is it a she? I'm assuming it's the other woman – oh well, yes then, I suppose it's possible. It's a fair-sized bath, true enough." Macrae heard the business-like smack of the latex gloves and waited. "Well, that settles it, then. They'll have to be chipped out, won't they?"

Macrae replaced the receiver with a sigh.

"This is aiding and abetting," Macrae said. He looked

closely at Maria and wondered if she fully understood the implications of what she had said, or if she simply expected to be able to talk herself out of it. "You could be in serious trouble," he said softly. "Do you understand? Would you like to have your lawyer present?"

She shrugged. "Do you think I am going to say something I will regret?"

"If you lie to me about anything, it will be very serious," he repeated, and felt himself drowning again, not in his own failure to grasp what was happening, but in hers.

V

"We travelled. We went all over the world together, but it was in Luigi's apartment where we embarked on our greatest adventures.

"Our friendship was sporadic at first. We met for occasional evenings, delighting in the new culinary diversions Luigi created for us. In the beginning, it was the desserts we remembered him for. He was an exquisite cook, but the desserts – ah, they surpassed anything he ever did with lobster or chicken or Chateaubriand. Chocolate and liqueur mousses as rich in forbidden pleasures as a Paris bordello, so light they seemed to float on their own wickedness; chocolate sauces so rich and sinful you would drift down to Hades on them; ice creams so cool and silky they were as sensuous and thrilling as a first kiss."

Her eyes danced with light as she remembered, and Macrae felt the pull of her charisma, the animation of her speech, as she painted pictures of vivid scenes built around almost tangible chocolate centrepieces.

"Then he began to tease us. He made chocolate candlesticks – you probably noticed those on the mantelpiece, yes? – and produced tiny paintings and cameos, shell-shaped dishes holding green pistachios, drinks coasters, just to amuse us. He even replaced sections of the wallpaper patterning ... yes, you have noticed those, too.

"We brought back chocolate board games from Spain – draughts and chess and backgammon, we sat in cafés in Barcelona and Madrid, in San Francisco and Chicago, Berlin and Vienna, tasting and sampling and laughing and enjoying each other, and storing ideas for our own explorations at home."

She regarded him with amazement. "You have no idea of the power chocolate can exert over you," she said. "You cannot imagine how much it is a part of so many pleasurable things and psychological associations until you learn how it has worked its way through so many different cultures, stimulating and comforting and creating happiness and a sense of wellbeing. We trekked through the jungles of Ecuador to visit ziggurats where chocolate was used in religious ceremonies and sacrifices, we drank it as the Incas and Maya would have taken it, bitter and made frothy by pouring cacao liquor between two jugs. We ate it ground into paste with chillies and thickly coated around chicken breasts. We discovered the very roots of *xocolata* in South America, then travelled to Switzerland to see how the concept has been refined and purified by modern societies. It is like meeting someone, becoming an acquaintance and then a friend, then a lover, then someone who cannot be separated from you. The story of chocolate is like a developing personality, but it is also more than that. It is a social icon, it touches us in many ways of which we are not even aware.

"One evening, we surprised him. We gave him the idea for his death masque, although we didn't know it at the time. We painted each other's faces – trying to use the chocolate as if it were make up, but it didn't work. We tried to create abstract masks, but the heat of our skin melted them. So we used ordinary make up on our faces, but painted our lips and eyelashes with chocolate, and added beauty spots. And we painted our fingernails – " she flashed long, elegant nails at them – "and left off the varnish so he could taste something familiar in a new environment."

"And what did Luigi think of that?" Macrae asked, when the silence had stretched itself beyond a pause, and he was losing her to it.

She looked thoughtfully at him. "He kissed the chocolate from our lips," she said. "It was the start of a new phase, the one Luigi had so desperately wanted to enter. And it was the beginning of the end of everything."

"What happened?"

"Did you know that Casanova preferred chocolate to champagne as an aphrodisiac? So did the Marquis de Sade. That is very interesting. Casanova was considered Europe's greatest sexual athlete and exponent of the sexual arts, while de Sade was our greatest pervert, a man who twisted the principles of pleasure and pain, brought suffering into sexuality and explored the principles of degradation and corruption through striving to achieve physical ecstasy. Chocolate was so for Luigi. He loved it so much his body was corrupted by it, so that it tortured him as much as it had pleasured him."

"There was no question of turning back once we had started down the road to sexual awakening," Maria said, with some genuine regret. "We had devoted ourselves to the chocolate arts – tasting, melting, tempering, developing techniques such as the making of chocolate caraque and the creation of artistic *objets*. Now it was time to bring together our skills with the exploration of pleasure that went beyond the excitement of flavour and texture."

"So are we talking about sex or aren't we?" Macrae said in exasperation.

"You must judge that for yourself," Maria said. "We painted each other and photographed our work. We learned massage and arousal techniques and heightened the experience with chocolate." She caught Tess's smirk and withered her with condescension.

"Perhaps I am explaining it badly," she said. "But you cannot imagine what I have lost with the deaths of Luigi and

Juanita. I wish I had had her courage. I will never again know those feelings that make you revel in life and the inspiration of discoveries deep within yourself that enable you to touch the essence of pure joy." She was silent a moment, watching Tess's suitably chastened features, then said, "You cannot enjoy the summit of a mountain without first experiencing the climb. Modern enjoyment is so superficial, over in a flash, nothing anyone takes seriously anymore. When you eat a bar of chocolate in the car on your way to work, or instead of lunch, you have barely begun to know all the pleasure that it could release in you. I have mined it to its deepest depths. I know. You do not. And I pity the fact that you never will."

Macrae remembered the manuscript and flicked ahead. "Just a minute," he said.

I piped scrolls and scallop shells on their bodies. Sometimes it would take several hours of sketching to arrive at the design I wanted, then several hours more to transpose it to their flesh. At first, I did simple things. I anointed their nipples and traced delicate spirals on their breasts, or worked designs around their navels and necks. But soon I worked to cover them entirely in delicate filigrees and bold swathes of white and dark chocolate, fashioning living sculptures of them reclining or sitting, standing or entwined. The very act of creation sparked intense desires, which we held in check as long as we could. Our senses were heightened by the scented oils of lemon, almond or orange I would stroke into their skin, as an artist prepares his canvas, the rich aromas of the chocolate I applied to their bodies, the sensation of delicate brushes against their skin, my lips or fingertips. From the beginning, in the charged atmosphere, their physical interest in each other would exclude me, as I worked with brushes or spatulas, then hid behind the camera and its detached eye. I let them play, and joined in when my documentation work was done, sometimes kissing and smoothing away all trace of my work, sometimes creating new ways of loving, new ways of releasing the tide of ecstasy that would leave my etchings unscathed. Juanita was my firefly, with her delicate, dancing fingers, her hot honey eyes and her impatience, her capacity for an intense erotic rapture I could not achieve for myself. Maria smouldered longer and ignited a molten core deep within me when my passion was calmer and the first explosions were over. Sometimes these encounters would last for two days, leaving us utterly exhausted and replete. In the soft light of dawn, we would bathe in water scented with sweet almond oil and cinnamon bark, and dissolve into the deepest bliss I have ever known.

So what went wrong? Macrae's forehead creased with incomprehension. The man was so bloody happy. Two bowls of melted chocolate, a paintbrush and a couple of naked women and he was off. If only it could be that simple. The exotic language invaded his mind, loosening his grip on the real world as he had come to understand it, tampering with all his knowledge of death, unusual circumstances and the people involved in it. It was as if Maria and Luigi had draped his mind with chocolate cobwebs, obscuring his judgement with the complex strands of a tantalising fable of transcendental pleasures. He was caught in their spell, his investigative reasoning paralysed by their visions of pleasure, and a tiny, illogical part of him that yearned to experience it for himself.

Macrae leaned forward. "I have to be certain," he said, "that Luigi wanted to die, that he was not coerced into the actions that led to his death."

Maria shook her head. "Luigi did not *want* to die," she said. "Nobody *wants* to die. It was a circumstance forced on him, because to continue with the business of living would no longer be pleasurable to him."

Macrae raised his eyebrow, and she shot him an amused glance. "No, Mr Macrae. Luigi did not die of sex," she said disapprovingly. "He died of chocolate."

"What – bulimia? On chocolate?"

"No. He developed diabetes."

Now Macrae saw daylight, felt himself staggering clear of the cloying chocolate swamp that had clogged his progress so far. "Hence the insulin," he said.

"Luigi was devastated by the diagnosis. His personality completely changed. For a time he tried to live without the substance that had inspired him for most of his life. But it was too difficult for him. He was always so cheerful before, with so much energy and the ability to inspire others – as he did us. After the diagnosis, he would weep and rage as if he had been bereaved. His artistic imagination was soured by the corrosive longing for what he could not have. He made chocolate skulls like the Brazilian ones they use in festivals for the dead, and photographed Juanita with skulls covering her breasts, and set between her thighs. Sometimes, his rages would terrify us, but we could not leave him, we could not abandon him to his suffering. We knew it would have to end, and that we would be there for him when it did." She sighed. "You cannot imagine what torture it was to him to be denied chocolate in such a terminal way. He could not get better, so he could not even dream about one day being able to indulge himself again with his all-consuming love."

"But he might have found something else," Macrae said, still attempting pragmatism in the face of such irrational, devouring obsession. "He had both of you. Why was chocolate so essential to the equation? Weren't you wounded by that implicit rejection – that you weren't good enough to compensate the loss?"

"It was always understood," she said. "We were his instruments of discovery, but not the main focus of his passion. Perhaps, though, I understood that better than Juanita."

Macrae found himself staring down at the manuscript again.

When they created those first chocolate masks, it was as if they were opening themselves to my curiosity, and creating the bridge that enabled me to cross into unknown landscapes. Our kisses were gentle at first, and I saw my own needs reflected in their eyes. Then Maria opened her blouse and proffered a dark, swollen nipple, richly scented. As the chocolate coating melted on my tongue, I sucked again on the soul of my mother, and an understanding of my desires and deprivations burst upon me. Our first sexual union was savage and tender, painful and joyous, wonderful and troubling as I found myself for the first time thrust against the intense desires of this woman who had waited so patiently for me. As I neared the peak of pleasure, Maria ran her hands through my hair, gripped my head against her breast and whispered, "This is not chocolate, Luigi. This is the passion of a woman." Then she tensed herself around me and I released myself into her with a great cry. But when I kissed her afterwards, it was chocolate I tasted in her mouth, and chocolate I smelt on her flesh. We had shared our first passion, but I could not separate her from the substance I had loved all my life. It was as if she had become chocolate incarnate.

"So that's what happened to his mother," Macrae said to himself.

The sharp and sudden sound of the phone tore him out of the trance as he sensed something in his mind click suddenly into place. He picked up the receiver to hear Bruce's perplexed tones at the other end. When he replaced it, he looked grave.

"That was the pathologist," he said, and his voice was hard, as cold as the sunshine outside. "It appears Juanita drowned in the bath. There are indications it was against her will."

Against all his expectations, Maria began to cry.

Macrae persisted, recovering his usual gusto as he tore the cobwebs down and the chocolate bubble burst. "There's something not quite right here, wouldn't you agree?" he said. "Luigi creates a vision – an impression of drowning, but Juanita actually *does* drown," he said. "What were you trying to do – turn their deaths into some sort of obscure artistic statement – a double-take on the object as seen, and the hidden meaning of it all beneath the surface?"

Maria shook her head. "It wasn't supposed to happen like that," she said, opening her bag and groping for a handkerchief. Irritatingly, a bar of chocolate slid from its interior. "We didn't know it was going to happen until the very end." She shook her head again. "It was so horrible. I thought she was already dead. Luigi was in the bath, preparing himself. I had to do everything. Just an hour before, we had been all together for the last time. We were so happy, drinking champagne and eating chocolates and reminiscing about our adventures, we wanted it to be a proper, cheerful farewell. Then Juanita told us what she was going to do. I didn't want it – I didn't want to be all alone at the end. But just as Luigi could not imagine a life without chocolate, so she could not imagine life without him. I had not realised how closely she had come to depend on him. And she could not bear to see him die. She took the insulin first."

"Wait," Macrae said. "How did she get into the bath? Did you lift her?"

"No, no," Maria said impatiently. "She climbed in. We discussed how best to do it, and decided to curl her body in between his legs – like so – so she would be low down and not disturb the surface. But when I began pouring the chocolate in –"

"Luigi was still alive?"

"Oh yes. Alive and conscious. But Juanita was still alive, too, and when the chocolate covered her face, she began to choke. It was so horrible," she whispered, and Macrae saw it in her eyes, the sudden cruel intrusion of reality bursting in upon the confectionery world they had built around them. There was no nice way to kill someone, even if you used chocolate. "We decided the best thing was to hold her down and quicken her release. We could not go against her wishes, and it was too late for that anyway, and we could not disturb the final plans we had made for the finished tableau. So Luigi held her head and I held her arms. It did not take long."

"What if she had changed her mind?" Macrae said, his voice suddenly gentle.

She was defiant. "I am not ashamed of what I did," she said. "I discharged the wishes of my dearest friends. Luigi took the insulin shortly afterwards. When he slipped into the coma, I began my work."

"Why did you leave the spider?" Macrae said suddenly. "Didn't he spoil the perfection you were striving to achieve?"

She smiled. "I think he adds something to it, don't you? My first thought was to sweep him away, but he had landed so delicately on Luigi's shoulder and his feet stuck at once. I thought there would be worse ways for a spider to die than to be immortalised as part of an extraordinary sculpture."

"That must have been hard," Macrae murmured. "To lavish so much care on two people who had betrayed you."

"What do you mean – betrayed?"

Macrae shrugged. "That's what it sounds like to me. Your lifelong friend chooses to die with Luigi rather than live with you. Luigi chooses to die for chocolate rather than live for you. Didn't you blame him? Doesn't it make your loss so much more lonely?"

She shook her head, staring at him, her eyes wide.

"I would feel used if it were me," Macrae said. "To do so much together, only to find at the end that you were excluded – by Luigi's real passion that elbowed everything aside, including Juanita, and by the intensity of her feelings for him. How did you bear it, that sense that you had lived through something real and vital that was suddenly revealed as an illusion?"

As the sunlight shone in the room, now the colour of chilled champagne, Macrae's hunting instinct took over. Maria looked smaller, overwhelmed. He watched her, all pity and revulsion and compassion as he closed in on the events she had tried to both explain to him and protect from him.

Tess listened intently, recognising the cat paw tread of her boss moving in for the kill. With Macrae, it was his quietness that people who were questioned by him came to dread. His frustration, his inquisitiveness, his sharp questions – they could field those because they were expected, *de rigeur*, part of the cat and mouse game you had to play. But there was a moment when he stopped asking, stopped staring out of the window to collect his thoughts, and his voice dropped low – then you knew it was all over and he had you cornered.

"Let me tell you how I think it was," he said softly. "Luigi's statement – the folded parchment – refers to his dear friends, who have agreed to help him achieve a final tableau in homage to his lifelong love. He goes to great lengths to excuse you from culpability. He wants everything to be cut and dried, perfect, nothing loose or messy. *He doesn't know Juanita is dead.* He writes that message as if she is still alive. You killed her after he had gone into the insulin coma and heaved her into the bath."

"Why?" Maria said faintly, as if it was her turn to fall under

179

the spell of Macrae's voice, which had taken on a rhythmic, hypnotic quality. "Why would I do that?"

"Why did you kill her?" Macrae said, feigning surprise. "Oh come, Maria. Because you loved Luigi. You were the first to make the connection for him between his mother, and chocolate and sexual fulfilment. You completed the circle he had been trapped by, but in so doing you set him free."

The light went out of Maria's eyes as she gazed at him with utter exhaustion. Was he right? Or was she completely disillusioned by his failure to grasp what she had told him?

"He loved you for making him whole. You were his bedrock. Through you he was able to understand how his mother had made him a prisoner of her own obsession and depression. Like her, you used chocolate to draw him into your love, but the knowledge he had made him free – free to love Juanita." The silence stretched itself between them as Macrae leaned forward. "All you had to look forward to after Luigi's death was the rest of your life with a woman he had loved more than you. It wasn't Juanita who couldn't bear the thought of living without Luigi. It was you. Murdering Juanita was your revenge on him for his betrayal."

The laden silence seemed to settle in pools in her eyes as she stared.

"Am I right, Maria?" he said, and his voice was gentle, caressing, cajoling the truth she had buried to surface, leave her and come towards him. "Is that how it was?"

She stared, unable to speak, unable to tell the thousand and one stories he saw in her amazing eyes, of before Luigi, before Juanita and before her own passions released their destructive force through all of them. And Macrae liked her less than the woman who had walked in, walled up in a chocolate maze of want and jealousy, greed and vengeance that only now was melting down from its carefully constructed form to reveal the manipulative drives inside. Poor Luigi, the innocent centrepiece of his own story, but only a pawn in hers.

As the sound of Maria's anguished crying cut through the drab paperwork atmosphere of the office, Macrae felt the light around them dim and knew they had not yet got to the bottom of the chocolate and corpse-filled bath.

But that is another story.

VI

Later that afternoon, Tess Campbell sat before the Incident Book and unwrapped a Crunchie bar in an act of tongue-in-cheek scientific enquiry. She bit into it and let the golden honeycomb crack open in her mouth in a shower of blistering sweetness, like a split atom releasing a brilliant explosion of flavours and half-remembered sensations from childhood. The chocolate melted, a rich, warm, satiny lava flow over the crushed golden nuggets on her tongue. She sighed with contentment, opened the book, and began to write her report, aware that she was falling short of ecstasy.

8
END PAPERS

I

The doctors said it might be today. It could happen any time now. But they've been saying that for at least a week now, and they've been wrong. He's looking a bit better today, I think, he's got a bit more colour and he's sitting up, just look at him, and by the looks of the tray, he even took a bit of breakfast. So I don't think it'll be today. Of course it won't be! You spend so much time listening to them you start to think like them in the end, and that's the last thing either of us needs. He's got into this state in the first place because of people thinking like that. I was going to ring Janet and tell her to come in, but I don't think it will be necessary. No sense bothering people for no reason – she's got her own life to be getting on with.

"All right this morning, love?" He definitely looks more chirpy, look, he's trying to smile at me.

"I'll just straighten this pillow up for you, you're looking a bit lopsided sitting there like that. There's a dear, just sit forward for me, I've got you, you're all right. There, that's much better – more comfy now?"

Well, he's nodded, so that's an improvement, too. I thought it might do him good to sit up a bit, take a bit more interest in what's going on. I don't like to see him all listless, he used to be so busy all the time, always pottering about in the garden, listening to the radio, always keeping up with the news.

"Look, there's the gardener, can you see him dear?" No, he doesn't want to look, he's waved his hand, he looks annoyed.

"He's planting the bulbs, dear, daffodils I expect, for the spring. I bought a big sack of them the other day, crocuses this time, I thought it would be nice for you and me to plant them together when you come home – it's quite early still for planting, I'm sure you'll be well enough before they have to go in."

Oh, he looks so sad now, perhaps I've overdone it, I just don't want him brooding over being poorly, I want him to have something to look forward to. I don't know what they're doing to him in here to make him so miserable, all this lying about with nothing to do isn't good for him. I spoke to the doctor, I got quite cross, really quite annoyed. What's the good of keeping him here like this? I said. He'd be much happier at home. I'm sure he'd start to get better if he could just be at home, with the garden to look at, and he could plan his next planting round. He said months ago he wanted to change the herbaceous border and put in some buddleia, he always said he wanted something that would bring the butterflies. But all they do is say he's too ill now, and he doesn't want to be bothered, he wants peace and quiet and he still needs a lot of pain relief. Well, frankly I think they're giving him too much of that as well, poor man, looking like a zombie half the day, no wonder he can't think straight or apply himself to anything. It's not good for him, it really isn't. They don't understand him, they don't understand what makes him happy. An active man like that, the running he used to do, and the football, you can't expect him to be content with lying in bed all day, it's not right.

And he just lets them. Imagine! Fred Timprer, who never let anybody tell him what to do, and he lets them just boss him about, tell him what's good for him, why, he hasn't even got his television anymore, they took it away two days ago and said it was what he asked them to do. It must be something to do with cuts, Fred would never say he didn't want his television.

He used to love sitting down of an evening with a glass of beer or a whisky if he felt like it, and just relaxing with a good programme, he always said television was a great educator, and you always learned something new, every single time you switched it on. So don't try to tell me that he doesn't want it any more. I'm going to demand they bring it back – today. If nothing else, it'll take his mind off things and then he might see something that will give him his old spark back, and he'll turn the corner. There's been some lovely gardening programmes on lately, I wonder if he saw some of them in the evenings, I don't like to ask, he says so little, and he gets cross if he thinks I'm fussing about things.

He's still looking at me. He looks so sad, so fed up with everything. He hasn't spoken for two days now, just looks at me with this terrible empty expression. It's killing him, being like this, and I don't know what to do to help. Every time I suggest something, he just shakes his head, or looks away. Yesterday he cried, but he couldn't tell me why. He looked so agitated, so very upset by everything. It was when I said I was making plans for a little Easter holiday, just the two of us. I only wanted to cheer him up, give him something else to think about.

I'll have a word with the nurse when she comes in. I think it'll be Elaine today, she's a bit nicer than the others, a cheerful little thing, it must be nice for Fred to have at least one smiling face in here. I'll see what she thinks about perhaps putting him in a wheelchair and taking him out into the garden for a bit, just to get some fresh air, and maybe he'll see the gardeners working, and it'll give him something to live for again.

It's weeks now since I heard him laugh. In fact it's weeks since I saw anything except this lethargy. Elaine said it was normal when you were very ill to get depressed, and then she said something about perhaps he was starting to accept the end and that was why he was quiet. Well, I wouldn't hear of it, accept the end? I said. My Fred is a fighter, and he'll never just lie back and not get better. You don't know him, I said, he's got absolutely no intention of taking this lying down. He'll be back on his feet, just you wait and see. As soon as the sun starts to shine again, and the days start to get a bit longer. He always did like the sunshine, he said he got down in the winter when it was so dark all the time, especially when it was grey and raining a lot, and no clear, sunny frosty days.

It's this place. I never wanted him to come here in the first place. He was perfectly happy at the hospital, he'd got to know the staff, he had people to chat to on the ward, and then they said they couldn't do any more for him and he'd be better off at the hospice. Not so much couldn't as wouldn't, I said to myself. Their attitude really surprised me, after all they'd done, I expect it was to do with not having enough beds, it's so expensive when people are ill nowadays, you've only got to think about what it costs to get a prescription. I complained about it, quite high up I had to go, but it didn't do any good, and he came here anyway. I can't see they've got any more money than the hospital, they've probably got less, judging by the amount of fancy machines the hospital had, so I couldn't see why he had to be moved, and why they kept telling me he'd be better looked after. Something to do with beds, I expect. And anyway, a move won't do him any good, I said, and it's another bus for me, I do enough running around as it is, I said. And all this coming to a place to die, well it's plain morbid, that's what it is, I'm not surprised so many people die here if that's all they've got to think about. You need a change of attitude, I said, it's bad enough him being ill without you keep telling him he's on his last legs. All he's done since he's come here is get worse.

"Hello, Mrs Timpter."

"Oh, hello, dear. Look at me, daydreaming as usual." This is Elaine, she's a sweet thing, always popping in to check up on us and see if we need anything. I don't know how many cups of tea she's dropped off while she's been going about her business.

"How are you today, Fred?"

"Oh, I think he's looking better, don't you? He's eaten a bit of breakfast, and he's got a few roses in his cheeks. I think

185

the sun might come out in a while, and he always did like to see the sun shining."

She's taking his pulse now, it's a shame they disturb him all the time, he was looking out of the window, watching the gardeners, I know he was, and now she's distracted him and he looks tired and listless again. And she's moved him again, look at that, I'd just done that for him, and she bent over and had a little whisper in his ear, don't think I didn't notice – and now he's back where he was. They've got to have everything their own little way, haven't they, they can't just leave him be, everything I try to do, they just walk all over it and say they know what's best. Even Elaine's started doing it now.

I've brought my knitting today. No point sitting about doing nothing, saying nothing, is there? If I do say anything, he doesn't bother to reply, and then next time I look he's dropped off, so I'll do something useful, and you never know, it might make him remember there's more to life than lying about all day.

I wouldn't mind, but he isn't the only one feeling off it. I've come in sometimes in the past few weeks with terrible headaches and I get no sympathy, he doesn't even notice, even when one day it was so bad I had to ask the nurse for some aspirin before I left, did he ask how I was feeling? No. I've had to do everything since he went in, keep up to the house, the garden, sort out the repairs on the roof, finish off the painting he'd started, pay the bills, etcetera, etcetera. I'm worn out, exhausted all the time, I can't do with all these extra problems. He can't help being ill, I do realise that, but starting to paint all the window frames just before he collapsed was ridiculous – they didn't really need it, and all it's done is make extra work for me, on top of all the other things I've got to do. I wish he'd thought things through a bit more.

And all this talk of him not lasting much longer, well it's just making a meal of it, isn't it, encouraging him in all this attention seeking. It's pathetic in a grown man, it's about time he pulled himself together. Listen to that, he's reading my mind, he's started making little whimpering noises now

Elaine's come in, and she's off for the pain killers like a shot out of a gun. He's got no self-respect, one murmur and he'll be full of all that stuff again and he won't know whether I'm here or not. I don't know why I bother sometimes, I really don't.

Oh, look, the doctor's come in as well now, all this fuss over an injection – it's not as if she hasn't done it fifty times before, is it? Probably increasing the amount, not that he looks any different to yesterday, I expect it's easier for them if he's drugged up to the eyeballs all day – they can get on with more important things, can't they? Well, we'll soon see about that. Fred might be taking all this lying down, but I don't have to. Do I?

II

I told them straight. We had one of those case conferences, you know, where they chat about the patient and what he's doing, and what kind of treatment he's on. There's been quite a few of those, I suppose it makes you feel included, as if you're joining in with what they're doing, but I don't think they actually listen to what you say, or take you up on any of the things you suggest. I'd had enough this morning, enough of seeing my Fred looking as if he was at death's door. I told them I thought it was all in the mind. A bit of fresh air, a bit more cheerfulness and positive thinking about the place, something to occupy his mind and they'd notice a big difference. They said it wasn't like that.

One of the nurses was very nasty. Said what about my headaches – were those all in the mind? Very aggressive, quite uncalled for. I never thought much of her.

Listen, I said, why not let him come home for the weekend? It's Tuesday today, so there's plenty of time to make arrangements. I'll look after him and you can send a nurse round if you like, just let him come home and see the garden and it'll do him a world of good. The nasty one, Claire they call her, rolled her eyes when I suggested it, and one or two of the others looked uncomfortable, a bit shifty, like people do when they know something you don't. They kept looking out of the window and down at the carpet, and eventually one of them said, "I'm sorry, Mrs Timpter, but it wouldn't be in Fred's best interests if he was to go home."

I was on them like a shot. If there's one thing I've learned, it's that you never get anywhere if you let people walk all over you. "Why ever not?" I said. "You're always letting people out. I've seen them – some of them are practically on stretchers when they go. It's in your leaflet – you're always on about how good it is for them to go home. Why not Fred?"

"Fred is very ill –"

"Oh, don't I know it!" I said. "That's all I ever hear about. You'd have him dead and buried with all the talking you do about it, never mind anything else. I'm his wife. I've known him a lot longer than you have, and I say a weekend away from all this miserable attitude would get him back on his feet." I sat back and looked at them. There. I'd said my piece. What did they have to say to that?

The doctor sighed and shuffled his feet, and looked across at the Sister, and then he sat right forward and put the ends of his fingers together, then raised his head. You can tell when they're going to say something you don't want to hear, it's what they call body language. I was reading about it in a magazine, you can tell people's feelings from how they sit and such. I do read a lot, I'm not thick, I like to know what's going on in the world. I do quite like this doctor, he's called Andrew, and he's very modern, always up to date with the latest ideas. I don't know what he's doing here, he'd be much better off in a new hospital where they're interested in making people better. Him sitting like that unsettled me a bit, all of a sudden, so there must be something in all this body language business.

"I'm sorry to have to say this, Mrs Timpter, but you really must try to understand what is happening to your husband," the doctor said. "Fred probably won't live to see the weekend. He's very weak now, he needs a lot of pain relief and he's asked to be kept quiet, in a room with reduced lighting. That's why we took away the television set. We weren't being unkind, or saving money or anything like that. He simply can't cope with extra noise, or excitement, or any kind of change. He's ready to slip away now, and he needs your permission to go."

I admit it knocked the wind out of me a bit, hearing that. He was trying to be nice, I think, the doctor, but I couldn't help thinking it was their fault he'd got into this state in the first place. My eyes started to water, and I had to look for a hankie. I don't like scenes, getting upset in front of people, it's not right. Elaine gave me a pat on the hand and said, "It's all right, Mrs Timpter, lots of people find it very hard to accept and react just like you have. But we have to think of Fred, and what's best for him."

When she said that, I thought of the daffodils again. I couldn't help it. I could see him, clear as day, bending over the sack and planting the bulbs out – it must have been fifteen years ago, and every year we've had more and more of them. We had a single line going all down the path, and now they're in great clumps, round the garage, round the pond, Fred always loved the daffodils because they meant springtime. I couldn't bear the thought of him not being there to see them this year, not being able to plant the new crocuses. They've done for him, I thought. Good and proper. They've drugged all the life out of him and made him not care. I went from feeling upset to blind fury in half a minute.

I asked them what they thought we should do, just to keep them happy. The doctor looked relieved, and started talking about what they thought should be happening over the next few days, but I wasn't really listening. I just nodded a lot, and they thought I was too choked up to say anything. At the end, I asked if I could spend some time with him on my own, just to chat quietly and start to say goodbye.

They didn't suspect a thing. I set off down the corridor, trying not to walk too quickly. It's a good job they couldn't see my face. My mother always said she could tell when I'd made up my mind about something, because my jaw stuck out, and it stayed like that until I'd got my own way.

I marched into the room and gave Fred my best no-nonsense look. He teases me about it all the time, *Oh look now, she's got her tail up and her no-nonsense face on, he'll say, she means business and no mistake.* He was flopping on the pillows, there's no other word for it. Flopping. I was so angry I felt myself go hot. I took him by the shoulders and hauled him up into a sitting position. His eyes rolled and he let out a strangled little cry.

"Now listen to me, Fred Timpter," I said, "I'm done with your whining and your camping out at death's door. They might be falling for it, but I'm not. You always did lay it on a bit thick when you were poorly. If you don't fight now, you really will be in trouble, do you hear me? You're coming home with me right now."

I dragged his legs round so they dangled towards the floor and I got each of his arms and threw them over my shoulders, then I braced against the bed and tried to lift him. He let out a very loud noise and I got him away from the bed.

"This is the cause of all this," I shouted at him, kicking the bed leg. "All this lying about. It's pathetic, Fred, I won't stand for it. If you're not going to do it for yourself, I'm going to have to do it for you."

I was sweating with the effort – even though he's lost so much weight, I'm not as fit as I was, and all this extra strain has worn me out. "Look what you've done to us," I shouted at him, and I tried to swing him round towards the door. "I just want you to try, for my sake. One way or another, we're going to sort this out now." The door opened just as I lost my balance and we both fell over.

"Mrs Timpter!" It was Dr Andrew.

"Get away from him! He's going home. He's not staying here in this bad atmosphere. He's got a life to live and if I've

190

got anything to do with it, it'll be me he'll have to thank for it."

They weren't listening, of course, because Fred was on the floor groaning and they were paying attention to him. But at least I'd said it. I felt a lot better for just saying it, even they weren't listening.

By this time Elaine was in the room as well, and Claire, and Sister. I expect they'd heard me shouting. They all rushed to pick Fred up and put him back into bed, and then they started running around again, getting instruments and needles and goodness knows what else, and it was quite a time before anyone thought of giving me a hand to get me up on my feet. It was Elaine, showing me a cold little face, very different to all the smarmy hand-patting I'd been getting in the conference.

They're all the same, I thought. All up on their high horses, all thinking they know best, coming between us at the hardest time.

I was quite all right by the time I sat back in the chair. I like visitors' chairs in hospital, they're nice and roomy, aren't they, and comfortable to sit in. I was a bit shaky, you know, but that was the exertion. All in all, while I sat catching my breath, I was quite pleased I'd stood up to them and shown them they weren't going to push Fred and me around. I'd shown them how important it was that he went home.

Fred was quiet after that, full up of morphine again. They all walked out after a while except Dr Andrew, who sat by the bed holding Fred's hand. I couldn't bear that. I got myself out of the chair and went to the other side, by the big picture window. His eyes were very calm, and when he turned his head, he looked at me so that I got quite a shock – he hasn't really *looked* at me for weeks now. He didn't say anything at first, but I felt his hand squeeze mine – a tired, thin little squeeze, but something all the same. I smiled at him.

"I'm sorry I gave you a shaking," I whispered. "But it's brought you round, hasn't it? That's the most awake I've seen you for days." I tried to make a little joke out of it, you know, because I was feeling awful about it then, but as soon as I said it, and gave him a smile, he shook his head, looked at me sort of disbelieving, and then turned to Dr Andrew. Dr Andrew dropped his head, and then went over to the window, and stood looking out at the big trees on the lawn.

"Dorothy," Fred said. His voice was scratchy and feeble, and I hadn't heard it for a while.

"Yes, love, what is it?" I said. I hoped the doctor was listening. I was going to fall over myself to be reasonable now, just to show them.

"I'm tired now," he said, still looking at me. "I'm tired. Do you understand?"

I tried to answer him, I really did try, but all of a sudden this terrible choking feeling came up in my throat and my voice started shaking so badly I couldn't say a word. I squeezed his hand and nodded, and all these tears started running down my face. I don't know what happened, I completely lost control when I was supposed to be taking charge of everything.

"I don't want any more fuss," he said. "I have a lot of pain now. I don't want to see you hurting as well."

"I'm all right," I said, trying to sound a bit more brisk. "You know me. I say my piece, and then we can get on with things."

"It's nice and quiet here, Dottie, it's just what I need. I don't want to go home anymore. Can you understand that?"

"I just thought the garden – "

"No, no," he said, and he squeezed my hand again. "Not any more, Dottie. Not now."

III

So in the end I did need to call Janet because Fred died later that evening. She'd just got the supper things cleared away and all the family settled, so it wasn't too much of an inconvenience for her to hop in the car and run up to the hospice –

it's only a couple of miles, and she always said she'd be glad to help out if she could. It's just that I didn't feel like catching the bus.

It wasn't like I thought it would be. Dr Andrew was there at the end. We left the curtains open because they have lights in the garden at night and for most of the time when he wasn't sleeping, Fred seemed to want to watch them. He was very quiet, but he didn't seem to be troubled anymore. I was thinking how thin he was, such a lot of weight seemed to have fallen off him in the last few months, and nobody could get him to eat, he didn't want anything, not even his favourites. Now I think of it, it was almost as if he'd resigned himself, a long time ago, to what was going to happen, and eating was just going to drag things out for him.

Perhaps I should have given him more credit for understanding. I thought about a lot of things all that day, and if I'd made things better or worse for him. But that little performance before they got him back into bed for the last time, well, in a funny sort of way it seemed to sort things out. I shouldn't have done it, but it was when I stopped fighting it, and started to see things from Fred's point of view. It was upsetting, him dying, don't get me wrong, but that last afternoon was one of the most contented we'd had since he got ill.

He got a bit agitated at about five o' clock, when the light was dying, and Dr Andrew gave him an injection and he fell asleep. He muttered quite a bit, mostly things you couldn't understand, but one or two things about things that were on his mind, special times we'd had and odd things. He told me not to forget the volcanic ash when I was planting the new bulbs, and told me where the BabyBio was for the cheese plant and the hyacinths, but most of it was rubbish, really, just things he was going through for himself.

At about eight o' clock, he came out of that, and opened his eyes and stared out at the lights. It was a very cold night outside, a very black sky with a few stars. I got up to go for a tinkle – I was only gone a few minutes, I told him I wouldn't be long. I stopped by the drinks machine to get some orange juice, because I hadn't had anything since just after lunch time – and when I got back, Dr Andrew was standing by him and he was gone. I asked Dr Andrew to double-check, just to make sure, but I saw for myself his eyes had lost their shine, and he couldn't see anymore. The doctor said it was very peaceful, what he called a good death, Fred had just suddenly had trouble breathing and he had given him a shot to relax the muscles, and he stopped struggling very quickly and that was it.

The nurses were very good about sorting everything out, they all came in and said how sorry they were, he had been such a pleasant man, no trouble to them at all. I stayed quite a while, they brought me a cup of tea and said there was no need to rush off, I could say goodbye as long as I liked, so I rang Janet at about half past nine.

She was very good, she came and sat for a while and we had a little weep together – she had quite a soft spot for Fred, he used to pop round and do little jobs when her husband was away on business, she was always appreciative of that. But that was typical of Fred, he used to help out whenever he could.

IV

We had the funeral a few days later, quite busy it was, with all his friends from the football club and the neighbours and that. Dr Andrew came with Elaine and so did our GP, and the vicar was quite good, he said he could tell from the number of people who turned up that Fred had been a popular man, and would be sadly missed. I had him cremated, I didn't think I could cope with a burial, all that morbid stuff standing round the grave, I didn't want that, and I didn't think Fred would, either.

I did the tea afterwards with Janet, bless her, and people

stayed and chatted until about six or seven o' clock, and then we tidied up together and I finally got to sit down in front of the telly at about nine.

I got my knitting out, I was on the third row before I realised it was a jumper for Fred. You clot, I thought, he's not going to wear it now, is he? So that set me off for a while, I had a really good cry about it all, but I pulled myself together and gave myself a good talking to. *Now look, I said, you've got another twenty years in you yet, you can't spend it all crying over spilt milk.* I had another look at the knitting and I thought, look, I've nearly finished it, I've only got one sleeve left, and it's such a nice pattern. It'll do for Jack, I thought, it'll be a way of saying thanks to Janet for helping out over the last few days.

It's only when it's all over that you realise how busy you've been with someone who's ill. I never seemed to have any time for sitting about in the last six months, it seemed that as soon as I'd got off one bus, I was jumping on another, it's been non-stop all the time. I used to think I'd be glad when it was all over and I could have a bit of peace.

I've got all the peace and quiet I can take now. I don't get so many headaches, so it was obviously all the tension causing those. Mind you, my legs have been aching terribly now I come to think of it, I've had one or two quite uncomfortable nights, and I'm wondering if I've let myself go a bit these last months, not taken enough care of myself. I've been so busy for Fred, so busy making sure he had all his things clean, I haven't been paying attention to what's going on inside *me*.

Well, I can be as poorly as I like now, can't I, now I'm not needed. I made myself chuckle when I came up with that one! Just fancy, I thought, Janet would have a good laugh at me, looking forward to being tucked up in bed poorly. I'm owed a few days' rest, that's for sure, all I've had to put up with in the last weeks, it'd be nice if someone was looking after me for a change.

Perhaps I'll go on holiday for a while, get all the spring planting done for Fred – not forgetting the volcanic ash – bless him! – and get things sorted out for the summer. It's the least I can do – if the poor old love's looking down from heaven, seeing the garden all nice will cheer him up no end. After that, well, who knows? I could go on one of those coach tours, I've got plenty of savings, I might go somewhere really exciting, abroad, go and see other countries and see what they're like. I might make some new friends, you never know.

But not at the moment, I don't think it would be quite right just now. Apart from the fact it would be disrespectful, I need time to get my strength back, look after myself a bit, spoil myself with a few treats, finish off the house, then we'll see. There's just me to do for now, so I'll have plenty of time for making plans. There's all sorts of things I could do now, anything I fancy, now all that catching buses and running around and hand-holding's over and done with.

In fact, I'll tell you the very first thing I'm going to do, and I'll do it first thing tomorrow morning. I'm going to get an appointment with the doctor and get myself sorted out with a tonic, and start building myself up a bit. I'll have a proper medical and a good checking over, and make sure I'm all right. It's my turn for a bit of TLC now, and if I don't get it for myself, no one's going to get it for me.

Times change, don't they? Last week I was a wife, now I'm a widow. I wonder sometimes if I'd have done it again if I'd known how things were going to turn out. No one's ever been able to see into the future, have they? We all just have to take our chances, hope for the best, and wait and see what happens. I've got my share of happy memories, but I've still got a lot of life in me yet, and I don't really know what I'll end up doing with it.

Oh well, I suppose that sounds ungrateful, especially when I think of what Fred's just been through. Poor Fred. Poor old thing. You think you'll be glad when it's all over, you don't realise how much you're going to miss them, and how busy you were, until it's too late.

But there you are. There's days to be filled now, plans to be made, all different routines to work out.

Life goes on.

9

DON'T SIT UNDER THE APPLE TREE

I

When I started this job, I used to dress for it. Sometimes I still do. Don't get me wrong, I love my work. But sometimes it's difficult to hit the mood, get the voice just right. I have this wonderful black silk baby doll with a lace G-string and a butterfly embroidered over the crotch. If it's a warm day, I can lie on my bed and perform, and watch the breeze playing with the lace curtains that hang full length in the French windows, and know I'm doing a good job. The headboard of my bed is in the shape of a butterfly too. I've got a thing about them. It's the way they transform themselves from a non-descript bug to a flittering shimmer of jewel-like colours. It's the way they shed their clumsiness, after hobbling along on all those short legs, all those spare tyres welded together into a sausage. And then they sleep, and when they wake, they can dance through the air, transient as light and shadow in a sunlit forest. Ever since I was small, I've longed to shed this prosaic body that traps my true spirit, and become delicate, fragile and beautiful enough to make little girls cry. One day soon, it's going to happen. I'm going to fall asleep for a long time, and when I wake up, I'll be transformed.

This is a luxury, a thrill, that most of you will never know. Which is a pity, given the burning desire most of us have to be transformed in some way.

Though in another way, everybody's being transformed.

Only it's such a slow change, we don't notice. It's partly an evolution we can understand, the physical tweakings and fine-tunings and readjustments that Nature makes to all her species. Evolution responds to desires – eventually. I believe that. But Nature's slow, serene way of achieving change isn't nearly fast enough for the techno age. This is the quick fix society, where all of us want it all and want it now. My upcoming sex change operation is a case in point – it will be pretty much instant, and it will give me the kind of radical change that will enable me to start an entirely new life, a little death followed by rein-carnation.

The change I think our species is heading for is altogether more radical. We're already beginning to lose our desire for physical form. Our bodies are always letting us down, looking all wrong, under performing, killing us. So few of us live up to Leonardo's ideal, and the cosmetics industry is huge as we all try to cover up what we really are, hide the lumps and bumps and blemishes. The fitness industry is huge but it's just a fad, too much like hard work. And most people's bodies are beyond hope. Sometimes you hear people talking as if doing a bit of running or a few workouts is going to give them an extra six inches, or stop them being bandy-legged, or work some other implausible change to what Nature has handed out. So when those things don't happen, it's too easy to give up and go back to dossing on the sofa with a box of choccies.

My friend JayJay says I'm talking rubbish. What about athletes, he says, all that honing and training they do – that's love of the body and striving to achieve its potential, isn't it? No, I say, it's the opposite. Athletes are dissatisfied with their bodies too, that's why they take drugs to try to change the chemical balance of their bodies. They don't want to celebrate the achievements of flesh alone – they want to be cyborgs, a synthesis of tissue and chemical and performance enhancing implants – six million dollar men and women who view their bodies with their imperfections as placing limitations on their ability to achieve.

I think that because we're so aware of the fact that we

can't be perfect, we're programming ourselves to lose the need for our bodies altogether. Just think about it – there are so many sedentary activities, linked to cerebral activity. That's why we watch so much telly. People think telly is a political weapon, the opium of the people, but it's a spiritual weapon, making us more reliant on our minds. You might scoff, and say nobody's going to become enlightened on the Jerry Springer Show and Blankety Blank, but you have to start somewhere. If there are good spirits and evil spirits, then there must be clever and stupid ones as well. That's why we talk, isn't it, to communicate thoughts and ideas. That's why we read and write. The body is becoming irrelevant, revealing itself as the clumsy, old-fashioned repository of the ideas and emotions that make us what we are, creatures rooted in the mind.

People keep saying we've already evolved, as if it's a process that stops. But evolution doesn't stop. When you think about the way procreation is all of a sudden not something you have to do in person, and the way that society is deciding that parenting is far too demeaning a task for mothers and fathers to be bothered with – boy, are we evolving!

What are we going to look like in half a million years from now? We might have merged with technology, or discovered that technology is organic, like we are, and it's capable of independent evolution. I believe that soon we'll be able to transfer what we're thinking straight to computers, and then each other, and then the need for speech and motor skills will go, too. We're definitely on course for spiritual essence.

JayJay thinks I'm just bitter and twisted with a warped view of bodies because I hate my own, but it's not true. I'm looking forward to being a woman, but I have a sneaking feeling that when the first thrill has worn off, I'll be just as discontented as everyone else, and wish I had better legs, or bigger boobs, or a thinner waist – the human condition, don't you know?

I've spent years not exactly killing off my sexual identity, but putting it to sleep for a few hours. Finally, I've got close to committing the ultimate assassination. I'm going to push the boundaries, experience the thrill of crossing sides. Of course it's a lot easier for me because I'm not dying in the physical sense, I'll be transforming.

Extinction is part of evolution as well. We can't imagine the harm we might be doing by clinging on to our last few pandas, our Siberian Tigers and killer whales. Who knows what marvels are waiting in the wings to replace them, hindered by the last few stragglers being kept alive by a human race dedicated to saving only the beautiful and magnificent? We are *so* shallow. It's so easy, so transparent to see why we love the handsome Siberian Tiger, the cute and cuddly panda, the sleek killer whale. It's the same reason the nation went mad with grief when Princess Di copped it. We can't see any further than what's put in front of our eyes. When Mother Theresa died in the same week, it was as if God was playing a particularly bad-taste joke, or making some kind of moral point. Here is someone who held a few hands, here's the one who spent her lifetime squeezing pus out of boils and picking maggots out of wounds. And we all spent our grief on the pretty one, blinded like rabbits by the dazzle of her blond hair and blue eyes.

You've only got to look at the panda to see that it's not the least bit interested in being saved. They've stopped eating meat – that's a big no-no on the Wanting To Survive scale – and made themselves entirely dependent on bamboo shoots, probably the poorest nutritional source ever actively selected by anything, ever. Plus the bamboo shoots are in increasingly short supply because the habitat is shrinking. Which creates another problem. More and more pandas are being squashed into a smaller and smaller area, and they don't like company. When pandas are forced to meet in zoos, they don't rush at each other like Cathy and Heathcliff, they sulk and go into separate corners. And they can only mate once every two years. They have to *really like* the other panda to give their consent – so they're obviously not that desperate to procreate and maintain the species. If ever a species has pressed its own self-destruct button, the panda is it. But do we respect that? Of course not. Why not? Because the panda is Cute and Cuddly, a dumb animal that doesn't know what's good for it – and it must be saved by the human race!

Man created God to give himself a standard to live up to, and eventually has decided that he can do a better job himself. Rather typical of us, don't you think?

I used to exhaust myself wondering why it had to be me, why couldn't I be a man and be happy about it, who the hell cares that I want to be a woman? What significance does it have next to third world flood and famine – how dare I consider myself important?

Well, this is what I've learned. If you're unhappy, then you do become important, and self-obsessed, and a prisoner, and to become unimportant, and free, you have to become happy. And do you know something else I've learned? You have to find out what makes you happy, and then do it, whatever it is, without compromise, without regard for what other people think.

So while I wait for my transformation, I have to make a living. Hence the bed, hence the sexy underwear, hence the voice.

II

I've practised hard at the voice – it's been one of the most difficult things. One of the reasons I love my job is that it's a short cut to being the woman I nearly am. It's great voice practise, except in day to day life I try not to over breathe as much. It's not appropriate.

When you don't realise you're a transsexual, you take all kinds of paths before you get on the right track. Cutting off your willy isn't the immediately obvious solution. People say to me, it's hard enough finding the right clothes, the right make-up, the right image – and you have to decide that you not only don't have the right body, but it's the wrong sex as well! I tried everything, believe me, before I arrived at the right conclusion. At first I thought I was gay, so I started dating men, but it felt all wrong. Then I thought I was a fetishist. So I did that for a while. I tried group sex, dressing up in chains and leather, doing things with a dominatrix, half-strangling myself. You name it, and I've probably done it, although I did stop short of nailing my balls to planks of wood – even JayJay wouldn't try that one! It was all great fun, but none of it was quite right.

Mind you, all of this has been very useful in my job. Because I've dabbled in all these things, and I'm not frightened of them, I can tell what my callers want, and I can take them exactly where they want to go. At one time, I thought seriously about training to be a psycho sexologist, because I know all this stuff. Anyway, I eventually tried cross-dressing, and something clicked at last. I thought I might be happy with pretending to be a woman, and for a while being a chameleon was fun. But I came to realise that I'd have to go for the real thing. The whole idea of being a phoenix was fantastic.

JayJay has been brilliant. I met him right at the beginning, when I was trying to be gay, and we're still best friends. JayJay takes terrible chances, he's lucky to be alive. He'll do anything for pleasure, and I mean anything. The last time he went up an apple tree, he ended up being cut down by an ambulance man. Another minute or two and it would have been too late, he would have been a martyr to bad timing. He still jokes about it, he says if Isaac Newton had sat under that particular apple tree, he'd have got more than an apple landing on his head. It frightened me to death, but he can still remember it being the best come of his life. I find it unbelievable, that he retained such a strong memory of the payoff instead of the risk he took, but he's always been like that, no matter how big the cloud is, he can always see the silver lining. *Remember,* he said to me afterwards, as I sat by the hospital bed raging at him, *I was up the tree getting the big thrill. I took my chances. I'd a million times rather I died in the aftermath, rather than sat sensibly on the ground underneath being showered by someone else's joy juice. Do you understand?* His throat was black and purple and swollen and his voice rasped like a torn violin bow – but he was doing his best to smile. I lost my temper all over again.

Have you noticed how sex is our benchmark for how good something is? *Better than sex*, we say, when we clinch a good deal, or unkindly score points off a rival, but we know we're exaggerating. We still need to push that joy button – sex connects us powerfully to the body at the same time it sets us free of it, and makes us imagine that even greater pleasures are possible. If mere mortals can attain such heights, imagine what we could be missing! We never believe in the ultimate – whatever we achieve, we know that if we've got that far, there must be another step up, just as there's always another step down when you don't think you can sink any lower. It's as if we perpetually define ourselves as underachievers, so there's always going to be something else to discover.

Last week we went to see that trendy arthouse film, *Walking*. We still can't work out why it was called that. We went because JayJay had heard about this auto-erotic asphyxiation scene, and he fancied both the actors in it, Hannah Dell and Matt Jordan.

"Soooo melodramatic," JayJay chortled as we walked home afterwards, arm in arm. I was in my woman's gear – I've had to be for the last year, in prep for the operation, and to satisfy the psychologists that I'm serious – and he looked, as ever, like a glorious mutant of Quentin Crisp and Ziggy Stardust. He loves the movies to bits, but he wasn't impressed by the sex and death gig acted out in the half-lit apartment. "They took all the fun out of it," he complained, deliberately too loudly, as we sauntered through the cinema foyer. "Richard Knott should know better. He's got so stuffy of late, his early films were much more fun. I bet anything he was getting off on that – I wonder how many takes the poor things had to do?"

"Well, it's a risky thing," I said. "I wouldn't have liked to try and get that past the censors. And it worked for the film. It was very sexy, in an overblown kind of way. I thought they did it quite well."

JayJay snorted, and tossed his head like a petulant pony. "But it's not just dangerous," he insisted. "It's exciting, wild, it's something you don't tell all your friends about. But there isn't all this terrible drama about doing it – isn't it funny how people in the movies take sex so *seriously*? Auto-E isn't serious – it's ridiculous! The only reason people will think that scene was sexy is because it was artificial, and they don't know any better. It's a raw, basic thing, not something you design and intellectualise. And it's delicious." He paused, and I knew he was thinking about the apple tree. "That's what was missing," he said, his eyes sparkling. "The *deliciousness*."

"It nearly killed you," I pointed out tartly. I'm very fond of JayJay, and I wanted him to show some – not remorse, exactly, just some understanding of how close he came to dying for the sake of deliciousness. But I knew I was wasting my time. He's got the recklessness I'll never have.

I feel there should be an explanation for why JayJay flirts with risk so much, but I don't think there is. He just seems to have this incredible awareness of the brief nature of life, and the unfairness of it.

When I first met him, we used to meet in a graveyard. That sounds awful, doesn't it, like we were cottaging or something, but it was a very special place, full of huge Victorian monuments and great patches where it had been left to go wild, so it was full of small animals and birds, and the fattest, juiciest blackberries you ever saw. That's corpse power for you, JayJay would say, as he picked them to make jam. JayJay said he found it peaceful there, and we used to stroll round, admiring the architecture and reading the headstones. We used to work out how old people had been when they died, and it seemed to strike a chord with JayJay that vibrated between us as we walked the wide avenues or headed off into some of the less easily navigable older parts of the cemetery.

On one of our visits, we found the grave of a young man who had died at the age of twenty five after a sudden illness.

JayJay kept repeating the dates as if he was trying to understand that one day, his own life would be compressed between a similarly terse grouping of figures. Then he took my hand and said, "It just goes to show, doesn't it, that if you wait and plan for something, it might never happen. What plans might this boy have had, that never came to fruition? You can waste a lot of time waiting for the moment to be right, and in the end, it might never even come." His grip on my hand intensified. "We should promise each other that if there's ever anything we want to do, anything at all, we should go for it, do it as soon as we possibly can, because you never know what's coming."

That experience seemed to clarify something for him, about the way he approached his life, and why he lived as he did. Ever since he's been both more aware of the preciousness of life, and more inclined to savour it more fully – which is his rationale for taking risks in apple trees. I think he finds it easier to swing on the fun parts of life because he knows how close all of us are to losing our grip and plunging into tragedy.

III

But now I'm being interrupted by business – my first call of the day. I've just switched on, so I'm on duty now, and the first client of the evening is calling me up for an arms-length trip towards sexual fulfilment. If we're going to be strictly accurate about things, I suppose you always do wank at arm's length, don't you? Anyway, aside from being facetious, what I meant was, more and more people these days are getting off on virtual stimulation. I can tell by the volume of calls. My disembodied voice constitutes a virtual sexual experience for anyone who dials my hotline. You can have the biggest dick in the universe, and most of my callers think they have, but it's the brain that's the most active sexual organ – you can't come unless you're concentrating.

You get the connection, of course – it's back to evolution, isn't it? Sex is beginning to disengage itself from the physical, and is almost completely divorced from its original function. Thinking about sex as a means of procreation is such a poor second in people's minds that they apply themselves to the act completely differently when they're thinking of making babies. And unless you're on fertility treatment, you still have to do it the old-fashioned way.

All right, all right, we've always had wanking and dirty pictures, but people are choosing this more and more, preferring it to the good old bump and grind, the sweaty thrill of in-out, in-out. Now you've got me on the end of a telephone, or girls at a safe distance on the Internet. You don't have to have a shower afterwards – unless you've aimed badly - and you're not going to catch anything. The point is, it proves that we don't really need the body to get off – everything is happening in our minds. It's almost a clue, I think, Nature saying to us, *look, you don't need all this flesh – it can be just as good, better, even, without it. The flesh is out of date, learn to discard it, fly towards enlightenment and freedom.*

Which rather puts me at the cutting edge of sex. I transform into whatever my callers want me to be, I can help them imagine whatever pleasures they want to experience – and they don't even have to mess up their hair. With me, they can fly to Borneo, make out with a group of naked tribal women (very popular) and arrive home after a phenomenal come, just before their date arrives for dinner, or they pop out for last orders. It's so convenient. It's very satisfying – I can make all that happen for someone, just with the power of my mind.

There's one Golden Rule. Whatever strange perversion you get breathing down your ear, never be cruel about the people who pay your rent – rent boys, as JayJay slyly calls them – unless they become abusive, or are ringing up for a lark. The majority of callers are deadly serious, and you have to respect that.

I'd tell you my trading name, but it's risky – my callers, and

I have several regulars, would be horrified if they knew I was still a man, with abnormally high female hormone levels and a dangler just like them. They'd probably call Trades Descriptions and send in the police, regardless of the fact that they'll hang up well satisfied when I've finished with them.

The best woman I ever heard doing sex calls was the one who gave me the job. She used to walk round the house with a headset and keep herself busy at the same time. She told me the first time she took a call, it was two o' clock in the afternoon and she wasn't expecting it. She was in her worn old leggings, and a baggy sweat shirt, she hadn't washed her hair, and she was washing jumpers in the sink. She told the caller she was in the bath with a dildo. He came in about fifteen seconds flat, and still rings up three times a week. That taught her a lot – anything is possible when you can't be seen. She lost all her self-consciousness in five minutes, and never looked back.

Twenty minutes is about average for a call. You have to be realistic – you can't block up the line for too long, but on the other hand, I don't like to rush them along. I try to be considerate and give them some foreplay, in the hope they might pick up some useful tips if they already have, or ever get, a real live girlfriend to practise on.

Over the months I've been doing the job, I've developed a little interview so I can find out what each caller wants and how he wants to be satisfied. I ask how long they've got, and what they want to do, and what their favourite fantasies are – then when I've got everything I need to know, I start properly. I say 'he'. I do get some women, and that can be quite challenging, and quite sexy for me, but in the main, I pleasure men. It's exciting for them when I say I'll do whatever they want, I'll be whoever they want, I'll even invite a friend round to fill out the numbers. JayJay has helped out on occasion, but he giggles too much and pulls faces to put me off – if the punter hears you laughing, it's all over.

The most difficult ones are the ones with an unexpected fetish. It can be really hard to keep a straight face. Sometimes people call in a terrible state because they've been ridiculed by another operator. They want to share their kick with someone, and then they feel betrayed if the other person can't see the serious side. The minute I answer this call, I know it's one of these.

People are so afraid of the unusual. I'm sure so many of us spend our lives perpetually missing out because we lack the courage to stand up and say, *This is what I want. You can laugh at me, you can sneer, you can be as disgusted as you like, but this is what I want, and I'm going to have it.* There're boundaries, of course there are, but in the main, what do people do for pleasure that can really be that shocking or distressing or harmful to people whose business it isn't? And what damage do we do by depriving them of it and making them feel guilty and frustrated? Life's so short anyway, isn't it, without living it in a state of denial. So I feel sorry when people call me and can hardly bear to tell me what they want me to pretend to do with them. You mustn't ever try to guess. If you start off by, say, asking if they want chocolate smeared on their bottom, you'll almost certainly be wrong, and they'll be thinking, *"Oh my God, it's not chocolate, that's so normal, what's she going to think of me when I tell her it's actually cold mashed potato and custard?"*

I get comfy on the bed while I'm counting the number of rings. I don't answer straight away because it either panics them, or cuts down the sense of anticipation. If I leave it too long, they bottle out, or get impatient, and then they're in the wrong mood. Four is about right. When I pick up, I try to sound quite normal – if you go straight in on the breathy lust ticket, you're taking control of them, and that's not what they want – not at first. And there's an outside chance they've dialled a wrong number – they'll get a real shock if I ask how I can bring them to orgasm when they're actually looking for car insurance.

So, this is how it goes for Caller No. 1:

Me: *(warm, reassuring, sexy if you're looking for it)* Hello? This is Katrina (it isn't really, but I told you I wasn't going to say). What can I do for you today?

Caller: *(very nervous)* Oh! I – sorry, I –

Me: How about telling me your name? Then we can get to know each other better.

Caller: *(whispering, hunted)* Tim. It's Timmy *(loud clattering sound)* – oh God –sorry? Did you get that? Oh God, I'm sorry. I dropped the phone. Are you still there?

Me: *(very friendly, gentle)* It's OK, Tim. Yes, I got your name. I'm here to have a good time with you, that's why you've called me. So what can I do for you?

(long pause, during which I work out that this is going to be an unusual one, and decide to forget the interview – we're going to have to wing this)

Caller: I'm sorry. I don't think I can do this. *(half-sob)* Oh God, I hate this. I can't tell you. You sound so nice. I can't bear it if you laugh at me.

Me: *(soothing)* Sweetheart, I promise I won't laugh at you. Listen, I'll tell you something. I'm wearing black underwear and stockings and my hair is all down round my shoulders and if you don't talk to me, I'll be all dressed up with nowhere to go. So please don't be shy. Tell me so we can enjoy each other.

(even longer silence, some controlled gasps in the background – he's working up the nerve)

Me: *(gently, but encouraging, with a touch of firmness)* Timmy, I can tell by your voice that we're going to hit it off just fine. And I want us to do whatever makes you happy. What makes you happy, Timmy? Just tell me.

Caller: *(deep breath)* Oh God – *(whimpering)* I want this so much. You swear you won't laugh?

Me: No, no. I want to be with you too much, Tim, I can tell we're going to be good together.

Caller: *(blurts it out)* Eggs.

Me: *(Aha – I know about this – I can do a lot for this caller)* Do you like them cooked, Tim – or raw? *(a lot of breath on the last word)*

Caller: *(relieved, I didn't laugh, allowing himself to let go a bit)* Raw, Katrina. *(strangled)* I like them raw.

Me: *(whispering, settling into it)* What do you want me to do

209

with them, Tim? *(as if guessing inspiredly)* Are they still in their shells, Tim?

Caller: *(breathing heavily – it's normal the first time – this isn't going to take long)* Oh God – yes, they're still in their shells.

Me: Where are they, Tim? Do you want me to put them somewhere? Somewhere naughty?

Caller: You're holding them, Katrina, you're warming them –

Me: *(softly, just a hint of a gasp)* Between my breasts, Tim? *(some mutual sighing)* I'll be so careful not to break them.

Caller: *(well gone, voice trembling)* You're putting them down my pants now, next to my sex machine and round my cheeks . . .

Me: *(into this now, he trusts me, we're going to be all right)* They're so smooth, Tim, so fragile, so perfect. It's exciting listening to you getting so turned on, do you know that? What do you want me to do with them?

Caller: I'm going to sit down – *(pause, heavy breathing, then fast, very fast)* Describe it to me, Katrina, tell me what it's going to be like, tell me you like it too. Come with me. *(breaking up – almost there)*

Me: *(on the home run – doing my best to give him value for money)* Very slowly, Tim, very slowly. I've put my hands over your buttocks, I can feel the eggs hard against them, like you are against me. I'm excited, Tim, I'm trying not to break them too quickly, but I can feel the first one crack and the warm goo is spreading over your skin, and sliding between my fingers. And now I'm pressing on the second one . . . and the third – Oh, yes, I can feel how close you are . . . it's too much for me, I'm going to come now, Tim, I can't hold it any longer – I've cracked the last egg and it's sliding between your cheeks –

Caller: *(lost it)* O-O-Ohhh –

(silence, with breathing)

Me: *(mission accomplished – giving him time to come down)* That was so good, Tim. I really liked it. Are you happy now? Did I make you happy?

Caller: *(pulling himself together)* Thank you Katrina. Thank you.

Me: You're very welcome. *(reinforcing the fact that I'm not disgusted)* I liked it too.

Caller: Katrina? Can I call you again?

Me: *(sighing, happy, chalking up another regular – repeat business is the most satisfying)* Oh yes, of course you can. I'll really look forward to it, Tim. And the more we do it, the sexier it'll be, I promise.

Caller: *(replete)* Okay. Okay. *(pause)* Katrina? Can it be jelly next time?

Me: *(delighted surprise)* Oh! That would be such fun! *(reluctant, longing, but realistic)* I have to go now, Tim. 'Bye till next time.

Click.

That, in a nutshell, is my job. The next caller could want a threesome, a same-sex interface, the promise of a good spanking or sex in a space shuttle. You have to be able to think quickly, be creative, and get as close to that person as you can. It's rewarding – it gives people pleasure, it's challenging, it develops interpersonal skills – and how many jobs can you do where your clients are so pleased with your services that they end up coming?

I wanted to ask Tim if he ever actually did it with eggs, but it's too soon, on the first date. I'll find out when he's rung me a couple more times – I could lose the business if I'm too hasty.

I had another egg man a few months ago, which is why I could handle Tim's call so proficiently. It's quite a common thing, with variations like warm custard and porridge, and urinating in your pants. Something to do with babyhood, I expect, and memories of warm, wet nappies. The other man's wife was getting suspicious about the bits of egg shell she kept finding in the washing machine, so he chose his eggs over his wife and left her. He told her it was for another woman, so she wouldn't guess what was really going on. Of course, now he can egg up as often as he likes, but he still calls me occasionally when he wants to imagine sharing his gooeyness with someone else. I'm quite flattered.

It's sad, isn't it? Not that Tim has a thing about eggs, but that he sets such store by something so little, and suffers so much for it. It's only what we all want, after all, the temporary transformation into the state of bliss, the exquisiteness of a little death, a little escape from our bodies and the fears we have about our foolishness.

IV

So, I'm about to be transformed, without having to die to lose the body I feel so uncomfortable in. That makes me the luckiest man alive – reincarnation in the same time, the same place, with the same lovely friends.

I'm lucky in that I'm not too tall, and have a nice covering – I've already got wonderful knockers, thanks to the hormones, and very kissable lips. My little sister is *so* jealous of my boobs – I can't tell you! She's always been flat chested, she keeps threatening to get silicon ones now, to outdo me! And I don't have lots of body hair, so I don't need to spend a fortune on depilatory creams. I think I'm going to be the voluptuous type – you know, great cleavage, curvy hips. Hips are a problem, of course, because men don't really have any, we just sort of go straight up and down, but you can cheat. The operation tends to concentrate on the bits between the legs, refashioning everything so that the penis becomes a vagina. It's very complicated surgery, you can't afford to have a knife and fork surgeon, so I've saved and saved to go private. Actually, I'm really looking forward to my first full sexual experience as a woman – they leave the root of the penis intact, where all the nerves are, so you have a real clitoris, and the orgasms are supposed to be fantastic! And before you ask, I definitely want it to be old-fashioned, physical sex, with sweat and everything – in fact, I can't wait!

So I only have a couple of months to go, although even

when it's all over, I'll still have to pay regular visits to my special shop. JayJay found it for me – it's where transvestites and transsexuals can go to get the clothes and accessories they need to complete their feminine look. A lot of men just give up and go to Marks and Spencer, but they miss out on a lot of tricks. If you see a transvestite in the street, you can usually tell it's a man, even if you can't quite put your finger on it. That's because men's bodies are different, you can't just put on women's clothes and expect it to be enough. For starters, the panstick we're forced to wear, especially the more hirsute of us, has to be one step away from cement just to hide the stubble. Then there's your hips. You might not have any of your own, but you can get special pads to wear – and then you look right in tight skirts and denims. Shoes are another thing – my special shop cuts them so they flatter my great big feet, and shape my ankles. The woman who runs the business used to be a man – that's why she knows these things. She's great to chat to, and I know she'll be a friend to me when I'm going through the change.

The best fun of all is choosing wigs. I'm already thinning on top, so wigs fit really well. My favourite is my newest one, a long, brunette tumble – it completely changes the way I look and the way I feel about myself. When I'm dressing, I always put it on last, and that's the moment I transform, become somebody different, become the woman I want to be, become Carmen. The hair joyously confirms my femininity, my new life, it denies my maleness, signals the coming death of the person I used to be.

A strange thing happened to me when I bought it the other week. I was leaving the shop – I was dressed as Carmen, so I had another wig on, a curly auburn one – and a funeral cortege was going by. Inside the hearse, the coffin was decorated with four objects. A single white lily, a piece of what looked like granite, a peculiar thing the colour of sandstone, that looked like fossilised cactus, and a large piece of polished crystal, creamy pink in colour, which caught the sunshine and sparkled softly with a gentle radiance like a guiding star. It was so beautiful, so touching to see a coffin, which even though it contained a spent life with its light extinguished, still shed the light of rebirth, of transformation, which would never diminish. I didn't know who it was, but I knew the person was being honoured in a very specific way that would have pleased him or her. What lovely people they must be, I thought, to choose this way to remember their friend.

It made me think of JayJay and the grave of the young man we'd found. Somehow, I knew the person in that hearse had died young, and I felt sad for them, as if in some way it was my own loss. It's true, you know, you never know when your time will come – you really do have to seize the day, and let the rest of the world go hang.

One day, it'll be me riding through the streets in a wooden box, and Lord knows what my friends will put on the coffin to commemorate me! A black leather basque, a feather boa and a whip, no doubt, with *Venus in Furs* blaring through a loudspeaker. Now *that* would be a great way to go. It was a sobering, but also exhilarating thought as I stood and watched the hearse go past, that soon my male self would be dead, and a new woman would rise out of his ashes.

I took a firm grip on my special shop carrier bag, and strode towards the car as if it was my mode of transport towards the future. Watch out, world, I said, and felt the joy of being alive, and hopeful, with my torch burning strongly with the light of change.

Carmen is coming!

10
BURNING

I

From the beginning, Malcolm Defries did not want his sons to follow in his footsteps. It wasn't that he wasn't proud of the family business (established 1883), and it wasn't that he wasn't proud of his offspring. It was just that he didn't want to raise another generation of undertakers. This would be the fifth, and not a single male heir since 1892 had defected to other available careers. Sometimes Malcolm thought that death was inherent in the genes, so deeply embedded it seemed to be in the family psyche.

Given that there was already a certain irony in despatchers of the dead choosing to procreate, Malcolm did not harbour any ambitions for his offspring to follow his example and endlessly tread the gloomy path to the cemetery. But he and his wife Gertrude were blessed with two sons, the first of whom showed early inclinations to inhabit the world of the dead. Maurice took to death like a duck to water. His first word was *ashes* and for weeks, his doting parents thought he was imitating a sneeze, until they noticed the word was always accompanied by a brief scattering action of the right hand. When he was older, his favourite game was funerals, and his bewildered friends – he didn't have many – joined in the endlessly invented scenarios, squabbling about who they were going to be – corpse, minister or weeping relative. Maurice was always the funeral director. Nobody even bothered to argue that one. Childhood games are usually associated with escapism; with sinking heart, Malcolm realised that Maurice's creative play was actually preparatory.

As he got older, and showed promise in mathematics and sciences, his despairing father tried to derail his interest in undertaking by talking of the attractions of accountancy and banking. But Maurice, who at fifteen already sounded like an undertaker, with his carefully pitched voice and measured speech, would have none of it.

"I'm not interested in money," he said in his infuriatingly quiet, respectful way. "If I worked with money, what would my challenges be? Money on its own does nothing but turn itself into more or less."

"What about corpses?" Malcolm said, with a sudden vicious disrespect that would have his grieving clients reeling in horror. "They just lie there." He leaned forward, pleading. "My boy, for over a hundred years our family has grown rich on life's most profound sadness. I want my sons to grow rich on its joys."

Maurice considered this point with his customary tact, but he already had his answer. "I know what life has to offer," he said, with a confidence verging on the arrogant. "But death always surprises you – by whom it chooses, by its method, its speed, its timing." He warmed to his subject. "You know this, too, Dad – you never know what's going to come through the door on any given day – and it makes a good living as well. I'm sorry, but I want to carry on in my father's line. I just find death endlessly fascinating."

"So did the Yorkshire Ripper," Malcolm said in exasperation.

Maurice saw his chance. "Exactly. So be grateful I have the opportunity to explore my fascination within a legitimate career structure."

Malcolm nodded with resignation and utter sadness, the way undertakers do, and gave up his son to the family business. Maurice would be a good undertaker, he had an instinct for it, and Malcolm had to be grateful that his son had inherited a gift he could develop to make a useful, contented life.

He had never understood the attractions of undertaking. It was an interesting and unusual career, but it worried him that he got such profound job satisfaction from such a morbid occupation. When he told people what he did for a living, they were immediately fascinated, but also repelled. It had made finding a wife a difficult business, and yet somehow he and all his predecessors had married happily and produced children with no difficulty. He wondered if they all suffered from a strain of Munchausen's Syndrome, or if they just wanted sincerely to help people survive the most traumatic and stressful experience of their lives. He still wasn't sure which it was.

It wasn't that undertakers didn't know how to have fun. Like girls, like doctors and nurses who dealt daily with human distress, funeral directors knew how to have a good time and compensate for the misery inherent in their daily working lives. But you had to be careful to socialise with people who would not be calling on your services. This was difficult, as everyone Malcolm met was a dead cert candidate for the mortuary – it was just a question of where and when. If you went to a party, got pissed as a fart on champagne, and ended up doing the funky chicken with your mistress's knickers over your head, you would be unlikely to pick up business from the hostess a week later, when her husband dropped dead in the street from a heart attack. She would not be able to bring herself to arrange the funeral with someone who danced badly and couldn't be trusted with other people's underwear. So, like closet transvestites who always go clothes and accessory shopping a hundred miles from their homes, undertakers were careful to let their hair down in nightclubs and suburban houses far away from the hushed stillness of their funeral parlours, with people who already had an alternative undertaker in mind.

Maurice left school when he was seventeen, and immediately entered his father's profession. Like a human bitten by a vampire, he descended into darkness. He learnt about the twilight world of the mortuary, the darkness of human despair, the sombre mien of the conscientious undertaker, the secret skills of preparing bodies for burial, the dark corners at the end of life where few people in the western world ventured. He applied time and motion principles to the business, learned how to keep a steady flow of bodies going through the system, what to do in times of plenty when facilities were stretched and the holding bays full. He learned from watching his father about economy of speech, that an undertaker could bow his head, clasp and unclasp his hands and say "Ah," in an almost infinite number of ways, to an almost infinite number of remarks. He learned the low-key vocabulary, the modified body language, the strict dress code, the detailed manoeuvres.

He learned the discreet appreciation of the winter boom period, when flu and the bitter cold drained the life from the elderly and frail and filled the coffers. He studied flow charts breaking down the year into typical causes of death related to season – an increase in road mortality in the good weather, more deaths from sickness in the winter. The variations came with sprinklings of non-traffic-related accidents, beatings, regrettable communication failures, the odd murder, a few suicides.

He learned about cost analysis, kept abreast of new product development, learnt about combustion, synthetic materials and different woods, their properties and how they responded when subjected to extreme heat. He familiarised himself with the trade journals, entered debates about the virtues of the new synthetic coffins. He shared anxieties about the trend for DIY funerals and the devaluation of the profession, but like most of the industry, felt powerless to act against it. If it continued, they'd be back to the good old days of families washing down bodies on the kitchen table and laying them out in the dining room – it didn't bear thinking about, if people's growing cynicism regarding professional input spread into the world of the dead.

As his practical skills and confidence grew, he spent more time away from the mortuary, dealing with necessary PR and expanding his knowledge. He mollified the secretary of the local golf club, who complained that black smoke caused by melamine coffins belched out over the fairways from the crematorium chimney when important visitors were halfway through their eighteen holes. He travelled to America to see revolutionary bone-grinding machinery. He visited ladies who turned glittering phosphorescent remains into attractive pottery. He met mortuary cosmetics experts who routinely broke the jaws of the dead, wired them back together again, and stitched the sagging lips into unnatural smiles for the benefit of their grieving relatives, and was grateful for English reticence. He accepted the stifling restraint, the damping down of an industry whose very name is a euphemism, that deals in death in a culture that has no honest vocabulary for it. There was no doubt about it, Malcolm was forced to acknowledge with a degree of pride – Maurice was a born undertaker.

Ian, the youngest, was different. An averagely noisy, healthy little boy, he played ghoul games, trampled graves to spook his friends, and blew raspberries down the freshly dug ones, daring the ghosts to rise and haunt him. He was adept at taking the wilting remains of flowers and fashioning them into surprising decorations – a gift that Malcolm should have taken more heed of than he did. But he also played games that did not include the cemetery, took childish flights of fancy to Mars, the Antarctic and the Wild West, had a wide circle of friends, showed an early gift for drawing and painting and was generally interested in style. It did his father good seeing a completely different set of talents emerging; when he discussed career possibilities with his youngest son, there was none of the foregone conclusions he had experienced with Maurice. He couldn't imagine what Ian's talents would develop into, as if he was trying to stare at too bright a star.

"An artistic career," his father said enthusiastically, grasping at the opportunity like the accountant who yearns to be a liontamer. "You have undeniable talent."

"Oh, I'm an artist, true enough," Ian said, in his cheerful, rather offhand manner. "But I don't know where it's going to take me."

"South America, Paris, the Far East," his father twittered exuberantly.

"I didn't mean that," Ian said. "Travel's part of it, but it's what I want to work with – that's what I don't know."

"Pottery, wood, precious metals, paints – " His indefatigable father should have heard the distant warning bells tolling in Ian's persistent vagueness, but the dream of a roving artistic son, out on the sunlit plains and mountains, had struck him deaf as well as blind.

"Maybe, maybe. Something 3D, at any rate, I think."

The lurking dilemma that Ian couldn't articulate was linked to the family business. Like Maurice, although he expressed it differently, Ian was interested in death – but not in the emotional, psychological or abstract concepts that so tantalised his brother. Ian was drawn to the artistic elements that surrounded it. The corpses, the mourners, were peripheral to the ideas he had begun to develop. He had begun to make `a connection between the word funeral and the concept of design. Best not say too much, until you can define your thinking, he decided.

Too debonair for this business, his blissfully ignorant father thought. *Too lively, too connected to the finer things of life, too imaginative, too ambitious – qualities that were singly inappropriate for the world of the dead.*

Oh, how wrong he was.

II

Jana died, sinking below pain in a deep, rocking sea of analgesics and opiates. She drifted in a pool carpeted with water lilies, surrounded by smooth sandstone pebbles, dusky pink banded with dark mauve, and shielded by jagged cliffs of agate and quartz, pyrite and marble. She completed the landscape herself, creating the scenario she wanted while she still had the power of imagination. For a while, the fantasy location sustained her interest in things terrestrial, but the time came when she began to fall away from the impossible beauty of the towering rocks and white flower heads, and did so gladly, wrapping herself in the dream of endless sleep. Down she went, past the trailing roots of the water lilies, sliding into the cool, chocolate-coloured silt, immersing herself in the thick mud. Her lungs solidifying, her body moulding itself to the contours of the underlying rock, and finally, merging with it, as the cold, the comfortable, binding weight, took her down to the centre of the earth.

She didn't struggle anymore, the fighting analogies she and most people employed to describe the relationship between the sufferer and the disease seeming curiously redundant and inappropriate. Because she had tried to fight, she ended up having to contemplate defeat at the hands of a merciless victor, as if she was somehow to blame for slacking on the job. It just made it worse, dying of cancer and then being made to feel culpable. She had lived her life like an underwater swimmer, rising briefly to the surface, gasping in the air, taking in the sunshine and scenery and any opportunities that happen to be passing, and then breathing out and submerging again, deeper than before.

She had begun to will herself to leave, wanting the seepages, the smells, the rotting, the organics to cease. Her flesh, corrupted by tumours engorged with her blood, reeking of the sourness of decay, became a thing of horror, something she wanted taken away at any cost. She began to long for the day when her pure, opal-white bones would glisten amongst the decay and damp of the soil – the hardest part of a human, the closest she will get to assuming the clean, hard-edged dignity of rock.

In the room across from her, Dorothy had died a fortnight before, a victim of her refusal to accept what was happening.

Jana saw at first hand the cruel futility of denial, how much additional pain could be caused by mental torment, how much Dorothy was demeaned by constantly asking for the impossible, and it scared her. The nuns tutted sadly, powerless to help. Dorothy's only visitors, her neighbour Janet and Dr Sheila Mooney, had their attempts to communicate with her stifled. She didn't want to know. She complained about the nuns, the medicine, the standards, the lack of understanding, the lack of sympathy. She died still pretending it was all going to go away.

The turning point for Jana came when she realised it wasn't going to get any better, and her quality of life had plummeted to the point where a good day consisted merely of being largely out of pain. Sometimes her visitors seemed a long way off, and she was too tired to swim back to the surface of her conscious mind and acknowledge them. Towards the end, she was dimly aware of Carrie, suddenly larger than life, bouncing her impressive baby belly at the bedside, indecently proclaiming the new life burgeoning inside. *It's like a trade,* was one of the thoughts that drifted idly through her head. *I go out, this one comes in.* She had a vague recollection of lazily lifting her arm and passing her hand across Carrie's belly, and Carrie pressing her hand against a lump that suddenly kicked against her. Her hand registered the sensation, then her fingers splayed and held themselves briefly over the moving leg before falling back towards the bed. *Like a blessing,* Carrie told the baby later, in a private moment at home.

A good job the declining Jana wasn't there to hear *that.* The pressure of reassuring the ones being left behind was bad enough, without being credited with the power to distribute divine favours. In an odd way, she knew there was a funny kind of role reversal going on and she was somehow looking after them, that her moods and general physical state dictated how her family and friends felt while they were at her bedside. She constantly had to play down how she was feeling so that her visitors would not suffer on her behalf, found herself worrying about how they were coping with the extra burden her dying was placing on them.

It was a slow process, dying. She felt she was ready to go a long time before her body relinquished its fierce grip on the present and began to think in terms of stopping. But she wasn't ready. Sometimes she'd panic, suddenly catch herself drifting off to sleep and drag herself back, sweating and excited, as if she had saved herself from the final exit. She realised as long as she was still aware that she might die at any moment, she would fight against it. She didn't have any of those prophetic dreams about doors at the top of spiral staircases, the ones people report afterwards, saying they could see a tree on the other side, and knew that if they went towards it, that was them. She wouldn't have gone through the door for a tree, although an interesting geological specimen might well have swung it for her. Eventually, it was Terence who had made her want to go – but even that took time. She had hated him for it, but hate was just part of the process of denial, of fighting, of making it harder for yourself in the long run. Her circle was complete, it was time to swing out in a new arc. She wondered if the whole idea of seeing death as a journey, leaving everyone behind, was designed to instil a sense of adventure in the dearly departing. Perhaps it was supposed to make them look forward to it, leaning eagerly over the ship's railings and waving at the people left stranded on the quayside, as if they were lucky to have got a ticket for the early sailing.

Not yet.

III

At what point does the body switch over from living to dying? Where exactly is it that the points flick over, without you noticing? Are you driving to work, cooking dinner, reading a book, loading the washing machine? When does it change, when does your body, having failed to alert you to the approaching crisis, give up the ghost and accept the inevitable? When the sorrowful doctor completes his examination, and utters the damning words, however gently, *You should have come to see me sooner* – how much sooner should that have been?

She wondered how much God could be implicated in her untimely demise. Was he busy the day her tumour slid from being not particularly dangerous into lethal mode? Did he glance away from the monitor at the wrong moment and fail to see what was happening? Was he sorry for his negligence when he saw her dying? Did anyone up there appeal on her behalf, citing her thesis as a major argument, only to be told that God was too tied up interviewing important people?

We like to think we can look at our life and see a pattern in it, a purpose and meaning, so we try to rationalise someone's death as a logical full-stop. We cling to the hope that people will only die at the appropriate time, when things are convenient, and their story has been properly told, with a beginning, a middle and an end. What's interesting is that each death does indeed acquire its own individual logic when the story of the life preceding it has been told a few times, as if in the telling of the tale, it has begun to assume proper dramatic form. We like the idea of being organised, with all our full-stops and commas in good order. On the other hand, if we knew exactly when we were going to die, that we could say, *Well, I can't have lunch with Clarrie this Thursday, because I'll be dying of an aneurysm on the Wednesday evening, just before the end of Coronation Street*, we would be petrified.

So, without the (dis?)advantage of foresight, the best we can hope for is that our loose ends are all tied up, and it doesn't happen somewhere embarrassing – on a public toilet (doesn't bear thinking about), in the middle of a civic lunch (dreadful to upstage the guest speaker) or halfway through unloading the trolley at the supermarket check-out – just think of the queue building up behind you while the staff try to rescue you from where you've fallen, headfirst down amidst the grapefruit and Jaffa cakes! Or just after we've put the bread in the oven, just as we're about to score the winning point at badminton, or just as we're roaring down the third lane of the M1 at ninety miles an hour.

Even though we all know it happens all the time, death still takes us by surprise. It happens, quietly, unexpectedly, not to mention inconveniently, thousands of times a day, to any one of us. And when it comes to people we know, even though we know it's part of life, we are still affronted, angry and bewildered, and want to apportion blame.

Of course, if you're ill, like Jana was, then things are a bit different. You do get time to prepare, and if you don't go into denial, the chances are things will be a bit more organised, a bit more like we expect. For Jana's friends, colleagues and relations, there was no shock factor – she'd hung on quite a long time, and was in danger of becoming a bit of a joke. *She's not still here, is she?*

But then again, that didn't prevent the familiar feelings of devastation, especially given her youth and talent. The sense of loss is always exacerbated by the feeling you've also been robbed. For herself, she was pissed. Pissed at being too young, pissed at drawing attention to herself, pissed at everyone who had nothing wrong with them – just generally, bitterly, furiously pissed. She waited for acceptance. It never really came. She waited for the fear to subside. It never really did. She waited for illumination to give her peace. No bloody chance. The grateful dead? I don't think so.

Light to dark. Seeing to sightless. Speaking to speechless. Hearing to deafness. Living to leaving. Resistance to deliverance. Sensate to withdrawn. Blown apart to centred.

This was the good thing about dying, the compensatory factor, God's apology. The leave-taking was accompanied at last by the sensation of becoming whole again. The cancer had knocked out her centre, shifted her focus away from not who she was, but to what was destroying her. In the final stages, when she was stroked by the transforming hand of death and was at last appreciative, she became whole again, transcended the ravages of Terence and his marauding gang and experienced the solidity and liberation of restoration. She fell

225

as if she was made of gold, a goddess throwing herself with gusto into the fathomless luxury of a bottomless featherbed. She went all the way back to herself, choosing the direction, walking the path, no longer someone skittering drunkenly away from it, a scared rabbit of a person frightened of dying, knocked off course and decentralised by seepages and excrescences. In the end, at the very end, she went with good grace. Welcome to the next stage, the next new beginning.

And farewell.

IV

So now there is the funeral, and Jana would be curious indeed to see what kind of full-stop her family and friends and colleagues are about to put on her life, what kind of logic they will apply to it.

She felt bad that in the end, she had failed to come up with the music for her funeral. After all, it wasn't as if she didn't have plenty of time to think about it. In a way, she had too much. Unable to make the decision herself, she eventually passed the bucks – four of them, one for each piece of music, and asked the people who would be listening to them to choose for her.

She had tried to do it, to be helpful, making up several shortlists, and always changing her mind the next day. She thought how silly it was, and how egocentric, to be worrying so much over something she wouldn't even hear. *What does it matter? Is it image I'm worried about, how the rest of the world will judge my final gesture of self-definition? How stupid of me, if that's the case.*

Four pieces of music, selected with no conferring, to be heard at the funeral. One chosen by her family, one by her work mates, one by her girlfriends and one by the nursing staff. One person nominated within each group, no arguing. She stressed the fun element. *This is supposed to be fun. It isn't a*

226

test. It's not going to stress anyone out, because you've all had plenty of warning. No one is to fall out over it. This is for you more so than me, and whatever you choose will be fine. You place your requests with the funeral directors in a sealed envelope and they sort it all out. She trusted them enough to feel it unlikely that she would end up being lowered into the ground accompanied by *Shaddup Your Face.*

What is it about a funeral that compels everyone to think about the dead person in terms of music? What would you play if the corpse in question had previously owned a record collection which in its entirety comprised *The Chicken Song* and *Agadoo?* Do you play to their taste – or do you play to the occasion?

V

The Sinclair family had chosen Malcolm Defries and Sons as their funeral director, in accordance with Jana's wishes, and against their better judgement, for the establishment had in recent years acquired something of a reputation for being out on the edge. The funeral director, Ian Defries, was a surprising, dapper little man, full of sparkle and energy, and quite candid about his desire to give the cadavers in his care the very best sending off possible. They had heard of Ian Defries. Few people in their area hadn't. He had returned to the fold, was the prodigal son, but no apologetic recalcitrant. He was on a mission, the reforming angel storming the House of Death, brandishing the Sword of the Clean Sweep.

Following school, art college and a scholarship in a prestigious Italian university, he had returned to his roots, and declared his intentions to his father, who was aghast. The dead had seduced him after all, but he came to the business burning with the cleansing fires of change. He wanted partnership in the business with Maurice, he wanted to take the funeral by the scruff of the neck and drag it into the next millennium.

227

Death became his friend too, securing him a good income, enabling him to meet a wide variety of people and apply his considerable creative skills to the management of the formal rite of leaving the human world. It hadn't worked out for him in the world of the living. Like the rest of his family, generations of living with the dead had soaked him in its rituals and fabrics, its subdued colours and shaded light, so that he was centred on death, and there was nothing to be done about it. The harder he lived, the more he sucked energy into his preoccupation with death. He stopped fighting. He had been born into a family of undertakers, and death was written in his destiny.

And then out of the darkness, Ian Defries came into the light. With all the rich possibilities of the world spread before him at the age of twenty-five, there seemed no challenge more tantalising, more seductive than the reform of the undertaking business.

He began to think about his father's business. It was steeped in self-effacement, had no energy, no drive, no vision – absences that would kill any other enterprise stone dead within three months. There was no competitive element, no-one dared to dream, no one was brave enough to offer mourners an alternative to what they had been dished up for countless generations. It didn't need to. Despite their best intentions, people were always going to die, and they would always need undertakers. Why waste money advertising, ramming this uncomfortable truth down your prospective clients' – and they are all your prospective clients – throats?

Ian proposed working with his brother, offering a range of both traditional and modern funeral services, to meet the differing needs of an eclectic marketplace. After his high hopes of an artist in the Defries family had been dashed, Malcolm found the prospect of a radical undertaker in the family business at least intriguing, at least offering a different slant on the familiar patterns. Maurice was poised to take over the business from his father, and more surprisingly, he, too, accepted the proposition. His position was pragmatic – the threat of the DIY funeral still hung over him, threatening his livelihood, and Ian's plans offered the potential to broaden the business and widen its appeal. By this time a thoroughly self-effacing fully-fledged undertaker, he accepted his filial trainee, and for three years Ian learnt the practicalities and fundamentals of the business he was planning to change.

Ian had the utmost respect for his dead clientele, took pains to learn about them, build their ended lives into their departure and feed the information he gathered to the person in charge of the funeral service. What had saddened him about his job from the beginning was the morbidity of it. He hated the fact that his clients were always in varying stages of the worst negative emotions known to man. His first conviction was that not everyone wanted to leave this life accompanied by depressing music and draped with half the contents of Kew Gardens.

By the time he was thirty five, he had spent most of his working life on a largely unsuccessful reforming crusade, trying to encourage his clients – the living ones, at any rate – to be less obsessed with formal ritual and express themselves in ways compatible with those of the deceased. How many deceased people had begged their families not to turn their funeral into a miserable occasion, but use it as a means of celebration and farewell? How many found themselves on the receiving end of a bland, depressing farewell, steeped in the grief of the people who missed them? It was selfish, it was morbid, the way people wallowed in self-pity and misery, failing to notice the artfully trailing flowers, the sensitive lighting, the meticulous attention to detail that would have singled out Ian Defries as a remarkable talent in any other creative profession. He thought about instigating an awards ceremony, to honour funeral directors who distinguished themselves with a range of imaginative client services, and raise the profile of the industry.

How many funerals lacked any sense of personality, and seemed to be held for the benefit of the wooden box, and not the person inside it? Time and again he watched young, bright, vivacious people sent on their way amidst the dreadful gloom of grieving families and friends, with dreadful, gloomy music, dreadful, gloomy lilies, dreadful, gloomy clothes and a dreadful, gloomy presiding minister, who frequently knew nothing about the deceased and despatched him to Eternity with a dreadful, gloomy and inappropriate speech. In a chillingly clinical crematorium, with its cold white walls and the next batch of mourners lining up outside, the roll on roll off funeral was becoming a familiar and wretched way of sending loved ones on their last journey.

He wished he could meet the end-user of his services before they actually needed him, but that idea filled the profession with horror. He had suggested it when speaking at conventions, and they were scandalised. Might as well have the Grim Reaper standing over them with a sharpened sickle, as a funeral director asking them how they wanted to be treated when they'd gone. But, he had argued to a frosty and disapproving audience, it would make the task so much easier if people did, if he wasn't kept away from the dying like a bad smell, as if his interest in them would somehow hasten their final departure. His speech created interest, controversy – how many funeral directors' conferences make the papers? – but little support. It seemed the world was not yet ready for his ideas. Try telling an industry that earns its living from tragedy that they should see themselves not only as funeral directors, but also as funeral designers. The increasingly frustrated and volatile Ian nearly came to blows over the notion at the Funeral Directors' Association Christmas party.

Ian would be the first to acknowledge that his radical approach wasn't always feasible. In real life, you couldn't always deliver the concept funeral in its purest, most well thought out form. Sometimes, you were faced with a sudden, harrowing bereavement – a child killed in a road accident, or an unexpected heart attack for a father with young teenage children. With a family reeling from the impact of unexpected, shell-shocking grief, and all the painful and venomous emotions that often came with it, you couldn't start talking design. You had to get them through it as professionally, as sensitively as possible. So often, the responsibility for making a fitting end to a life fell to people too wracked by sorrow, or handicapped by shock, to do justice to the job. Ian Defries saw his role as filling that gap.

In these circumstances, the business of nitty-gritty, of the funeral director's profit, and the practical choices to be made, was hateful. There might have been a small *avant garde* movement which bought its own cheap coffins and used them ostentatiously as coffee tables until the fateful day dawned, but in the main, people in a funeral parlour were bewildered, resentful, irrational, hysterical, gripped by a powerful feeling that they shouldn't be there. And at their most vulnerable, you had to ask them to hand over their money so you could put their loved one into a box. What kind of coffin would you like? Wood or melamine? Brass handles, satin linings, lead, ornate mouldings or plain? Half the people said, *Who bloody cares? Our darling is dead, nothing else matters, bury her in a shoebox if you like.* The other half took you seriously, took enormous comfort from throwing themselves into the details, the fripperies, the idea that you could give someone the best sending off in the world by throwing a lot of money at them.

Ian had strong feelings about coffins. He showed families the cheapest and the most expensive models. He said, *Whichever you choose, we can make it look just as you want it.* He tried to say, nicely, that the view from inside them was exactly the same, whether they cost £50 or £5,000. The dead didn't give a damn either way – families were actually buying coffins for themselves. Sometimes Ian told them that he and his wife have agreed that whoever goes first, the one remaining will do a cheap, simple funeral, and then spend a great deal of money on a lavish holiday, as thanks for the continuing gift of life. Ian toyed with the idea of being dropped from a light aircraft high over the Pacific, but the costs were prohibitive. The reactions to this revelation were often interesting.

Going about his daily business, he tried hard not to whisper. He believed in respect, but didn't see any point in pussy-footing round the funeral parlour as if a strident voice would bring the corpses springing back to life. There was a business-like edge to him, which some people found offensive. It was part of the way he tried to remind them that once this is over, there was still the business of life to attend to – it wasn't just going to stop because someone had died. At some point, you're going to have to pick up all the pieces and carry on, because that's what life is all about.

That was perhaps why Ian Defries was particularly good at funerals where a high degree of flair and stage management was expected. He had a few celebrity funerals notched up, people who wanted to go out on a high, or do something out of the ordinary. It looked good for the cameras, and it made other people think that maybe they didn't have to conform rigidly to the old-fashioned ways. And, the shrewd Maurice couldn't help noticing, it was undeniably good for business.

Rebels attract a certain type of client. With gradual, but increasing frequency, Ian had been able to persuade some burying parties to acknowledge the passing life in a real, genuine and applicable format. Funerals were not just about saying goodbye, he told his clients. They were also about saying thank you. How can you say thank you properly with a monk on?

He had buried a middle-aged Hell's Angel, orchestrating funeral corteges with chopper bikes, coffin drapes with elaborate patterns in acrylic paints, adorned with heavy metal studs and accompanied by *Born to be Wild*. He had encouraged mourners at the funeral of a *Star Trek* fanatic to come in appropriate costumes, play the theme tune and sing a Klingon anthem.

Last month, he hit the Big Time. He had attracted the interest of a film company shooting *Death by Chocolate*, the story of South American serial killer and chocoholic Maria Ramirez. He immediately saw the creative potential of shifting from the real world to the false, where grieving is carefully controlled by scripts, distraught families keep their emotions for the cameras, coffins are empty, budgets are generous, and the flamboyant, the wild, the unexpected are not only acceptable, but mandatory. The producer had invited him to design the funeral scene, and he had accepted the commission with relish. His initial proposals were already drafted – everything was still very much in pre-production – and had got an enthusiastic reception. There were simple things like silver trays of chocolate truffles for the "mourners", and more ambitious things – he planned to deck the coffin with a superbly sculpted chocolate flower display, commissioned from one of the country's leading chocolatiers. He also wanted to ensure that at least a few of the more prominent mourners wore elaborate hats with intricate chocolate decorations, even suggesting that his chocolate anorak sub-contractor should make a breathtaking chocolate veil for one of them – his sketching skills had been invaluable. To be absolutely truthful, the chocolatier was doubtful that a real chocolate one could survive the lights, even after tempering, and they might well have to substitute a flexible latex for the actual shoot – but still, the principle was sound and it was worth a shot. Even allowing for the possibility of this small cheat, Ian felt that Luigi would be proud of him. Ian had done his homework – he read the book, he researched the various locations the producer had described. As a final flourish, he planned to commission dozens of chocolate skulls to be scattered on the coffin when it was lowered into the grave, in tribute to the ancient funeral customs of Maria's homeland. The project had fired him up, consumed him like a crematorium incinerator, made him see with searing clarity what could be done with death if you got real bodies, real relatives and real grieving out of the way.

The meeting with the producer was the most liberating afternoon of his life. He felt as if for the first time, he was free to explore the pure artistic forms of a funeral untrammelled by feelings of guilt, and accusations of inappropriate behaviour. He met an American funeral director, who made him wish he'd set up in business over there, where funerals had made the shift towards movie mentality decades ago. He got on with everybody – he was an approachable person, it was his job to be. He met Hannah Dell, deep in preparation for her role, got the idea that there could be a few very interesting offers for similar projects if this one turned out OK.

So the Sinclairs were lucky to have him at this important juncture of his career, before his exalted ambitions took flight, and there was the strong possibility he would branch out into a totally different direction.

The Sinclairs were there because Jana had heard about Ian Defries, the country's first celebrity undertaker, who swept away the dull, predictable morbidity, listened to people's wishes and respected them. She talked enthusiastically about him to her friends when she read about him in the paper, even before she was diagnosed. Being good friends, they had remembered, and being local, original and sharing her hatred of morbidity, Ian was their natural choice.

When her body arrived on the premises for preparation, he did what he always did – sat with her and studied. Victims of cancer always moved him. Her body was eaten away, disfigured, the face calm after the long struggle. He wondered where people got the will to hang on for so long, when they knew the outcome in advance and were up against a foe that didn't know how to lose. Or perhaps they didn't want to stay and fight, it was just that the disease was sadistic, and gave them no option.

When her relatives and friends began to visit, he began to amass information about her. What did she like? *Rocks*, they said, all of them, without hesitation. What did she hate? *People making a fuss*. He asked about music, and they told him about the playful task she had set, and asked whether they should be worried about it. Was it right, posing conundrums for people plunged into the preparatory stages of mourning? *Certainly*, Ian said gently. *She is making you think about her in a positive light. In order to choose the music she wants, you have to remember things about her which make you happy, which are good. It's a positive step towards healing your grief. It's never too early to have a happy memory. It's never wrong to look back on a funeral and remember it with affection, as well as sadness.* He smiled, liking her for it, and asked what they had chosen. They didn't know yet. Nobody did. Over the four days preceding the funeral, each of the four nominated people arrived with their sealed envelope, which he didn't open until he had them all. He conferred and consulted, listened and thought. His funeral concept was simple, dignified, full of what Jana loved and what she would have wanted. This was an occasion for understated creativity. Above all, not fussy. A lasting gift to the family and friends who mourned her.

VI

Everyone agreed that Jana would have liked the coffin. Faced with a deceased who loved rocks above all else and loathed fuss in equal proportion, it was the university department who had suggested to Ian that geological specimens might be more appropriate in her case than botanical ones. That gave him the spark he needed to develop his ideas. A blow for freedom from Kew, too.

After the slow journey through the streets, past the park, past the roundabout, past Tristan with his new wig in its bright and glossy carrier bag, past the war memorial, past the Pig & Whistle. And finally, at the steps of the 12th century flint Norman church, Jana's father, himself a geologist, her mother and sister each carried one of the rocks inside and reset them on the coffin for the service.

As Jana's faculty head Rupert, earnest, dignified and bearded, explained in his eloquent address: *The Lewisian Gneiss was Jana's favourite rock, and her foundation – the centre of her thesis, the object of her fascination and the grounding of all her original work. She loved the fact it had survived over millions of years, which is doubly poignant as we reflect on her own brief existence. We balanced the gneiss with rose quartz, for its ability to cleanse and purify, and for its soft light which shines on in Jana's absence. She would have hated us for choosing anything so corny as a flower to represent the fragility of her life, so we were delighted when, after much fruitless discussion, Carol suggested the desert rose and saved us all from cliché. The desert rose is formed from sand and symbolises to us Jana's return to the elements of the earth she loved. If you're listening, Jana, the lily was purely for decoration, okay, and has no hidden meaning that might make you cringe.* He was rewarded with a laugh.

Later, at the graveside, while everyone stood respectfully around, Jana's father crumbled the desert rose over the coffin. Later still, he and all who visited the grave would be able to see the handsome piece of Lewisian Gneiss and the delicate rose quartz set into the polished granite headstone.

Everyone cried at the service, expressed their grief. Of course they did. Ian had worked to eliminate not sorrow, but morbidity from death. He worked to connect people with the person who was leaving, instil in them a sense of remembrance linked to their own relationship with them, not a hazy memory of ubiquitous flower arrangements and well-worn hymns.

Carrie was there, close to term, the piece of rock from Jana's bedside held firm in her hand. She made a point of thanking Ian afterwards for a service that had gone some way to restoring Jana to her friends and family in the way they wanted to remember her.

So, what music did they play at Jana Sinclair's funeral? Her friends had chosen Mozart's *Requiem* – rather grand, but Jana's all-time fave rave classical piece, one that she called, puzzlingly to some people, the musical equivalent of a rock. Her colleagues played Elton John's *Rocket Man*, because Jana had a thing about planets and the fact that she would never get her hands on a rock from Saturn's rings. Her mother chose Ennio Morricone's *Harmonica Man* theme from *Once Upon A Time In The West*. This was the music Jana played when she was battling her personified tumour, Terence – and her mother wanted some acknowledgement of the pro-active stance her daughter had taken in her last two years. Finally, the hospital staff chose Frank Sinatra's recording of *It Was A Very Good Year*, because Jana asked to listen to it frequently towards the end. They didn't know why, but everyone else did. There was an additional piece – impishly, her friends had also requested *Tiptoe Through the Tulips*. It made everyone laugh as well as cry – it's that kind of tune – because it was a wind-up, and was related to an incident that is deeply imprinted on the memories of everyone who knew Jana well.

You may not know the tunes, and they may not mean much to you, but never mind. On the sunny day that her friends and family bade her goodbye, everyone wished that her favourite music went with her, with love from them. As Jana officially began the long journey away from them, they made the shorter, earthbound journey back to a different life, and began the business of living without her.

11
THE MEANING OF LIFE

I

It's the instinct that gets you in the end, the sexual imperative, call it what you will. I understand that now. I thought, when I found out how it was going to end for me and all the others of my kind, that there was a strong argument for change. But you can't fight against what Nature intended. I was pretty certain that when I told everyone what I had discovered, it would have to change, but even knowledge can't achieve victory over the basics of what you are. I understand that now, too. I would have been better off not knowing, and I regret the sharing of my fear and outrage and determination to secure reform. Reform! *It appals me now, the sheer scale of my arrogance and naivety – I actually thought I could reform Nature!*

The mistake I made was in assuming that the Females enjoyed their dominance over us as a privilege. Women have the upper hand in our society and their behaviour is – well, it's consistent with that state of affairs. They're physically bigger than us, they're better dressed, they're equipped with impressive defensive weaponry, which they use at their own discretion, without consultation. They have a devastating psychological advantage, they live longer, and they make no allowances for the weak and small. Which is us. Even our entire species is named after them. I have to say that on the whole, they do a good job without us, which adds to the general sense of gall. There are a few slack mothers, a few who get carried away and destroy their eggs as well, but in general, they take the responsibility of nurturing the next generation of little black widows pretty seriously. It is, after all, what's really important. My point was simply that if we introduced a few more sharing and caring type principles into the natural order of things, and lost some of our primitive barbarism, we'd all enjoy better quality of life as well. And us males wouldn't be eaten alive at the point where we've just fulfilled our most important role.

You wouldn't like it, would you? If you give your best all your life, you expect a golden handshake, a designer watch to help you monitor the time remaining after all your good service. You wouldn't want your dick pulled off, your head bitten off and the rest of you devoured without even the courtesy of a thank you very much or the nicety of a garnish – would you?

I found out because of Reggie. Reggie was trying to get me to go on a double date with two of the Females. Reggie was my best friend, and we did everything together. I knew that once he mated, I wouldn't see him again. Nobody ever worried about this, it was just understood. You grew up with your mates, you met a Female, you went off with her, you made babies. Well, fair enough – so far, so par for the course. Because everyone was so relaxed about it, it never occurred to you that anything nasty was going to happen. Perhaps it's living in close proximity to humans that gave me the wrong idea. You know – grow up, mate, have babies, grow old together. That equation seemed about right to me, and I expected all species to more or less play the game of life by the same set of rules. Although I had to admit that I was still trying to work out how humans managed the mating slash babies part – none of them ever seemed to have any. I put two and two together and came up with about eighty-four.

Anyway, Reggie was up for this date and wanted me to go along, too. I wasn't sure – I knew I hadn't yet got all the tackle I needed, and I didn't fancy getting on the wrong end of an irate Female I couldn't satisfy. But Reggie was all there, and he wanted to go for it and, well, somehow I got talked into it.

It was pretty hairy, meeting a Female for the first time – I mean, not just a baby out of the nest, but a fully grown woman. Margie and Fran were beautiful – long, sleek black legs, nicely sharpened pincers, and a surprisingly frail mating call designed to lure us to our private trysting place. Remember, it's the Females who call the shots. They call, we do whatever they say, and we might get our shot in, but they always win the final showdown. Margie was looking at me a bit doubtfully, as if she guessed she was out with a lemon, and I wondered if I'd live to tell the tale.

We strolled over to a quiet corner of the wood pile, sat under the stars together, ate some bugs and then Reggie and I said goodbye, and he and Fran went to somewhere a little more private. Mine looked me up and down a bit, and when she asked if I was up for the job, I lied. Well, you do, don't you? It's bad enough being classed as the inferior sex, and lugging round all the attendant baggage that implies, without them implying you're incapable as well. I might look small, I bragged, but I've got enough juice to father the next three generations. You _all_ look small, she said, rather sniffily, and started pushing me over to the place she'd spotted.

Well, you can imagine how things went. It was apparent pretty soon that I was pitifully short in the lunchbox department, and her frustration was awesome to behold. At the time, I thought she'd eat me alive, she was so livid. She said something I didn't understand at the time, when I begged her not to kill me. _You're not worth killing_, she hissed, nipping me spitefully with her pincers. _You haven't done your job yet._ In the end, she let me off with a couple of vicious little jabs in the leg which left me lame for a while, but I soon had more to worry about than a war wound. I was limping away – not easy, not with eight legs, you tend to lose your rhythm and trip over the other seven – and I happened upon Reggie and Fran. Or, that is, I happened upon what was left of Reggie.

At the time, I thought I heard the most terrible, blood-curdling shrieking, but I couldn't have done, because Reggie had already lost his head. Fran held him in thrall, in a tight grip between her pincers, and he was getting smaller before my eyes because she was eating him, right down to his freshly polished antennae and the last undigested bug.

The treachery of the Females burst upon me as I watched, rooted to the pile of wood shavings in terror and shock. No wonder they always wanted to go somewhere a bit more private. When Fran looked up and saw me, Reggie's blood dripping from her mandibles, and her eyes glazed with a kind of sated lunacy, I thought I'd be next. I pulled myself together and legged it as fast as I could, dragging my lame leg and blinded by the horror I had just seen. Thank God neither of them knew where I lived – I'd seen Fran committing the vilest atrocity I'd ever seen, and Margie had left me in a fury determined to satisfy her drives with someone else more developed. I tore down my web, grabbed a small store of food, and fled into the woods.

As I ran, I thought that perhaps Fran was a one-off, a freak psycho who preyed on unsuspecting males with that high-pitched voice and those long, slicked legs, but I knew in my heart of hearts that to run from her was to run from my destiny.

II

I've always been an idealist at heart, so once I'd recovered from the trauma, I began to think that there must be a better way. It seemed such a terrible waste of young life, so unnecessarily barbaric. I mourned the passing of my elder brothers, all of whom I'd waved off cheerily as they scurried off over the woodpile behind their alluring Females towards a new life. I felt foolish for imagining them spinning their webs together in some quiet corner, raising their children and enjoying all the little intimacies of family life. How heartbreaking it was to realise that all of them had met the same terrible end, butchered by their partners when they were at their most vulnerable, and the evidence of the crime destroyed forever.

I didn't know what to do. Tell all the males and frighten the life out of them? Confront the Females? Try negotiation? (*Look, girls, couldn't we just try mating without the penectomy and cannibalism?*) It was worth a shot. They couldn't treat us with any less respect than they already did. Ignorance might be bliss, and knowledge, while it might be painful, could surely be turned to the advantage of the whole race? I tried to think things through, come up with an alternative that meant everybody would be happy. About the only conclusion to emerge from these ruminations was celibacy – withdrawing mating services, just as a short-term tactic. If the males refused to mate when the Females approached them, the Females would soon realise they couldn't have it all their own way. Then they might just be ready to talk about methodology.

I don't know why I questioned it. Nobody else did. Maybe I'm just weird, or a coward. Maybe I just saw things differently. Most of the other males I discussed it with already knew, or had an in-built instinct that something of that sort was on the cards. And they had that built-in sex drive as well. Seeing Reggie being eaten alive had kind of hurled my sex drive head-first against a wall, and I wasn't confident it would ever come out of the coma.

That was *it*, I thought. Overcome the sex drive, the need to procreate, and you've cracked it. The males were their own worst enemies, obsessed by the Females, with one-track minds heading straight for that suicidal rendezvous. But what could I offer as an alternative? Live a life of creativity, of contemplation, live longer, and maybe leave something worthwhile behind. It didn't sound very exciting, and even to me, it had that vague, unspecific quality of an argument that doesn't hold much water.

"But you can't," my friends pointed out patiently, as if I was a few strands short of a cobweb. "You won't live long enough. Haven't you noticed? When you're born, there's no one bigger than you about. If there is, they want to eat you. Christ, Frank, if your mother eats your father alive, what's she likely to do to her kids? It's all been worked out, man, so you don't have to think. All you have to do is eat, sleep, fuck and die. What else is there?"

I detected a certain degeneration in the levels of expectation nursed by my fellows. I dropped from the esoteric to the basic. "Well, how about more fucking?" I countered. "Fucking for pleasure, like the humans do –"

"They do *not*!"

"I've seen them," I said. "I've got a web up at the top layer of their nest. I've been watching them. They mate without producing young. And the males don't get eaten alive, either. I think that's why they call themselves Superior Beings."

This got them thinking, but they were so strapped down by What Nature Intended for them, they couldn't get to grips with it.

"Just imagine," I said persuasively. "Sex when *you* want it – not when the Female says so, not when Nature says so, but when *you* say so. How would that be?"

"Look, Frank, it's just not possible. We're born, we eat, we sleep, we fuck, we die. That's it. End of story. Anything else is fantasy."

"I'll prove you all wrong," I said, turning my back on them. "You *can* live a worthwhile life without being eaten alive just when you get to the best part. I'll work out how."

So I became a recluse, living alone in the woods, away from the rest of the community. Now and again, one or two curious young males would make the trip to visit me while I was developing a programme designed to broaden our thinking and change the natural order, and we'd hang out for a while and talk about the difficulties we faced. Even a few Females came by, but I refused to enter into conversation with them until I was ready. Even while I knew I couldn't turn against them completely for practical reasons, I wanted to come up with a new system that would help them change the way they saw life. If the will was there, the rest would follow.

243

After some time, enough of the younger males were convinced we could be the architects of a braver new world, and started persuading me to go public with my reformist philosophy. It wasn't the cowards who joined me, it was the visionaries, the ones who just saw that there was a possibility of changing the natural order to make things better. So I became an activist, covertly at first, then with increasing confidence as my following grew. Our slogan was *Choose celibacy – choose life!* and it became a rallying cry amongst the more hip males in the communities round the wood pile. My strategy was simple enough – to try to get them thinking of something other than sex. I thought, when they knew what was in store for them, it would be easy. I had a feeling the Females were going to be pretty pissed about all of this, and I was surprised and somewhat deflated when they seemed cool about the whole thing. They knew how powerful Nature was, how difficult it was going to be to subvert her. I didn't.

Eventually, my pride was wounded enough by their lack of interest for me to open up a dialogue with them. To their credit, they did listen to me, my anxieties about the male lot, and my hopes of a more enlightened future, but while they agreed that yes, the males got a pretty rough deal, they couldn't go so far as to support my petition for change. When I suggested mating for pleasure, with no attached parental responsibility, they were completely uncomprehending. What would be the purpose of such an act? *Pleasure*, I said, brightly, seductively, challengingly. *What's Pleasure?* they said, grimly. *There is no Pleasure. There is only Purpose.* They came up with a lot of impressive logistics – food availability and population ratios, the problems of supporting an ageing male population that had shot its bolt. They couldn't see a way around eating us. I countered with proposals for research initiatives into new social structures and behavioural studies to see if we could break the destructive cycle. The head Female crossed her long black legs and nodded sagely, but stuck to the Nature line. Disappointed, I thanked them for their time and returned to the males. It was going to be up to us.

I went about it all wrong. I tried to bulldoze Nature out of the way. I tried to encourage creativity, open the male mind, expand their horizons. Look at the state of our webs, I said. No form, no balance – perhaps neater construction techniques would give us more pride in our work, and catch more food as well. I tried physical training, hunting exercises, dangerous forays further into human territories, where I hoped to show them mating without being eaten, and inspire them. I tried to develop sex aids as well, false male appendages that the Females could pull off and destroy without getting anywhere near the real thing. We even asked a Female to try one out for us. Arnold didn't get eaten, but the Female went off in a terrible rage and devoured three of his best friends to drive home the point that she had not got a lot out of faking it.

My most controversial initiative was the introduction of homosexual practices. The Females *were* unhappy about this, regarding the preference of the inferior sex as an insult to their status. There were isolated incidents of disgusted Females destroying their eggs, saying they would rather the species died out than harboured males with such defective behaviour patterns. There was web vandalism, some males had their legs cut off, there were a few demonstrations and for a brief period, a state of anarchy threatened. There was even a rumour that the Females would talk terms. This was satisfying, but short-lived. The panic receded when it became obvious that males experiencing the frustration of unrequited mating tended to seek out Females all the sooner, and throw themselves desperately, penitently and unquestioningly into their murderous embraces.

I couldn't blame the males. It wasn't easy being gay. When all your parts are hairy and scratchy, and your member ends in what is basically a spike, sexual gratification with your own kind is virtually impossible. If we used our legs, we fell over, and very few of us would attempt an anal insertion, not when you knew one of you was going to get the equivalent of a scorpion's sting up your arse. And, as several of the males could be heard muttering, what was the fucking point? So what, you might get a quick thrill, but where was the fun in that?

And then I had an unexpected success. On our outings to the human nest, we had got into the habit of trying different foods as we worked to out-spider our thinking and experience. We tried meats and dairy products, foods with high vegetable content, fats and carbohydrates that charged our minds, but made our bodies dull and sluggish, and a dark, shiny, cloying, caked resin called chocolate that the Female in the human nest particularly enjoyed.

There was a substance I wanted to find that eluded me on several visits, although it was in evidence in almost every part of the nest. The humans absorbed this fine white powder by sucking it up through their noses in tiny quantities, after which they felt exceptionally well. They also shook it over themselves in profuse amounts when they had bathed, and incorporated it into their food. It took several attempts at raiding the food store before we happened upon it in its raw state.

So it wasn't the foods that began to seriously undermine Nature's ambitions, and it wasn't the tapestry, meditation and PT I was teaching. No – it was the sackfuls of the white, grainy substance that sparkled like raindrops and melted between our jaws into a divine sweet liquid.

Sugar. At first, we all got high on it. But before long, I had a major habit on my hands. The males seemed unable to break their dependency, and started making dangerous trips at all times of day and night to bring back as much as they could carry. One day, I found a particularly bad case up to his knees in a ghastly brown puddle. I struggled to free him, but he was trapped. "Leave it, man," he drawled, his brain all furred up as he sunk his head into the sticky swamp. "This is top drawer stuff. The humans call it molasses. It beats sugar, and it beats anything the Females can cook up for us, that's for sure." Soon after, I found four of them on their backs, legs curled up in a pool of the stuff, and I knew I had to put a stop to it.

But there was worse to come. Because the humans noticed their stores being stolen, they attacked the woodpile with poison gas. Most of us got out, but the addicts simply lay back in the sugar and died with terrible inane grins on their faces.

My movement was in ruins, so was my credibility, and that's when the Females stepped in.

"I think this proves our point," the head Female said with stinging contempt. "You've failed to find a more meaningful solution than the one we've had in place since we began. Any more nonsense from you about sugar or celibacy and you'll be taken by force."

And if I hadn't met Susie, I probably would have been.

III

My position was becoming hopeless. I was trying to find something that was more macho than weaving and intellectualism, but stopped short of needless risk and drug addiction, and I was beginning to think it was an impossible ideal. How else could we prove ourselves and give meaning to our lives? I knew before I finally gave up that the only thing that fitted the bill was a terminal meeting with a Female.

In the beginning, I had loathed the Females for their deceit. Their coy looks, their sweet siren songs, their reeking sexuality that spelled ruin for us all.

But then I got to thinking about how it was for all of us, males and Females alike, and how difficult it was for any of us to make sense of anything when there were never any adults around. Where do they all go to when you need answers to important questions? Like why am I here, how long does it last, what constitutes the living of a good life? All I remember about being a kid is all of us running around together, doing our best to find food, trying not to get eaten and wondering what the hell happened next. Just as you got around to wondering if there was more to life than eating, spinning and sleeping, the Females started to grow noticeably larger, with deeply curved bodies, that exotic erotic blood-red mark, and the poison fang. Ask any adolescent male what turns him on most about the burgeoning Female, and it's that poison fang, the long, sensuous hooking claw that you fantasise about clacking gently against your mandibles while they run their long, satiny black legs over the back of your abdomen. And the questioning and wondering suddenly distilled itself into the solution of sex. It just seemed too obvious, too crass, too trite.

The two humans living near us had made the woodpile where most of us hung out. Their complicated nest, of several layers, was built down a hard, black pitted track. It seemed ridiculously large for the two of them, so my continuous expectation was that there would soon be hundreds of babies crawling around the vast interior spaces. Towards the end, it was my habit not to immediately head for the food stores in the lower areas, but to climb to the highest layer, an expedition which took several hours. I would spin a web in the eaves, where I had a good vantage point looking through one of their glass panels into the space where they slept.

I saw several things I couldn't explain. The Female was smaller, fleshier, with heavy, drooping appendages the males seemed to like. She dominated the nest. I knew this because several activities I saw seemed to require her consent. Behind the glass, they often shed the colourful skins they wore outside, and grappled with each other.

I still clung to the belief that this was mating, and, having got my sugar habit under control, and still not having much appetite to go the way of all the rest, I asked for Mark's opinion on the activity. He had stuck by me through all the trouble and had recently come, through his own deliberations, to adopt the position of healthy sceptic. He watched the grappling bout with detached interest, then shrugged.

"It's obvious, isn't it?" he said. "It's not mating. They're feeding."

"But – they feed off all those stores in the lower parts of the nest," I said.

"It's got to be feeding," he insisted. "Look – all that work with the mandibles at different body sites. It must be some kind of mutual cross-digestion process of previously ingested matter. It probably increases the nutritional value of the stored foods." He shuddered. "How they survive without live food sources is beyond me."

As we watched, the Female sighed and let out a moan. Mark tapped his front legs thoughtfully on the glass. "Now that," he conceded, "does sound as if it could be mating."

Much as I hated to, I had to disagree. "No, it's feeding," I said. "I've studied the Female closely. It's the same sound she makes when she's eating chocolate."

In some peculiar way, I knew that the Female's consumption of chocolate was linked to the strange grappling behaviour. She did not seem able to combine the two activities, and I had seen her reject the male's presence while she was eating chocolate.

"That'll be chemical," Mark said knowledgeably. "Probably the substances have to be at least partly ingested before they can be mutually beneficial. The Female must have to break them down."

"Perhaps that's what the chocolate's for," I said. "Only the Female ever eats it. And the male gets angry when she eats it, because she won't grapple."

"Well, there you have it," Mark said triumphantly. "She eats chocolate to facilitate mutual feeding. The male gets angry because he's frustrated that he can't feed. He's hungry."

I watched the humans again, until they fell asleep. Please note: *they fell asleep*. Something about it all still wasn't right. Eventually, we climbed down, arguing.

"You'll never convince me," Mark said flatly. "If one of them ain't dying, then they ain't fucking."

"But if that isn't mating – what is?" I said.

"Perhaps they don't mate," Mark said, in all seriousness, while I scoffed at the notion. "Perhaps they don't need to."

While I was turning over this novel idea, Mark said, "Jeez, Frank, you've got to stop seeing mating in everything you look at. Only a guy who's never going to get it would be this obsessed."

I conceded the point, and felt bitterly let down. If humans didn't mate, whether for pleasure or purpose, and didn't produce young, then life had to have some other meaning, one too obscure for me to fathom. If it wasn't sex, and it wasn't feeding, and the humans displayed no great drive to achieve anything, what was I missing?

IV

Not long after this, Mark came to tell me he'd decided to run with Nature. "It's been cool, man," he said, "but all these other things we've been doing, well, there's something I still feel I gotta do."

After the sugar fiasco, this was a speech I'd heard a lot lately. I was beginning to think I'd be making it myself before long, if I could find someone to listen to it.

But then he invited me to watch. "I know it freaked you out," he said, "but maybe there was something you missed. When I go over the pile with my Female, you follow, and take notes if you like, and maybe something might click into place. I'm sure hoping it does for me."

There were tears in his eyes as he walked away, and I thought sadly that before I had made my great revelation to them, all the males had approached their mating with eagerness and pleasure. I watched them, Mark and his rather neat, petite Female, head towards one of the recesses at the edge of the pile, and followed.

I soon saw the tenderness with which the Female handled him, and the way his initial apprehension melted into desire and then boiled up into a sudden, savage want that consumed both of them. Mark was right – this is what I had failed to see. I watched, enthralled, and heard his high, shrieking cry as the Female gripped his sex in her wild passion and tore it from him. I shuddered, but before his head disappeared between her frantic jaws, he threw it back and cried, "Frank! If you only knew what ecstasy this is! To die without knowing would be ... would be ..."

Then words failed him in a horrible gargle of blood, which they tend to when someone rips off your head. I picked my way back across the pile and spent the rest of the night huddled in my messy web. The night passed in contemplation of my abandoned attempt at a three-dimensional hexagonal web, my ideals of perfecting the arachnid arts, my rudimentary dildos, my spidery attempts at writing, and a small crumb of chocolate from a recent night raid. Its melting sweetness afforded me some small comfort, but I was haunted by Mark's last words, screamed at the height of his erotic transport.

My efforts were doomed to be ephemeral because we could not form an alternative culture without access to our history. With no forebears to learn from, we had no example to follow, and no rules to break but our own. No one would hand down stories of what we had done, no one would learn lessons. We had the choice of following the path laid out before us, or coming up with an alternative that would not survive us.

That night, I knew that I, too, would be lost to Nature.

V

I met Susie not long after. Her name reminded me of the soughing sound of her legs rubbing together, when she was cleaning or attracting. Susie, with the shiny, delicate legs that looked too fragile to support the deep curve of her abdomen, heavy with eggs, and taut, erect thorax. Her hour-glass mark, red and tantalising as ant blood, was perfectly formed, and her eyes, black as the night sky, black as the hopelessness of unrequited love, gave me their promise of the savage ecstasy of death.

"Perhaps there are many things we won't understand until it's happening," Susie said, as we shared our last meal of bugs on the woodpile.

"I just wish I had found something else," I said, brushing the last remnants of carapace and antennae from my mandibles. "I wanted there to be a mystery, something else other than the obvious."

"The obvious can also be a mystery," she said. "Why do you still want what Nature wants for you, even though you understand what it will mean? Why did you travel so far from your destiny, only to return to the same point? And why will I want to devour someone I have come to care for?"

In the thoughtful calm before the sexual storm engulfed us, we talked of our eggs, and what lay in store for our children, and I was grateful that I would not be there, with my awful knowledge of the dark side of pleasure, to spoil it for them.

And I was spared knowing that all the males who had fallen into sugar abuse had become sterile, that we would all die in fruitless ecstasy, that Susie would die, content in her ignorance, near a nest of eggs that would never hatch.

Such was my legacy. Such was the meaning of life.

12
LIFE'S A BITCH AND THEN YOU DIE

I

She's standing in the valley, 17,000 feet up, and Changabang, the Glass Mountain, is before her, rising into the sapphire sky like a crystal sculpture, torched to translucence by the scarlet fires of sunset. Its slopes are so sheer and perpendicular it looks as if it's free-standing, independent of the rest of the rocky piles towering around it.

This mountain has become an obsession. Her dream is to climb it. Maybe, one day, once this is over, she will. She eases the rucksack from her shoulders and sits on the long grass by the path. The Indian alpine flowers wink in the sunshine, the breezes lift the humidity she has walked through for days.

She's never been there, and she probably never will. But that isn't the point. This way, she gets to romanticise it, there's no dysentery or berry-berry, no farting Sherpas, no unnecessary clutter, no possibility of plunging to a horrible death from Changabang's slippery slopes. There's just her, the picture-postcard image of the slender, elegant mountain, the sunset, the breezes, the flowers. She chose this scene because she had to imagine it, paint her own picture, fill in the details, the brilliant colours of the flowers, the kindling power of the sunset. She thought it would make the whole exercise more effective, having to make her own contribution, she thought it would be more distracting.

As she prepares to move forward – oh Jesus Christ, it's coming again, why is it always this part – why can't she ever get any further than this next –

She's wrenched back from her stronghold in the

Himalayas by a sudden, gripping pain across her abdomen, a contraction of such savagery that her muscles harden like steel. The air turns blue: she copes by swearing.

It's killing, this business of giving birth. The contractions – agony, the bastards are running straight into each other now, there's no pause, no time to catch breath, no let up in the pain, which is so strong, she feels it's capable of lifting her bodily and throwing her around the room. She's looking at her feet, and they're arched in a massive cramping spasm, but the vice gripping her swollen belly, powering the baby down towards the exit, has bludgeoned away any finer sensitivities. She can't feel a thing except this awesome, all-consuming pain, the only pain in the world that doesn't mean there's something wrong. Anyone else going through this would be dying.

She's running against the usual form. First babies normally take much longer to deliver. She turns out to have a super-efficient body, which has taken to the task as if it's been waiting forever to get the show on the road. In a way, it has. She's no spring chicken at thirty-four, and for at least half the pregnancy, this baby was on a losing ticket.

But the baby has made it, and is on its way, and she's hurting. All things must pass. She has to remember that. This is going to end, it's not going to be forever. Pain ends, life ends, everything ends. The glass is half full. She has to re-member that, too. The glass is half full because the pain is positive, healthy, everything is going swimmingly. She tries to be grateful for this, tries to feel compassion for people who are having tougher times down the corridor, who have been in labour for twenty hours and are facing up to forceps and pinking shears and Caesarians and God knows what else.

She thinks how much the last four hours have redefined her attitudes to how much she can actually cope with. And it's not going to be forever. When it started, when the con-tractions began to build in power and she first began to feel uncomfortable, she'd been thinking of Jana, and how scared she was of having to face prolonged pain. Seeing Jana slide towards death, she was afraid that giving birth would be the same, the same horrifying descent into an abyss that was only alleviated through drugs that severed the connection between you and the rest of the world.

But it wasn't the same. What she thought she saw was not what Jana was experiencing at all. Jana argued that she was being born into a different state, and that the pain of transition was only to be expected. When you cling so jealously to your body, she said, it stands to reason it's going to hurt to let it go. When you are dying, if you don't let go, the pain only becomes worse, literally eating you away until your mind is swamped by it and nothing else can penetrate. When Jana began to go with it, when she stopped fighting it, she was allowing herself the freedom to achieve her rebirth through death. And it seemed to hurt less.

Jana talked about pain moving in circles that completed themselves and then faded, like ripples on a calm pool. She tried to imagine it – she could either be inside the circle and surrounded by it, or outside it, where she could detach herself from it, and roll it away from her like a wheel.

And now Carrie understands the difference. There's the kind of pain that ends, and there's the kind that doesn't. Sometimes, for the pain to end, everything had to end. So in the final analysis, it doesn't have much to do with the pain itself. It's more to do with what's going on in your mind, and what the consequences are going to be. If that sounds both glib and obvious, try putting it into practise when the contractions are coming every minute, stacking up like some mediaeval torture device, and you have no say in what's happening.

She could blame the midwife – that's always a good one. She could blame Paul for being so bloody fertile. She could blame herself for ever thinking that having a baby was a good idea. It's got to be someone's fault, after all. But the midwife, Debbie, is a great lady, cheerful, efficient, and Carrie can't find it in her heart to blame her, even though she's infuriatingly relaxed about watching Carrie suffer contractions. *You smug bitch, I know it's not happening to you, but do you have to rub it in so hard?* If she thinks this, she's certainly not stupid enough to say it. The midwife is her chief carer, and you don't want to run the risk of her turning nasty if you accuse her of not doing her job properly. It occurs to her that men at the bedsides of labouring women are at least good for that – at least they feel bad it isn't them, and stick up for you when you're screaming for pain relief. It's their job to shout at the midwife, in the role of anguished male protector.

Debbie knows it actually isn't all that bad – she knows when women are really in distress, and she can tell that Carrie isn't suffering all that much. Oh sure thing, it's hurting, but Carrie isn't displaying signs of psychological distress – that's the thing to watch for. Carrie is still responding to stories, still hanging in there. There's a determination about her, and above all, she isn't scared.

Debbie told her a story about an African tribe. When a woman went into labour, she said, they sent her into a birthing hut and gave her the end of a length of string to hold. The string went through the door and round the corner, into another hut, where it was attached to her husband's dick. Every time the woman had a contraction, she yanked on the string and the husband got a painful tweak, so he could participate in the suffering. Carrie liked that – it made her laugh, even in the middle of a contraction, and it sounded a lot better than middle class men going to relaxation classes and pretending to push alongside their partners.

What was the point of empathising? Hell, it was ridiculous enough for women who hadn't had children to grasp the enormity of the experience. It was stupid, trying to get men to understand what labour was like. It was physically impossible – far better they didn't know, didn't empathise, and got on with the business of being supportive. Lying on their backs with cushions up their jumpers, doing breathing exercises – it was a joke, like people who went on concentration camp holidays to try and empathise with the victims of genocide. You can bet the holiday version didn't include stripping, starving and gassing. It was like people holding hunger lunches in homage to famine victims. It was an insult, foregoing your cheese and tomato sandwich at one o clock, knowing full well you could pig out in the evening on a three-course dinner as a reward for your earlier abstinence.

Paul, of course, was not there to be supportive, or to have his willy tweaked. Carrie had not informed him of what was happening, did not want him to be involved. He had left the morning she had checked into the hospital the first time, fifteen weeks ago. She had had to push him so far, right to the brink, to get what she wanted. He wasn't there when she got back, he had packed his bags, the flat was emptied of his stuff, he had assumed the outcome. She hadn't bothered to disabuse him. At first, she intended to. She really did. Put him out of his misery. But she saw at once what that would mean. He would come back, demanding his father's rights. And she would have to go through it all again, without the advantage of time on her side. She would become a martyr to a relationship she no longer wanted, and her baby would have a father she didn't want it to have.

She had felt guilty at first, imagining him licking his wounds, grieving for something that hadn't happened. *There's got to be a point where you stop being nice.* Who had said that to her? Probably Jana again, who had come out with all sorts of things before she died. *There's got to be a point when you stop being nice, and think about yourself.* She understands about Paul now, that he was a survivor like her, the weak exterior was emotional blackmail, a cover to make her feel guilty if she ever thought about striking out for her independence.

She didn't feel that she had actually made the decision against the abortion that morning. Probably she was too exhausted, but when the Sister asked her if she really wanted to abort the baby, the first word that came out of her mouth was *No.* It surprised her. She decided to chill out, like Jana suggested, and trust her instincts. It had been a lot easier to say *No* than it had been to say *Yes.* When she said *Yes,* she had to go on to justify it, had to argue her case. But then she said *No.* It made her feel instantly better. It sounded, at last, as if it was the right thing to say.

There are other kinds of pain, Jana said to her, when she returned to the hospice the next day, subdued but already different, stronger, reconnected to the baby inside. *This is a pain that will stop, and no harm will come to you. Having the baby will be much easier than anything you've faced during the pregnancy. You'll do it, Carrie, you will.*

The rest of the pregnancy was so much simpler. She went home after work, cleaned the flat, moved the furniture around, completed the business of erasing Paul from her living space, grew strong on her own independence. She booked her bed at the maternity hospital, went to groups frequented by other pregnant mothers, read magazines, attended clinics, had her blood pressure taken, her urine sampled. She bought maternity clothes, packed her hospital bag, went for long walks, took up swimming, practised relaxation, talked to the baby, played music to him or her. She bought a bouncy cradle and a push chair, a cot and a leaping fish mobile, then sat looking at the bouncy cradle in her cosy front room, and tried to understand that in a few weeks, someone new would be occupying it.

She ate a lot. The first few months, she hadn't been able to eat anything except bananas. Everything else tasted of metal. Then she decided she wanted an abortion, and she couldn't eat anything at all. In the second half of the pregnancy, she ate for England. She listened to the healthy guideline recommendations, but basically, she ate what she wanted. She had unshakeable faith in the baby's ability to survive. After all, she'd almost killed him or her – if it could survive that, it could survive anything. When you've looked abortion in the face, the odd glass of red wine and chocolate are laughable candidates for life-threatening forces.

Chocolate was the thing. Truckloads of it. Bars and boxes of it, cakes, sauces, puddings – Carrie was unashamedly greedy, so gleeful in her over-indulgence, so happy after the dreadful beginning to everything, that no one would dare suggest she might be better off with a plateful of grated apple and cabbage. *Honestly,* one of her friends said, *I don't think you're going to have a baby at all. You're going to give birth to a giant chocolate cake.*

I ate healthily, Jana said one day, in one of her blackest of black humour days, *and look what happened to me.*

II

Close to the end of pregnancy, Carrie and a group of other mothers get to visit the hospital, to see the wards and the delivery suite and the gas and air and the forceps and the Special Care Unit for babies who are born into trouble. This is where you imagine the coming event, try to picture being in labour, and consider for the first time that things may not go according to plan.

This is the place where babies hover between life and death, sustained by complex machinery, egged on towards the living by the ferocious will of their helpless parents, who have been rendered useless by the power of technology. Carrie walks round in awe, looks in at incubators, machines that go *bleep*, wires, sensors, pressure pads, tubes that snake in and out of tiny bodies, the indecipherable paraphernalia of the business of saving tiny lives.

Now here's a thing. Spread-eagled on a Perspex-sided cot in the soporific warmth of the high-dependency ward, is a baby so tiny and frail it takes her breath away. It's a little boy – you know it's a boy because of the blue blanket – with a tube disappearing into his nose, an impossible array of wires and circular sticky pads linked to sinister monitors that *whistle* or *bleep* or *ping* at varying intervals. Sometimes the length of time between these sounds is disturbingly long, sometimes terrifyingly brief. He's an angry colour, somewhere between red and purple, and his scrawny limbs move feebly. The scrap of nappy taped around him looks gargantuan. His plum-coloured face is creased and now and again he makes a rasping, feeble *wail* that floats above the *bleeps*, *whistles* and *pings* of his mechanical nurses. His whole body is spiked with pain. There is a woman outside the room in dressing gown and slippers, taking a break, her eyes red from excessive crying. It's the kind of crying you are reduced to when you've done your best, which is nothing, and there is nothing else you can do except place your faith in a battery of machines that go *ping*. You hope the nurses can achieve by proxy what you can't do in person for your own child, and your vocabulary shrinks to a single word. *Please.*

Carrie stands before the window, reduced to the same wondering, desperate uselessness, her hands automatically circling her big fat baby belly as if to try and shield it from the possibility of something like this happening.

One of the nurses says at her elbow. "Born at twenty-one weeks – the mother couldn't sustain the pregnancy."

"Why not?"

"Sometimes it just happens that way."

Carrie stares at the baby. "Twenty-one weeks? And he's going to make it?"

"Oof – can't tell at this stage," says the nurse, who's seen a lot of premature babies in her time. "There's a long way to go yet, and even if he does make it, his life might not be worth living. Sometimes they go through so much in here, and they still die. But you have to give them the chance, don't you, if only for the mother's sake."

Twenty-one weeks. Carrie stands before the baby, humiliated, shaken. This little boy is younger than hers was when she booked in for her abortion. And here he is, thrown out onto the mercy of an outside world he isn't ready for, wired up to the mains, fighting for a shot at life against terrifying odds. Life's a bitch.

She turns away and the machines go *whistle, bleep, ping* in her wake.

The glass is half full. The pain is positive. Now it's nine hours after she went into labour, and the contractions are coming every minute. When she had read the baby magazines and the health pamphlets, she thought that meant you got a minute off in between. But she soon found out that the contraction lasts the whole of the minute, and before it's relaxed, the next one is coming. She keeps thinking, *If I could just negotiate here – if I could just have five minutes off, just to have a break, it's all I'm asking, just five minutes – please?* But her body has taken charge for the time being, is wagging its finger at her and saying, *I'm handling this, and we're going to do it my way. There will be no shirking, no let-ups, I know what I'm doing, you're just going to have to trust me. And cope.* She thinks about circles, the tightening bands around her belly, how deeply inside the circle she is.

She has her gift from Jana, clutched in her hand, the knobbly little rock that meant so much to her. During the contractions, her hand clenches around it and it is satisfyingly obdurate, not impressed by the fierce squeezing, oddly calming.

Carrie could not believe Debbie had left her, popping out of the room in her maddeningly cheerful way. *How could she leave me when I'm going through this? This is the worst thing that's ever happened to me.* Debbie comes back to check up on her after ten minutes, and Carrie glowers from behind her gas and air mask. Debbie tries to cheerfully whisk away the gas and air mask, but Carrie refuses to relinquish her grip on it, so they end up having a brief, undignified struggle. Debbie wins, her good humour momentarily coloured by a sudden show of will. "It's time you had some fresh air," she says, her smile ever so slightly grim. "I don't want fresh air, I want drugs," Carrie shouts. "Why won't you give me pethidine? Why won't you bang me over the head with a brick? Why – " That's all she gets in before the contraction removes her powers of speech.

Debbie glances at the clock. So does Carrie. It's five o' clock. Debbie smiles. *Everything's fine*, she says, from the irritatingly cheerful perspective of a woman not in labour. Then, tantalisingly, like a torturer promising to loosen the thumbscrews soon, she says, *I can't give you anything now because the baby will be here soon. Here's the gas and air. We'll have a look in an hour.*

In an hour. An hour bears no relation to the word *soon*. Debbie lied to her. Carrie sinks into the hollowness of betrayal.

She looks at the clock. The hands on the face click round, punctuating each circle of pain, sixty precise movements to each circle. Sixty circles of pain, and it will change. Carrie stares at the clock, all the numbers from one to twelve, the big hand and the little hand and the thin red hand jerking between each one of sixty black marks meticulously etched into the circular face. The thin red hand, clicking out the three thousand, six hundred seconds one by one. The glass is full of time. The glass is full of pain. She'll drain the glass of time and pain, throwing a hoop around it every sixty seconds. Sixty circles of pain.

Carrie watches the clock for the hour. The circles complete themselves and move on, roll away from her like a wheel. She stares at the clock as if her life depends on it. The first five minutes are the worst. Then she gets the rhythm of it, learns to split the circle into quarters, achieves each fifteen seconds by pushing the second hand forward, willing it round. Fifteen – thirty – forty-five – sixty. Another circle. Five – ten – fifteen – twenty. A third.

She should be visualising, of course, but visualisation has gone out the window. Too damn complicated. Changabang is as far away now as India. She has her own glass mountain to climb.

She empties the glass of time. All things must pass. This is the difference between the pain of giving birth and the pain of dying. You know it's going to end, and you know that you will be all right. Somewhere deep inside the circles of pain, you understand this and it keeps you going, gives you the strength to swear and rant, holler and yell. Soon, it will be over, and you will still be alive. Somewhere during those sixty circles, Carrie understands the way that Jana died, knowing that to relinquish the pain, she would have to give up life as well.

IV

In order for me to be born, certain parts of me have to die. Crossing the muscular threshold between warm and wet and warm and dry marks the single biggest change in physical circumstances any living thing experiences, until the end, when death sheds the body altogether and instigates a different kind of rebirth. Despite the fact that I've been busy growing for forty weeks, being born is the official beginning of life, what people recognise as the start of things. Which is why the unborn child – who is definitely alive, and certainly not as good as dead, as some people would argue – can be subject to the terrible risks that I faced, alive but with no mandate, inside my mother's body.

When I knew that I had been given another chance, I was hugely relieved. Of course I was. My mother and I left the hospital together, with a sense that we had both been through something enormous which had changed us and bridged the gap that had widened between us. For the next four months or so, that sense of unity became so precious to me that I dreaded the thought of leaving my charmed environment – I had not yet had enough of the loving acceptance my reformed mother showered on me in the aftermath of our near miss.

There was, however, a great deal of anticipation bound up in her revived enthusiasm for carrying me. While I relished every moment wrapped in the security of her body, she became more and more eager for the day when I would leave it, and she would know me.

There is a certain amount of romance attached to pregnancy – that if we are wanted, we are loved unconditionally and the essentially secret nature of our presence is a matter of great joy. I heard her talking about it to Jana – this exclusive relationship that mother and unborn child hug just to themselves, not knowing each other, but loving each other at the most basic, instinctual level, beyond the reach of intellectualising. I regard Jana as my saviour – I'm well aware of the irony that if she hadn't been dying, she might not have been. Dying changes your perspectives, no doubt about it – I sensed a reluctance in her to interfere, but being forced to give up your hold on life makes you see things for what they are – what matters, what doesn't, what's truthful and what isn't. You might not be turning into a guru as you approach the pearly gates, but what death does do is help you cut through all the crap. Because Jana was dying, she gave me the chance to live. But as I was saying a while ago, first I have to change and die a little myself.

I'll miss the camaraderie, and the music she's played for me, and the secret little chats we have in the middle of the night, when both of us are restless and keeping each other awake. But there's no reason to suppose those things won't continue once I'm out there with her – in theory it should get even better. One thing I won't miss is the chocolate. I've enjoyed it up to a point, but there are limits. I'm grateful she hasn't smoked, or subjected me to a tiresome litany of grains and vegetables, or overdone the garlic, but some plain flavours won't go amiss for a while. Chocolate is a pleasure I hope to reserve for the future, when I can have a little more say in when I take it.

It's happening, all right. Everything is changing around me, and now my state of mind is shifting to accommodate the new circumstances I must contemplate. I won't remember any of this, just like a dying person gives up on the memories of the life he's just lived.

Being born is a pretty noisy and uncomfortable process.

Not only do I have to contend with all the pushing and shoving as her body turns against me and starts the business of reclaiming its territory, but I have her yelling and screaming to deal with as well. I want to say, Oh, shut up, woman, it's just as bad for me – but of course I can't. I have to content myself with the knowledge that once I emerge, there'll be plenty of time to get my own back in the noise department.

Towards the end, it's the body that knocks both of us into shape, and forces us to comply with what both of us are resisting. My mother, swearing and screaming in a most undignified fashion, doesn't want to push me out in case I rip her apart. And I don't want to go through that impossibly narrow channel that changes irrevocably the relationship I have with her, strips me of my mental faculties and forces me to start the learning process, in a changed context, all over again. Despite all that, my head is being forced against the opening, my home is squashing me towards the exit, and both of us are falling prey to what nature demands of us. Fear of change is present at the earliest stages.

At least I know that when I reach the other side, I will be wanted. I fought hard for the opportunity to live in the next phase, so a little more struggle is not that big a deal. Having escaped death once, I still have to face it at some point, although not for a while now. This is my own little death, moving from the serenity of knowing – forgive the pomposity – to the indignity of being a screaming, uncoordinated, helpless mess, who knows nothing and makes a thoroughly indecorous entrance into the world, smeared with bodily fluids and greases, and starkers into the bargain.

As I start my descent towards the light, the familiarity of the landscape deserts me, and I begin to disappear inside the blankness that signals the approaching change. And I wonder if at the end of our physical life, there will be a mother waiting to sweep us up into her arms, comfort us for our loss, and make us welcome in our new place.

We shall see.

V

At six o' clock, Debbie says, "Let's see how things are going."
She does that, then calls in a lady in a green gown and begins
to put on a white plastic apron. Trays of frightening-looking
instruments appear, hard, cold, shiny metal. Carrie panics,
remembering the last time, the last time she was in hospital
and what she almost did. She starts to cry, sudden, hysterical
sobs, catching the midwife by surprise.

"Hey, hey, what's all this?" she says, pausing in her
business to take Carrie's hand. Carrie's grip is manic, fierce.

"The baby – it's all right, isn't it? There's nothing you
haven't told me?"

"It's fine," Debbie says, ultra soothingly. "It's on the
monitor, look – everything is ok, heartbeat's all right, no signs
of distress. You'll be cuddling him or her before you know it."

"What are all these for?" Carrie asks wildly, tossing her
head in the direction of all the metal. She knows she's
behaving like an idiot, but she can't help it. Up on the bed,
hurting, scared, she feels stripped, vulnerable, as if she no
longer has any say over what's happening. The fear that this
baby might suddenly be taken away from her by a vengeful act
of God is as powerful as it is irrational.

"They're for delivering the baby," Debbie says, laughing.
"Nothing nasty. Come on, don't go to pieces on me now,
you've done really well up to now."

The pain changes, shifts from her belly and moves down
as the baby starts forcing its way out. It feels as if it's coming
out of her backside, she doesn't want to push, it feels wrong,
but her body is bullying her along, thumping her haunches flat
to the bed and driving the baby down, down, down and out.
She makes indescribable noises, she's glad nobody she knows
is there to hear them. She thinks of all the actresses she has
watched giving birth in soaps and medical dramas, and how

deeply unconvincing they all are in the face of the real thing. Actresses are only pretending, of course – if a cameraman walked in here now, with her yelling, sweaty, undignified, legs hanging open, nightie stained, deeply embroiled in *the real thing*, she'd kill him.

She does exactly as she's told, she says afterwards that she had complete confidence in the midwife, but although that's part of it, she feels that she's got enough on her plate without trying to direct her own birth. Debbie is in a much better position than she is to see what's going on.

The head sticks in the same place, her lips are parted so wide around it she can feel them stretch to what feels like snapping point. This is when she remembers the threat of episiotomy. Never mind that some of her friends who've had one say it's tremendous, all of a sudden the baby just falls out and then you've only got to put up with the stitches, which you can't feel anyway because you're all numb. Debbie, who has been so great up to now, she really has, she can forgive the cheeriness, the totally in control thing, the depriving her for two minutes of the lifesaving gas mask. It's the thought of Debbie coming at her with a pair of pinking shears and snipping through that tough, elasticated band of flesh. To her, it sounds like the worst thing in the world – she'd rather have a Caesarian than be set about by a midwife turned mad axeman. But then again, the baby's head is stuck fast, and it hurts like hell and Debbie, her head bent over Carrie's groaning aperture, isn't doing anything, just letting nature take its course. *Oh for God's sake, do the pinking shears thing!*

Carrie screeches, it sounds shriller than a whistling kettle, but she can't stop it – it's unbearable, it goes on and on and on, the crescendo of pain screaming out of her steam-whistle mouth – and then suddenly, there's a rush of warm, slippery flesh slithering between her thighs, a gush of hot liquid, everything pings back into place and there's an immediate cessation of pain.

It's fantastic, the way it just stops. Just like that. Hours and hours of it, and all of a sudden, it's gone. She catches her breath, the glorious relaxation – oh, it's marvellous, never mind the sweat and blood and yuck – it's just amazing, it's all stopped, everything's stopped, the world stands still for just a few seconds while she stops hurting. Just like that.

The midwife is chatting, busy wrapping the baby, a quick check, but it's all okay, everything's okay, there won't be any stitches, they don't need any oxygen, there are no complications, it's perfect, it's all over. She's a mother. Just like that.

And here's the baby – *oh God, it's a little girl, just look at her* – squalling her outrage at being so roughly ejected from her domain, yelling blue murder at the world in her first few seconds, before her gaping jaws clamp shut around the new food source and she gorges on comfort. Carrie laughs with delight at this gutsy little alien life form, not got a bloody clue where she is or what's going on, but knows her mother, trusts her already with a blind, fierce instinct, to deliver the goods and see her right. She watches the greedy sucking, the jerky movements of limbs not yet acclimatised to the vastness of open spaces, feels her hanging on like grim death to the hard-won opportunity for life. She bends her head, whispers *Hello*, and *I'm so sorry*, and other things mixing welcome and apology and a yearning for forgiveness from this tiny bundle on whom she has no right to make any demands.

It's just beginning, this long road into the sunset.

She's got it all to come.

Acknowledgements

Thanks go to:

Tricia Feber for invaluable technical information and wisdom.

Carol Christies for forthright criticism and clear-headed comments.

My husband Mike, for hours spent discussing difficult subject-matter, and not pulling his punches